BUCK'S TONGUE TRACED
A TRAIL ACROSS HER THROAT

Every muscle in Amanda's body tensed. Waves of desire swept over her, and she looked into his eyes questioningly.

Buck cupped her face in his hands and lowered his lips to hers. Suddenly Amanda wanted him to take her—she wanted him more than she had ever wanted any man.

But after a moment, the kiss ended. His mouth hovered near hers but didn't touch. Only his steamy vapors caressed her, coaxing her desire to a deep, urgent craving.

Buck gathered Amanda against him. "I want you," he whispered.

Amanda knew that this was her moment of decision. Words of doubt and denial were there in her head, but they waned before the magnitude of what she felt. She knew the time had come....

ABOUT THE AUTHOR

An avid world traveler, Janice Kaiser says, "I hope to expose others to the fascinating aspects of various cultures through my writing." She's certainly accomplished this with the Thailand background of *Lotus Moon*, her second Superromance. Her fans will be happy to know that this California author's next novel, complete with another exotic setting, will be published in the summer of 1986.

Books by Janice Kaiser

HARLEQUIN SUPERROMANCE
187—HARMONY

These books may be available at your local bookseller.

Don't miss any of our special offers. Write to us at the following address for information on our newest releases.

Harlequin Reader Service
901 Fuhrmann Blvd., P.O. Box 1397, Buffalo, NY 14240
Canadian address: P.O. Box 2800, Postal Station A,
5170 Yonge St., Willowdale, Ont. M2N 6J3

Janice Kaiser

LOTUS MOON

Harlequin Books

TORONTO • NEW YORK • LONDON
AMSTERDAM • PARIS • SYDNEY • HAMBURG
STOCKHOLM • ATHENS • TOKYO • MILAN

Published April 1986

First printing February 1986

ISBN 0-373-70209-4

Printed in Canada

For Mortie, Papa, C.D. and The Trout, with love.

CHAPTER ONE

IT WAS MONDAY, and Buck Michaels was doing something he hadn't done in half a dozen years—he was taking a workday off. Leaning back in the lounge chair on the deck of his sailboat, he closed his pale-blue eyes and listened to the water lapping at the sides of the boat. If Kelly Wallace hadn't called from the office with word that a telex had come from Bangkok, he would be far out to sea by now. Instead, he was at his dock waiting in the sun, trying to enjoy the caress of the breeze blowing across Newport Bay.

Bangkok. The telex had to be from Kupnol Sustri. Months had passed since Buck had sent Sustri the money, and the telex had to be his report—undoubtedly more dead ends, more excuses. And all because of a damned woman.

Buck sighed in frustration as he remembered the sultry nights fragrant with the scent of the Orient, the river. It was all a long time ago, but he had begun thinking about it more during the past year. The woman, the faceless child and Bangkok. He was getting soft. He knew it.

"Hello, Buck," came a female voice from some distance.

He turned toward the house, but there was no one on the deck or on the lawn that swept down to the water's edge.

"Yoo-hoo, Buck!"

This time, he got a bearing on the voice. It was coming from farther up the shore. He sat up and saw Helene Daniels standing on her dock in her favorite string bikini, waving at him. "Hi, Helene. How are you?"

"Fine," she called back. "The question is how are *you*? I've never seen you home on a weekday."

"Just taking a day off," he called across the water.

"I didn't think the *Tribune*'s editor and publisher ever took a day off. They say that paper doesn't function without you!"

Michaels laughed. "Who told you that?"

"Bernie. Who else?"

Bernard Daniels, Buck's neighbor, was a friend and also a member of the *Tribune*'s board of directors. They were close. Unfortunately, Helene was a problem. Ever since Buck's divorce six years earlier, she had been determined to flirt with him at every opportunity. Buck had dismissed it as infatuation, but that didn't stop her from trying. Her favorite ploy was to sunbathe on her dock every time she saw Buck out in his yard or working on his boat. Whenever Bernie was out of town, she got especially aggressive.

Michaels discreetly watched the woman, who at forty had maintained her figure and was rather attractive. She had spread out her towel and, judging by the way she was moving and glancing in his direction, Bernie was out of town again.

As Helene Daniels preened, Buck closed his eyes and tried to forget about women and work and everything but the warmth of the sun on his tanned body. His imagination cavorted with the sound of sea gulls and the pungent smell of the ocean. After a while, his mind cleared, his body relaxed and he began drifting toward sleep.

"Say, Buck!" It was Helene again.

Michaels lifted his head and looked up the shoreline to where she was lying on the dock. "Yes?"

"You eating alone this evening?" she called across the water.

He eyed the woman who was on her stomach facing him, but at a slight angle. She had unfastened the top of her bikini. "Why do you ask?"

Helene daringly lifted herself up on her elbows. "I took a couple of steaks out of the freezer, forgetting completely that Bernie was out of town. Thought we could share them if you're baching it tonight."

"Thanks, Helene. I'd like to," Buck called, "but I've got a dinner date." It wasn't true, but it seemed like the most graceful way to decline the invitation.

She lowered her breasts back to the towel. "Another time, then," she called back in obvious disappointment.

"Yeah, sorry. It's a bad week, Helene."

The woman dismissed Buck with a wave of her hand, laid her head on the towel and stared out over the water.

Buck watched her a bit sadly. Helene always reminded him of Carolyn for some strange reason though there was little similarity in their looks. His ex-wife had been typical Beverly Hills chic, a woman who wore her sunglasses and her white linen suits like elegant armor. All they had had in common was their society backgrounds and his money. Now she had half the money, including the house in West Los Angeles.

Closing his eyes, he tried to recapture the relaxed state he had been in before Helene's interruption. He had just begun dozing off again when he heard footsteps on his dock. Buck turned and saw his secretary Kelly Wallace, a pert young woman with a cap of short dark hair, come walking up the gangplank. He was surprised to see that she held a tray with a bottle of beer and a glass. An ironic smile was on her face.

"And some secretaries complain about having to get their bosses a cup of coffee," she said. "Next time I'm up for salary review, remember it was me who delivered the beer on the boat—and drove all the way from Los Angeles to do it."

Buck laughed. He sat up and ran his hand through his dark hair. "What happened to Luisa?" he asked, referring to his housekeeper.

"She's in the house cleaning the kitchen. Since I was coming down, I volunteered to bring your drink. Luisa said you were probably ready for a beer." She handed him the tray, and Buck smiled. He immediately spotted the envelope next to the beer.

"This my telex?"

"Yes, Boss."

Buck reached over and pulled up a deck chair for Kelly. "Let me read it over and see if I need to answer."

Michaels took the telex that had been transmitted through the paper's communications center and tore it open. As he had suspected, the sender was Kupnol Sustri. Sustri had worked for Buck as a combination translator, secretary and office manager when Michaels had been the *Tribune*'s correspondent in Southeast Asia during the Vietnam War.

Have made many inquiries about Dameree. No success yet. I believe she is dead or has gone from Bangkok. She cannot be in the city while I look for her so long. I have spent the five hundred dollars for my expense in looking and to pay bribes for information. Although I give you my time to look further, I do not have great hope to find Dameree.

It is the same for the child, and even if Dameree is dead, the girl is old enough to be on her own. But by now, she could be in the streets, sold to a family or worse. There is one hope. From the brother of Dameree's first family, I am told the child was in some orphanage for sending Thai babies to America. I went to ask there, but even a bribe brings no good information. The administrator says my American client should ask to the American boss of the agency in your California at Los Angeles. It is a lady called Amanda Parr. Do you know her? She had many babies already in America. If you are of luck, Dameree's child is in America.

Kupnol

In spite of the fact that Kelly Wallace waited quietly nearby, Buck Michaels sat for a long time staring at the telex, an ordinary piece of paper spat out of some impersonal machine at the *Tribune* building. But, despite the dispassionate nature of the medium, the mind and hand of Kupnol Sustri were clearly in evidence. Michaels glanced out over the water surrounding his Balboa Island home, but the communication from Sustri had taken him back to Bangkok.

Three months earlier, Michaels had gone to Japan and China when the president made his state visit. At the end of the seven-day trip, he had flown down to Bangkok on an impulse, wanting to find Dameree and the child if he could though it had been about twelve years since he had lost track of them. It didn't take long to learn the woman's trail was much colder than even the intervening years would indicate. The experience had only served to heighten the frustration Buck felt over their disappearance.

Michaels did manage to find Sustri, who now ran an agency to assist Japanese and Americans doing business in Thailand. He, like his former boss, had come up in the world considerably, but he was still willing to do a five hundred dollar favor and try to locate Dameree.

Glancing down at the telex still clutched in his hand, Michaels tried to read between the lines. Sustri was never one to turn down a commission or to solicit one, even if it meant creating false hope. Another five hundred would be gratefully accepted and undoubtedly some effort would be expended to justify it, but Michaels sensed that the Thai's pessimism was a sincere attempt to discourage him from pursuing the matter.

Reading the telex again, Michaels began wondering whether the implied discouragement might not be some sort of deception. He knew Sustri was fully capable of taking money at the other end to report a negative result. Maybe he had found Dameree and she—or a protector—had paid him to conceal the fact. Twelve years earlier, Michaels had solicited Sustri's help in searching for the woman. A deception could have started as long ago as then.

The newspaperman rubbed his chin and glanced up at a jet headed west, out over the Pacific. It was strange, he thought, how easily one could be dragged into Oriental intrigues just by letting one's mind drift back. His years in Southeast Asia had been full of not only intrigue but much danger as well. The association fascinated him.

Buck Michaels looked again at the last paragraph of the telex. Sustri had been somewhat more optimistic about the girl though the trail he suggested was in the States, not Thailand. Three possibilities occurred to him. First, the story could be true. Second, it could be a diversion to direct his search away from Thailand. Or third,

Sustri might feel a little guilt at having spent the five hundred with nothing to show for it. The name he had given, Amanda Parr, might be nothing more than a token lead, a fragile reed of hope to assuage Sustri's conscience or to confound Buck. On the off chance it was legitimate, Michaels decided to check it out.

Kelly Wallace had taken the untouched bottle of beer, poured it into the glass and handed it to him.

"Thank you, Kelly. You're a doll."

She inclined her head to acknowledge his gratitude. "You sounded thirsty."

"*Sounded* thirsty?"

"At the office whenever you're the quietest and doing a lot of thinking, that's when you drink the most coffee. Judging by the silences, I can always tell when you're about ready for another cup."

Michaels smiled at the vivacious little brunette. "Ominous to be so thoroughly understood by a woman."

"Well, I probably know you better than anyone except for your mother and your ex."

"You may have moved into second place, ahead of Carolyn."

"Dubious distinction," she said dryly. She looked at the paper in Buck's hand. "So what's the decision? Any reply?"

"No, but I'd like you to do something for me. Got something to write on?"

Kelly pulled a notepad and pencil from her purse.

"There's a woman somewhere in Los Angeles named Amanda Parr—P-a-r-r—who runs an agency that deals with orphans from Southeast Asia. I don't know the name of it or where it's located, but I'd like to get hold of her. Would you see what you can find out for me?"

Kelly frowned. "That's not much to go on."

"There must be a directory or list of agencies somewhere."

She shrugged as if to say she'd try.

"Better yet, Kell, remember that series of articles we did last summer on war orphans fathered by American servicemen?"

"Yes, the one you got all excited about."

"Find out from Norm Harris who did those articles—I've forgotten—and check with the reporter. He or she probably would know of Ms Parr."

"Okay."

"Come to think of it, that was a hell of a good series. I ought to talk to whoever wrote it, if they're still with us. Make a note of that, too, will you, Kell?" Buck lapsed into a thoughtful silence.

Kelly looked at the expressive face of her boss partially hidden behind dark glasses. "The plight of those kids really got to you, didn't it, Buck?"

He smiled at her insight.

"You're just an old softy, you know."

Buck Michaels chuckled. "Don't count on that, young lady."

"Right, Boss."

He reached over and patted his secretary on the hand. "I appreciate you driving down here with the telex, Kelly."

She stood up and shrugged. "Just remember me at Christmas." She turned to go, then stopped. "By the way, your neighbor lady on the next dock must be awfully curious. She hasn't taken her eyes off us since I arrived."

"Oh, don't mind Helene. She has a prurient interest in everything that goes on over here."

"She probably thinks I'm your latest."

"There is no latest . . . at the moment." He smiled.

"What about Jillian?"

"Oh, we're just friends."

"I'll bet *that* galls her."

Buck gave Kelly a look but said nothing.

"Sooner or later," she said with a grin, "you're bound to get hooked."

"Don't hold your breath."

Kelly turned away, repressing a smile. "If I'm going to find Ms Parr for you, I'd better go."

"Here, let me walk you out," he said, starting to get up.

"No, you just stay here and relax. I know the way."

Buck sank into his lounge chair.

"See you tomorrow, Boss."

He gave her a wave, but she was already headed down the gangplank.

When Kelly had gone, Michaels made a mental note to think about his life. Perhaps he had let the past unduly intrude upon the present. After a moment's reflection, he relaxed. It was too late to go sailing now so he let his mind begin drifting back again to Thailand.

AMANDA PARR STOOD at the shaded entrance to the garden watching the children at play. The little ones were on a patch of grass throwing and kicking a large red ball among them. The adolescents, two girls and a boy, were sitting to the side on a bench talking quietly. The Thai nurse looked up from her chair and across the garden, and seeing Amanda, smiled broadly and nodded.

The children, all Amerasian, seemed to Amanda more relaxed than the last time she had seen them, several days earlier. They had been in the States for a week now and were gradually adjusting to their new environment. It was hardest for the older ones; Amanda could see the uncertainty on their faces as they whispered among themselves, not yet ready to deal with the wonders awaiting them beyond the garden walls.

The youngest stopped their play as Amanda came out into the sunlight. There was a touch of awe on their faces as they looked up at the tall slender woman with a cloud of soft red curls floating to her shoulders and gentle green eyes that smiled with her mouth.

One toddler playing alone at the edge of the grass craned her neck around to see what had caught everyone's attention, and in doing so fell onto her bottom. The child's face immediately screwed up, and tears spurted as she began to wail. Amanda stepped over and picked her up, brushing the tears from the little girl's cheeks with her fingers. She cooed a few words in Thai, and the child stopped crying. Seeing that all eyes were upon her, the toddler thrust all four fingers of one hand into her mouth, and the other children tittered.

With the girl cradled in her arms, Amanda walked over and sat beside the nurse, who had watched the episode in bemused silence. "Good afternoon, Mai," Amanda said as she shifted the child onto her knee.

"Hello, Miss Parr," the nurse replied in heavily accented speech.

"Looks like everyone is feeling a little more at home."

"Yes, Miss. Good children. They learn fast."

The toddler on Amanda's lap was looking up at her with wide eyes, and the other younger children began to resume their play. The adolescents across the garden continued to observe Amanda with shy curiosity.

"How are the older ones doing, Mai? I worry about them the most."

"Pretty good, Miss. They are a little bit afraid. They ask many questions, but they know their life is better here."

"Well, they'll feel much more comfortable when they've learned enough English to express themselves."

The nurse nodded politely.

Amanda looked at the serious little face and round eyes of the child sitting on her knee. "Aren't you a little angel," she said, tickling the girl under her chin. "But so serious. Can't you smile?"

The nurse said a few words in Thai, and the child turned away shyly. "She never see pretty lady like you before," Mai said to Amanda.

"I know my red hair looks strange to her."

"Not many red hair people in Thailand." Mai laughed.

Amanda was holding the little girl close against her now. "Whenever I'm in Asia, I do get the strangest looks from people."

"It's not just your hair, Miss," Mai said. "You are tall lady and very pretty. Skin like cream. Thai people think very pretty."

"Thank you, Mai. But I think the Thais are among the most attractive people in the world." She stroked the child's dark hair, which was gleaming with lots of highlights. "And these children of mixed heritage are gorgeous."

Mai agreed with a nod.

The toddler began squirming after a while so Amanda put her down, and the little girl tottered back toward the lawn.

"How are the medical exams coming along?" Amanda asked.

"One more day, the doctor say. That's all, Miss."

"Good. I'm sure the children will be glad to get that behind them." Amanda looked at her watch. "I'd better go back inside. I'm supposed to be meeting a woman from the *Tribune* here soon."

"Oh! Newspaper lady? Maybe you are famous already, Miss?"

Amanda laughed. "No, hardly. It's not for an interview, Mai. I'm not sure exactly why she wants to see me, to be honest." She smiled at the diminutive nurse and stood. "I'll see you later."

Amanda retraced her steps across the garden under the full scrutiny of the children. Even the nurse watched her long graceful strides with interest and approval.

Amanda remembered an experience she had had in a Bangkok orphanage when a little waif had asked if she were a fairy princess because she looked like the pictures in the school's book of nursery rhymes. Her work could be heart wrenching at times, but seeing the little creatures safely in the country of their fathers made it all worthwhile. Amanda turned at the garden gate, and on glimpsing a small boy in blue shorts waving goodbye, returned his wave and went to the office of the clinic.

KELLY WALLACE LOOKED UP when she heard the back door open at the far end of the corridor. From where she sat in the reception area of the clinic, she could see a strikingly beautiful woman enter. As she walked toward Kelly, the woman's fiery hair drifted around the tops of her shoulders. Kelly recognized a self-assured, businesslike demeanor in addition to the woman's obvious beauty. She wondered if this could be Amanda Parr.

The redhead gave Kelly a friendly smile as she entered the room, then looked over at the receptionist, a middle-aged woman, who glanced up from her typewriter.

"Oh, there you are, Amanda," the receptionist said. "Kelly Wallace is here to see you."

Kelly stood up as Amanda walked over to greet her. There was a genuine cordiality in the lovely green eyes. Kelly decided immediately that Amanda Parr was not a woman who used her beauty to intimidate. She gratefully returned the smile. "I appreciate you seeing me on such short notice, Miss Parr."

"No problem. I was planning on being at the clinic this afternoon anyway, and it's a convenient place to meet."

Amanda turned toward the receptionist, who anticipated her question. "You can use Dr. Boyd's office, Amanda," she said. "He won't be back for several hours."

Amanda took her briefcase from the corner of the receptionist's desk, then led Kelly into an adjoining office. She gestured for her to take a chair. Kelly noted Amanda's fine white silk blouse, her expensive pale-gray skirt and matching shoes as she moved behind the desk and sat down.

"From what you said on the phone, I gather you're not here for an interview," Amanda said.

"No, I'm from the *Tribune*'s executive offices, not the news department."

"I see."

"The reason I'm here is not company business but at the request of my boss, Mr. Michaels."

"Mr. Michaels? You mean Preston Michaels, the owner of the *Tribune*?"

Kelly smiled at Amanda's use of Buck Michaels's proper name. Everyone at the paper called him Buck—if they didn't call him Mr. Michaels—and he was fond of saying the only people who ever called him Preston were his mother, strangers and would-be friends. "Well, Buck doesn't exactly own the *Tribune*, he's editor and publisher, but his family does own a lot of stock.''

"I'm afraid I know very little about Mr. Michaels, other than what I've read in the papers, which isn't much.''

"No, Buck doesn't like publicity, even though he's in the newspaper business.''

"Tell me, then, Miss Wallace, what interest does a celebrity like Mr. Michaels have in our organization?''

The answer to Amanda's question was philanthropy, but after meeting Miss Parr, there was no doubt in Kelly's mind that Buck would be more interested in her beauty than in being charitable. In fact, if she had to describe Buck Michaels's type of woman, it would be Amanda Parr. *Oh,* she thought, *to be a fly on the wall when Buck sees this one.*

Kelly suddenly became aware of Amanda waiting for an answer to her question, and she covered the lapse by assuming a thoughtful expression. "I suppose you've heard of Buck's great interest in charitable causes....''

"To be honest, no,'' Amanda said, smiling. "But since we're totally dependent on public donations, I'm always interested in making contacts with public-spirited individuals.''

Kelly opened her purse and took out a plain white envelope. "Buck has looked into the Amerasian Children's Foundation and admires the work you do, Miss Parr. He asked me to give you this.'' She reached across the desk and handed Amanda an envelope.

"How nice! May I open it?''

"Sure.''

When Amanda saw the check inside, her eyes lit up. "How generous. I'll have to write him a note.'' She gave Kelly a look that made the secretary feel pride on Buck's behalf. "Please express my sincere thanks to Mr. Michaels."

"Yes, of course. Buck said to tell you that he might consider further donations, but he'd like your annual report and other information on the organization."

"Certainly. I can give you a packet to take back to Mr. Michaels."

"Also," Kelly said, feeling a little uncomfortable, "he wanted to ask a favor."

"A favor?"

"Yes, there are aspects of the organization that Mr. Michaels is very interested in, and he would like to meet with you to discuss them."

Amanda looked perplexed. "What aspects?"

"Frankly, I'm not sure. He didn't mention anything specific. But I do know he was very interested in the series the paper did last summer on war orphans, and he knows a lot about Vietnam and Cambodia, having spent time there himself."

"I see. What did he have in mind?"

"Well, he's a busy man, and he was wondering if it would be possible for you to come by the *Tribune* building. He thought you probably had reason to go downtown from time to time and—"

Amanda nodded understandingly. "Mr. Michaels has been very generous, and I am more than happy to accommodate his time constraints. In fund-raising, I meet lots of busy people. I know how it is. When does he want me to come by?"

"He's available any day this week after five, except Friday. He thought, if you don't mind, you could come by after work. You see, he's always in the office late unless he's got an appointment and, once everybody else leaves, it's less hectic."

Amanda gave a knowing smile. "Life in the corporate world," she said as she opened her briefcase and took out her calendar.

Kelly watched the beautiful woman studying the book in front of her, turning the pages with slender fingers tipped with perfectly sculpted nails. The long dark lashes looked to be her own, and Kelly felt a surge of jealousy.

"Would this evening be too short notice? I'm meeting friends for dinner in Santa Monica anyway, and that would save a trip later in the week. I just don't have anything scheduled for downtown in the near future."

Kelly nodded. "Okay, Buck said any day but Friday. What time can you be there?"

"Is six too late?"

"No, that'll be fine."

Kelly stood and Amanda came around the desk to see her out. Again the secretary saw the striking redhead through Buck Michaels's eyes and wondered whether it would be worth staying an extra hour after work to see the fireworks.

BUCK MICHAELS LOOKED OVER the half rim of his reading glasses at Kelly Wallace. "Tonight, huh? She doesn't let grass grow under her feet, does she?"

"She has a dinner engagement in Santa Monica and wanted to kill two birds with one stone."

"Oh, I thought maybe it was the thousand bucks."

"*Thousand?* You gave her a thousand?"

Buck smiled. "It's a long drive from Long Beach."

Kelly shook her head. "If I'd known, I'd have charged a commission."

"What do you mean, commission? You were gone so long I ought to make you stay late and catch up."

"Huh! I've already submitted the travel voucher to accounting!"

"Okay, Kell," he said, holding his hands up in surrender. "So tell me about Ms Parr. What's she like?"

"Oh, you know the social service type—white blouse, gray skirt and all that."

"Ugh! That bad, huh?"

Kelly had to bite the inside of her cheek. "No, Boss, she was very sweet...and grateful for the money. She told me to be sure and thank you. She seemed so thoughtful, she's even going to write you a little note."

"Oh, God. She sounds like my Aunt Grace. Was she old?"

Kelly had to turn to the window to cover a smile. "Not really. Those people that do that work are sort of...I don't know...ageless, I guess." She looked over her shoulder at Buck, who was preoccupied with a report on his desk. "Anything else, Boss?"

"What?" He looked up again over his glasses. "Oh, yeah. Would you call security and alert them to escort her up? The elevators will be on passkey by then."

"Sure thing." Kelly headed for the door, grinning. "Have a nice evening, Buck."

THE DOORS OF THE ELEVATOR slid open at the executive floor. The guard stepped out, holding the doors for Amanda. "Mr. Michaels's office is right through there, Miss," he said, pointing. "All the way to the end, in the corner."

She thanked the man and walked through the deserted suite. Amanda started feeling a little trepidation at the impending encounter. Meeting wealthy and influential people like Preston Michaels was hardly an unknown experience for her, but she always found the suppliant aspect of fund-raising the most unpleasant part of her job.

Having passed through the reception area and other anterooms, she came to a long line of glassed-in offices offering a spectacular view of the Los Angeles skyline. It was October and the sun had already set, leaving the sky pink above the bank of gray haze on the horizon. Although the overhead lights in the corridor compensated for the failing daylight, the individual offices she passed were comparatively dark and deserted. Only at the far end of the large suite did a warm glow of light emanate from an open doorway. Amanda assumed it was the private office of Preston Michaels.

The thick carpeting enabled her to approach in silence so that when she arrived at the doorway, the occupant was unaware of her presence. Seated behind a massive desk in the spacious room was a man in shirtsleeves bent over papers scattered in front of him. A desk lamp lit the otherwise darkened office, illuminating the surface of the desk, the white of the man's cotton shirt and a tanned face masked in concentration. Half-rimmed reading glasses rested at the midpoint of his nose.

Preston Michaels's image was most pleasing to Amanda. He struck her as surprisingly handsome though she had had no particular preconceived notion of him. She watched him without being seen, and the illusion of control that it gave her caused her to linger in fascination for a moment longer.

The man made little grimaces—perhaps in silent dialogue with the papers in front of him—and once pushed his reading glasses back up a bit from the end of his nose. She could see that the coal-black hair had clustered strands of silver at the temples, which together with the handsomely etched face told her he was probably in his late thirties.

Enjoying her candid observation with seeming security, Amanda was not prepared when Preston Michaels slowly looked up and stared directly at her.

CHAPTER TWO

INSTINCTIVELY, AMANDA'S HANDS moved to the opened door, and she tapped it with her knuckles. Preston Michaels pulled the glasses from his face and sat upright in his chair, smiling with seeming surprise and amusement.

"Yes?" he pronounced expectantly. "May I help you?"

With his blue eyes engaging hers and his finely sculpted face unmasked at the removal of his glasses, Preston Michaels presented such an attractive image that Amanda was momentarily struck speechless. "Oh...excuse me," she finally stammered.

He seemed both bemused and intrigued with what he saw. "Yes?" he asked again, waiting.

"Mr. Michaels, I'm Amanda Parr. The Amerasian Children's Foundation."

The bemusement faded from his face, only to be replaced with genuine surprise. His mouth even seemed to fall open as he slowly rose to his feet. "Miss Parr?" There was incredulity in his voice.

"Yes. You were expecting me, weren't you?"

"Oh, yes," he said, walking around his desk toward Amanda. "I was just, well, expecting someone a little different."

He was standing before her, taking her hand in both of his and looking down into her eyes. An easy smile spread across his face, and she felt trapped in his grasp. "Someone quite different," she heard him say.

Amanda felt besieged by the unexpectedly eager interest the man showed in her. It was flattering but a bit too presumptuous for her taste. "Different?" she asked, retracting her hand. "What do you mean?"

He laughed softly. "Do you want to know the truth? I was sure you'd be very much like my Aunt Grace."

"Your aunt?"

Smiling ironically, the man reached past her and flipped on the switch by the door, lighting the far corner of the room where three overstuffed couches formed a pleasant grouping in front of the expanse of glass. Gesturing for her to enter, he said, "My Aunt Grace is a lovely lady, really. You know the type—always writing thank-you notes—very considerate sort of person."

Preston Michaels was leading her toward the couches, his hand now firmly on her elbow. Amanda let herself be led, totally at a loss for words. It was unlike her.

Sliding around the coffee table, she dropped into the plush comfort of a leather couch. He was still standing, looking at her. He seemed almost delighted. "I suppose my impression was formed by what Kelly Wallace said about you. 'Sweet' is the word she used, I believe."

Amanda blushed. "Miss Wallace was very nice."

The *Tribune*'s editor and publisher sat on the edge of the couch opposite Amanda's. She felt his gaze on her even though she was looking around the room, avoiding his eyes.

"Look, I appreciate your coming up on such short notice," he said softly.

Amanda turned to him, suddenly cognizant of her purpose in being with this man. "I was happy to come,

Mr. Michaels. Your donation to the agency was most generous."

"Well, it's for a good cause. I'm happy to do it. But please, let's dispense with the 'mister' business. My friends call me Buck."

"Yes, I heard Miss Wallace refer to you as Buck this afternoon. I assumed it was some sort of nickname."

He grinned. "It was a name I picked up when I was playing football. Now only my mother still holds fast to Preston."

He seemed amiable, notwithstanding being rather self-possessed. His gentle, unassuming manner of speaking was disarming. But the almost proprietary way in which he looked at her and touched her induced concern.

Summoning her courage, Amanda returned his gaze, not entirely sure what they were talking about, uncertain whether it was her place to speak or whether she should wait and listen. Considerately, Buck Michaels resolved her dilemma.

"May I offer you a drink, Amanda? I've got a little bar over in the bookcase."

"Oh, no, thank you, Mr. . . . er . . . Buck. I don't think so. I—"

He was already making his way across the room. "Oh, come on, have a little sherry or something. I hate to drink alone."

"Perhaps some sherry, then."

After a few minutes rattling around in his hidden minibar, Buck returned with Amanda's sherry and a glass of Scotch on the rocks for himself. He placed her drink on the coffee table with a cocktail napkin, pulled a bowl of mixed nuts in front of her, then sat down next to her on the couch.

Amanda, feeling a little uneasy at his proximity, picked up her glass. Buck moved his toward hers as if to offer a toast. Their glasses touched lightly. "To my Aunt Grace," he said in a half whisper, "and to other pleasant surprises. May there be many more."

Buck's cologne, faintly lingering around him, touched Amanda concurrently with the soft resonance of his voice. The intimacy suggested by the sensations alarmed her. Somewhat flustered, she drank more of the sherry than she had intended.

He was watching her with rapt interest and Amanda felt the need to distract him. "Miss Wallace tells me you spent some time in Southeast Asia, Buck. Is that the basis of your interest in our agency?"

"Yes, in a way. I care about the people, but the plight of these racially mixed children concerns me in particular."

"Yes, we've seen some real tragedies. Fortunately, we've been able to help quite a few of them."

Buck took some nuts and popped them into his mouth. "I looked over your materials that Kelly brought back. I'm impressed."

"Thank you, but there's much more to be done, particularly in Vietnam." Amanda sipped her sherry again.

"Tell me, how long have you been with the foundation?"

"Three years."

"So you don't go back very far."

"No, not considering the agency's been around for more than fifteen years."

"Do you like the work?"

"Yes, very much." Amanda watched Buck take a long drink from his glass. He definitely had a charm about him. There was no doubt in her mind he was a ladies' man. "Kelly said you were considering further financial support of the foundation. Is there any particular information you require?"

"Not information, no." He seemed to weigh his thoughts before continuing. "Let me give you a little background on what has prompted this meeting, Amanda. Yesterday morning, I received a telex from a former associate in Bangkok, a man named Kupnol Sustri. He's a sort of unofficial private investigator who's been doing a job at my request."

Amanda waited as Buck took some more nuts.

"My associate suggested that you might be able to help me with my investigation."

"Me?"

"Apparently you're well-known by at least one orphanage director in Bangkok, and that seems to be where we've run into a stone wall."

"I don't understand. What would this have to do with me?"

Buck drank again, then leveled his blue eyes on Amanda in a way that seemed to penetrate her. "I'm trying to track down an Amerasian child, Amanda, a girl of about thirteen. My contact seems to think that she may have been brought to the States by your organization."

"I see."

"If indeed the trail has grown cold in Thailand, I was hoping that with your help, I might pick it up again here in the States."

Amanda suddenly saw the motive for Buck's donation and abundant charm. "Is that the reason for the thousand dollar donation, Mr. Michaels?"

The grin on his face dissolved. "It's still Buck, Amanda, even if the subject of money has come up." He drained his glass.

"I'm sorry," she said firmly, unwilling to back down. "But you must admit the question is reasonable."

"I'll admit that I didn't want to impose on you without . . . shall we say . . . cooperating myself. But to answer your question, I believe in your work and I'd like to help, regardless." Buck picked up Amanda's half-empty glass and went back to the bar.

"What is it, exactly, that you want of me?"

He looked over his shoulder at her. "I want you to help me find the girl."

"Mr. Michaels, we provide adoption services. We're not an agency that locates missing persons."

"I'm aware of that, Ms Parr."

Amanda watched him walk back with two fresh drinks. She had the distinct feeling that Buck Michaels intended to use her, and his charm and generosity had been carefully deployed for that purpose. As he sat down, he smiled as if to say, "I hope we understand each other." His arrogance annoyed her as much as his attractiveness intrigued her.

"I don't mean to seem ungrateful, Buck, but we have legal and ethical obligations not only to the children but to the adoptive parents as well. Disclosing such information from our files is neither easy nor an automatic thing to do."

"Then let me say if it helps, Amanda, that my objective is simply to locate the girl and verify her well-being. If she's safely here in the States, I don't have to worry about searching for her further in Thailand."

Amanda picked up her sherry and drank, telling herself that he had made a generous donation, and that she couldn't afford to be impolite or make an enemy. "Would it be indiscreet to ask the nature of your interest in the child?"

Buck's eyes bored into hers. He betrayed only the slightest hint of a smile. "Let's just say there are a number of people involved, and I'm not at liberty to be too specific at the moment. But when the time comes, you'll be told everything you need to know."

As she watched him, his expression reformed into a friendly guise. His eyes drifted down her body appreciatively, then met hers once again. Amanda tried to hide her annoyance with his lack of subtlety. "Well, if you provide me with the particulars, I may be able to confirm whether the agency handled the case."

"I'm afraid that's the problem. I have very little information, not even her name."

Amanda looked at his handsome face and experienced alternate waves of curiosity, attraction and antipathy. "I don't see how I could be of help, then."

"I'm in the process of getting together the basic facts. That is, I have Sustri looking into things for me. Perhaps you could give me a list of the data you'll need."

"It's not just a matter of data. Tracing a child can be very difficult. They sometimes come to us with sketchy background information or no information at all.... If you were able, however, to pinpoint the source orphanage and the date she was sent, we might be able to confirm the case."

Buck drew a long breath, apparently in frustration. "Almost sounds like you're sending me back to Bangkok."

"I'm sorry, but look..." Amanda hesitated, thinking of the large donation he had made. Feeling the need to make a gesture, she decided to placate him. "I'll be going to Bangkok myself at the end of next week, and I'll be visiting some of the orphanages. If you'd care to give me whatever details you have, perhaps I could make some inquiries on your behalf."

Buck's eyebrows rose in surprise. "That's very considerate, Amanda. I appreciate the offer." He paused. "In the meantime, I'll be communicating with Bangkok to see where things stand."

Buck fell into silent reflection, absentmindedly grabbing more nuts. Amanda sipped her sherry as she watched him. The request regarding the child came as an even greater surprise to her than did the man himself. She wondered what his interest in a thirteen-year-old Amerasian girl might be. Could the child be his? If he had spent time in Thailand, it was certainly possible. Thai women were among the most beautiful in the world, and Buck's involvement with one would come as no surprise.

He looked up from the nuts and saw Amanda watching him. "Sorry," he said apologetically, "I tend to get hungry this time of evening. I think I go through a ton of these things every month." He looked at his watch, then at her, scanning her body. "Hey, listen, why don't we go out and grab a bite to eat? We can compare notes on Bangkok."

"Thank you, Buck. I'd like to, but I have a dinner engagement already."

"Oh, that's right. Santa Monica. Kelly told me you wanted to kill two birds with one stone. I'd forgotten."

Amanda looked at her watch, too. "It is getting late. Perhaps I'd better be on my way. I'm sure you have plenty to do...." she said, her voice trailing off.

"Oh," he said with equanimity, "I could work twenty-four hours a day and never catch up. Of course, it probably doesn't make any difference. It's the nature of the beast."

Amanda rose as did Buck, and their hands touched. She sensed his physical awareness of her and pulled away, trying to maintain decorum. Amanda stepped around the table, but Buck had gone around the other way, moving intentionally into her space.

"Well, I'll walk you to the elevator," he said with a smile that she had to admit was compelling.

Buck took her arm, and as they made their way toward the elevator, she felt his touch more intensely than before. She wanted to be free of him but not quite enough to force the issue.

At the elevator, Buck pushed the button and stood there with her, his hands in his pockets, looking down at the carpet. "Listen, Amanda," he said, breaking the silence. "I'm having a little party at my place in Balboa this Saturday evening, and several of my philanthropic friends will be there. It might be an opportunity for you to line up a few more contributors."

The overture produced mixed feelings. The woman in her was instinctively cautious, while the professional weighed the opportunity he was presenting. She hesitated, not wanting to give him the impression that she could be manipulated. "That's awfully nice, Buck, but please, don't feel an obligation—"

"Nonsense, I'd like to see you again. Besides, we might be able to talk a little more about the girl."

Amanda paused, knowing she ought to accept.

"It's nothing fancy, just an informal gathering. And to be honest, I've already got a date, but I'd love to have you come. If you'd like, you could bring a friend."

The elevator arrived. "All right," she said, feeling the need to be decisive. "I'll come. Thank you for thinking of me."

Buck's mouth curled with self-satisfaction. "I'll have Kelly send you directions to my place and all the details," he said, grabbing the elevator door when it started to close.

"Thank you again for your generosity." Amanda extended her hand, which Buck gathered into both of his, drawing her closer to him. The persistent and firm way he held it seemed almost like an embrace, forcing Amanda to pull herself free.

With her heart pounding, she stepped quickly into the car, irritated by his presumption and angry with herself for not handling the situation better. As she looked up into his cerulean eyes and saw that he held the elevator door open, she realized the goodbye would be conducted at his pace and not hers.

Buck's smile hovered between amusement and triumph as he spoke. "Thanks for coming up to see me, Amanda."

She waited, feeling like a cornered animal, but managed to return his smile in acknowledgment. "Glad to do it."

Still he looked at her. He was clearly the most unsubtly charming man she had ever known.

"See you Saturday, then," he said and let the elevator doors slide closed between them.

Buck stared at the gray steel doors and listened to the car descending the shaft until he could hear nothing but the silence of the building. The lovely porcelain face of Amanda Parr was still before him as a twinge of self-doubt surfaced. She hadn't liked him. For Buck, the feeling was an unfamiliar one.

Wearily turning toward his office, he retraced the route they had just traversed together, thinking of the purity of her beauty and the hollow feeling her departure left in him. Buck was glad she had agreed to come to the party but wished it had been because of him and not the thousand dollars.

SATURDAY EVENING AMANDA DROVE down the Coast Highway to Newport Beach. She had flirted with the notion of inviting someone to go with her to Buck's party but abandoned the idea when the list of potential candidates failed to produce a suitable escort. Her most frequent date the past few months had been a rebellious young lawyer and would-be screenwriter named Steve Wilsey who mostly lived off his family's money. Amanda decided Steve had the pedigree for what she imagined a Buck Michaels crowd might be, but he lacked the maturity. In the end, she got into her Honda Accord and went to the party alone.

Thinking back, her meeting with Buck Michaels had been troubling. He had so flustered her that she had performed badly, which made her angry with herself and with him. Much as she hated to admit it, he had affected her. The explanation was plain enough. The man was incredibly attractive, and she had encountered him under evocative circumstances, alone in his office in the sky. She knew, though, his attraction was not the sort that meant anything.

She had no use for men who expected women to quiver when they flashed a smile, and she was sorry that his thousand dollar donation put her in a position where she had to accept his invitation. She'd had half a mind to turn him down anyway, but she hadn't, and that was probably wise. After all, Buck Michaels wasn't the first man to try to take advantage of her, and life being what it was, he probably wouldn't be the last.

Balboa Island, where Buck lived, was an exclusive enclave in Newport Bay. It was connected to the mainland by a short bridge across the encircling estuary that qualified it as a legitimate island. Newport Harbor was known as the yachting capital of the nation with more pleasure craft per square inch than just about anywhere else. The island itself was studded with million dollar homes; most were modern architectural wonders of glass and wood with hot tubs, saunas and, of course, private docks for sailboats or yachts.

Leaving the Coast Highway and driving over the bridge to the island, Amanda followed the directions sent to her by Kelly Wallace and soon found Buck's house. She parked her car and headed in the direction of the soft music and voices. The air was balmy, neither warm nor cool. Although it was fall, summer hadn't yet ended. The rains were still a month away.

Amanda stopped on the porch to take a last look at her reflection in the window. Her midcalf voile dress looked fresh and feminine, and the matching violet strappy sandals completed her outfit. Her only jewelry was a pair of gold hoop earrings and her tank watch.

She could hear the doorbell sound over the noise inside, but there was quite a wait before the wooden door finally swung open. Expecting Buck's face, Amanda was surprised to see an elegant blonde who looked as though she had walked right off the fashion pages. Her hair was combed up one side of her head and fell in a profusion of ringlets down the other side. Her shoulders were bare, but envelopes of fabric billowed around her body without completely concealing it. She looked chic but with the implied sexiness of a harem girl.

"Good evening," she said with a gracious smile and stepped back as if to beckon Amanda in.

"I'm Amanda Parr," she offered, entering.

The woman, who on closer inspection was younger than Amanda—probably in her early twenties, smiled warmly as she extended her hand. "Welcome, I'm Jillian."

Amanda took the hand, which was so slender it seemed almost bony and fragile. Looking into the carefully made-up eyes, Amanda could see fresh, youthful beauty through the glamorous exterior. She wondered at the way the woman had pronounced her own name, Jillian. Was it supposed to mean something to Amanda, as though she were saying "Jillian, as in Buck and Jillian"? The answer was not long in coming.

"I don't know where Buck is. He's around someplace, but why don't you make yourself at home. The caterers were late so I've been tied up in the kitchen trying to help organize." Jillian turned then, smiling on top of the smile that had never really left her face, and floated off to her duties. Amanda was surprised at the little twinge of jealousy she felt.

Turning, she looked into the remarkable house. It was so full of plants and greenery, her first impression was of entering a tropical rain forest. The center was dominated by a gigantic atrium two stories in height with a sloped ceiling of glass, now blackened in the night. Interior lights illuminated mature tropical trees and palms some twenty feet tall. The floor was sunk two or three feet below the surrounding rooms and was covered with polished stone. Several groups of people were standing about, the men in blazers or shirtsleeves, the women elegantly and expensively dressed.

Amanda slowly made her way through the atrium past a brightly plumed parrot in a large gold cage and into the living room on the far side. This room was also large, but the ceiling was low, and there were groupings of over-stuffed couches and chairs in warm colors that created a much more intimate feeling. There were people everywhere, talking and laughing, but other than a glance or smile in her direction, no one paid much attention to her.

She stood looking out the wall of glass at the deck and gardens that sloped down to the water and at the dock and sailboat that she had expected. All the sliding glass doors were open and half a dozen couples were out on the deck, drinks in hand, enjoying the air.

"Excuse me, Miss," a young Mexican girl in a white uniform said to her, "would you like a drink?"

"Yes, please. A glass of white wine."

"Chablis, Chenin Blanc, Chardonnay?" the girl asked.

"Chenin Blanc, please."

"I'll have a Scotch," said a voice, and an arm reached past Amanda to deposit an empty glass on the waitress's tray. "Excuse me." The man moved around in front of Amanda where he could see her. He smiled. "Hi."

She looked at the large, fiftyish man with soft gray curls—a rather flattering perm that complemented his masculine face—and realized she was on the verge of her first encounter of the evening. "Hello," she replied politely. His manner told Amanda he was on the prowl, probably between marriages.

"You aren't Jillian, are you?" he asked.

She couldn't help smiling. "No, I think she's in the kitchen."

"Oh, good," he replied. "I haven't met Buck's latest yet, and I didn't want to offend anyone."

"Offend?"

He laughed. "There's a little story to that. To be perfectly honest, I had too much to drink at one of Buck's parties and came on to Buck's date—not realizing who she was until it was too late. Fortunately, he and I are good friends.''

"I see."

He was still smiling. "I'm Alex Hamilton."

"Amanda Parr."

"Nice to meet you, Amanda."

Alex not too subtly looked Amanda up and down, then smiled again.

She glanced around, ironically hoping Buck might show up and rescue her. "It's a lovely house, isn't it?" she said.

"Yeah, it is. This your first time here?"

"Yes, I only recently met Buck."

"What do you do?"

"I'm in the social service field," she replied.

"Oh, really? I would have guessed you were a model, or did some kind of media work, show business or something."

The waitress returned with their drinks. Amanda was grateful. She wondered what excuse she could use to get away.

"Cheers," Alex said, and they drank.

Amanda was staring out at the darkness beyond the dock when she saw Buck Michaels suddenly step up onto the deck. In spite of their meeting at his office earlier in the week, she was not prepared for how attractive he looked to her. For several moments, she watched him talking to a couple, his handsome face expressive and full of pleasant amiability.

Buck wore a deep-blue polo shirt, white duck pants, topsiders and a gold watch. There was a clean, simple elegance about his appearance and manner that struck her. Amanda followed his movements with fascination, beginning to sense the danger signs in her feelings. *You know better than this,* she admonished herself, but she continued observing him anyway.

Alex Hamilton saw that something outside had captured her attention, and he turned to see what it was. "Oh, there's Buck."

"Yes, I haven't seen him yet this evening."

If the obvious attention she paid to Buck Michaels served to discourage Alex, Amanda didn't care. So much the better. They both watched as their host moved across the deck and came inside. He had not gone more than a few steps when he saw Amanda.

"Well, Amanda!" he exclaimed, walking toward her. "I'm glad you made it." Without the slightest hesitation, he leaned over and kissed her on the cheek, his hand gripping her upper arm firmly, his lips lingering an extra second or two. The cologne he wore had a delicious aroma, but she tried to ignore it.

She looked into his pale-blue eyes. "Hello, Buck."

"I see you've met Alex," he said, glancing at his friend. "He's one of the people I wanted you to meet." Then he turned to Alex. "Amanda runs this wonderful charitable organization that helps war orphans, Alex. I wanted her to come this evening because I thought she could meet some potential contributors. I chipped in a grand and thought you and some of the others might be interested."

Alex took a long drink, draining most of what was in his glass. "Yeah, I'd like to hear about it. Uh, let me run and fill this up and I'll be back." Without another word, he turned and was gone.

Amanda looked at Buck with a pained expression. "I think you might have come on too strong."

"Oh, I wasn't serious at all. Alex is *not* a potential donor. He's so tight he squeaks. Great guy, but there's not a generous bone in his body." He looked into Amanda's eyes and slid his hand up her bare arm. "I was getting rid of him."

It was all she could do to keep from trembling under his touch. "I hope I don't scare everybody away like that."

"No, don't worry. We'll pick our lambs carefully."

Amanda had to laugh at Buck's conspiratorial tone.

"Have you met anyone else?" he asked, looking around.

"Just Jillian."

Buck looked at her with a fleeting hint of uncertainty. "Oh, good."

"She's a lovely person and so beautiful."

He seemed to sense her manipulation and gave Amanda an ironic look. "Yes, she is, isn't she?"

"Funny thing," Amanda said, feeling suddenly courageous, "Alex thought I was Jillian when we first met."

"Oh? I guess Alex knows my taste in women."

Amanda knew she was venturing into territory where she didn't belong. His gaze was bold, triggering a daring impulse in her. "Do *you* find us similar?"

Buck responded with a wry grin. "Come on." He took Amanda firmly by the hand. "We've got to talk about my project before all these money wolves start clamoring around you to make donations." An instant later, they were out on the deck, then descending the steps into the garden. Buck ignored the few people scattered outside and walked briskly toward the dock with Amanda in tow.

Several men were talking at one end of the dock, but Buck headed straight for the sailboat. Up the gangplank

they marched, then around the deck to the other side of
the boat. There he released her hand and turned to face
her. "We can talk out here."

Amanda had followed along willingly because she
didn't want to make a scene, but she made no secret of
her annoyance now that they were alone. She glared up
at Buck Michaels in the moonlight. "Do you think dragging a woman off to your boat is a businesslike way to
behave?"

Genuine surprise filled his face. He hesitated before
responding. "Did I offend you, Amanda?"

His contrite tone made her regret she had said anything. "Not exactly offend..." His expression was
somewhere between concern and mirth. "Well, yes,
maybe 'offend' is the word I'd use."

He was actually grinning now. "I'm sorry."

Amanda flushed. It displeased her that he was so
damned good-looking. She wanted badly to get off this
personal track and onto the conversation his thousand
dollars entitled him to. "What is it you wanted to discuss?"

He eased closer to her. "Am I really that offensive,
Amanda?"

Her eyes flashed, but he paid no notice, slowly lifting
his hand and brushing her cheek with the back of his
fingers. She was sure that he was about to take her into
his arms, and in reflex, she turned away.

But his hand was immediately on her arm. He spun her
around so that she faced him squarely. Half hidden in the
shadows cast by the moonlight, Buck's eyes foretold a
hunger for her. His hands soon cupped her face, and his
fingertips slipped through the luxuriant curls at the nape
of her neck until they became entangled.

Though her face was filled with protest, he slowly lowered his head, and his mouth covered hers. Sweetly, his lips caressed her, taking her honey and savoring her flavors as though she were a succulent fruit. Amanda was momentarily stunned by the tender surprise of his kiss. When the reality of his transgression fully hit her, she pulled free and pushed him away.

"Why did you do that?" she managed.

Buck looked at her in silence, then sighed with exasperation. "I suppose because I wanted to." More silence. "Look, I'm sorry. I misread the situation."

Amanda scoffed. "Hopefully not due to anything *I* said or did."

"Look," he said abruptly, "I meant no offense, I just got carried away. Even though you might not see it that way, it's a compliment. But there's no point in going on about it."

Amanda tried not to let herself get riled, knowing she had the satisfaction of having made her point.

His voice grew calm. "I need to talk to you."

"All right. What is it?"

"I've spent the week trading telexes with Bangkok," Buck said as though nothing had happened, "and I've gotten nowhere. You know the pace at which they do things there. I've decided, though, that between my contacts there and you, I stand a good chance of finding the girl."

He paused, looking at her as a friend and ally though she had done nothing to warrant it. And as his charm washed over her, Amanda felt her sympathy for him growing.

"What I'd like to do," Buck said, "is to go with you to Bangkok next week and try to put the pieces together. I think if I'm on the spot, I can get it done."

Amanda was stunned. Only moments ago, she was worrying about Buck Michaels kissing her, and now he was proposing to travel halfway around the world with her. "Buck, I really don't think . . ."

She turned away from him, unable and unwilling to say more, but her mind screamed a thousand questions. Had he invited her here just because he wanted her cooperation, or had he some greater conquest in mind? Had Buck plotted seduction, or was he just unable to resist any ripe fruit he thought ready to be plucked? Could he really be arrogant enough to think his kiss would render her unable to deny him?

Before she could address the questions, Amanda heard a feminine voice calling from the other side of the boat. "Buck, are you out here?" They turned and Jillian Crane came around the cabin. "Oh!" she said, obviously surprised to see Amanda.

"Amanda and I were just talking about Thailand," Buck said as she approached.

Jillian's eyes went back and forth between them. The signs of female jealousy did not escape Amanda. She couldn't help but be amused at the irony of the situation.

"You met Amanda, didn't you, Jillian?"

The young woman gave Amanda a little smile as she sidled up to Buck, then slipped her arm around his waist. Buck looked a little uneasy but seemed to be making the best of it.

Jillian looked up at him and shivered. "It's chilly out here. Aren't you cold?"

"I am," Amanda said in a level tone. "I think I'll go inside." She gave Buck a brittle smile.

"Yeah, that's a good idea," he said. "Let's all go inside."

As Buck watched Amanda march off the boat with determined strides, he cursed his luck…and perhaps his foolishness. Jillian was watching him with uncertainty, but he knew he couldn't blame her—his honesty with Jillian was no guarantee she wouldn't feel possessive. Taking her by the arm, Buck steered her in Amanda's wake.

His eyes followed the willowy redhead on the path ahead of them. Her indifference was painful, and he wished he could talk to her, explain, apologize—somehow make things right between them. He knew that he had offended her, but the kiss had been spontaneous and not calculated though she would have no way of knowing that. But why was it so important to him that she understand that?

By the way she disappeared into the crowd of guests, it was obvious Amanda had no desire to speak with him again. After twenty minutes, he realized she was gone. Acutely feeling the sting of her rebuke, Buck knew he had no one to blame but himself. In the end, it only made him more determined than ever to see her again.

CHAPTER THREE

AMANDA PARR HAD BEEN pushing her suitcase incrementally toward the ticket counter with her foot as she gradually worked her way to the head of the line. When the plump little woman in front of her completed the check-in process and headed off, Amanda stepped forward and lifted her suitcase onto the scale. There was relief on her face as she handed the agent her documents.

"Ah, Miss Parr!" the man said after examining her ticket. "I've been waiting for you. I'm afraid there's a problem with your reservation."

She frowned. "What sort of problem?"

"Don't worry, we'll get you on the flight, but we may have to move you up to first class."

"Oh! That's not a problem."

"No, but unfortunately, we'll have to board you last so bear with us." He looked Amanda up and down, apparently taking pleasure in what he saw. She was wearing khaki pants and a matching jacket with a jade-green tailored cotton shirt. Under his intermittent scrutiny, Amanda touched the ivory beads at her neck. "The agent at the gate will give you instructions," he said as he tagged her bags. "Please check with him when you get out there."

"First class," Amanda enthused. "What a pleasant surprise."

The man smiled as he completed the paperwork and handed her a special boarding pass. "Have a nice flight, Miss Parr."

Half an hour later, Amanda watched the other passengers board the plane and felt a little anxious even though the agent insisted she would be on the flight. Finally, after several brief conversations on his telephone, the man sent Amanda down the jetway where a flight attendant, a lovely Chinese girl with a flower in her hair, greeted her.

"This way, please," the hostess said, taking Amanda's hand luggage.

She was led into the first-class cabin to an aisle seat. As the flight attendant stowed her bag in the overhead compartment, Amanda slipped off her jacket and glanced at the man in the window seat. His face was turned to the porthole, but the shape of his head and the dark, silver-flecked hair were familiar.

Buck Michaels turned and, on seeing her, smiled broadly. "Amanda! What a pleasant surprise!"

It only took her a moment to figure out what had happened. The man she'd been avoiding all week had outmaneuvered her! Amanda flushed at the realization. However, his endearing charm as he smiled up at her softened the blow, and she had to admit that she was secretly flattered. "Did it ever occur to you that I might not want to sit next to you?" she asked, dropping down beside him.

"Hell hath no fury like a man rebuffed," he pronounced evenly.

"I didn't rebuff you."

"You didn't return my phone calls all week."

"I didn't speak with you personally, that's true, but my secretary talked to Kelly. I was very busy. Besides, I knew why you were calling. I already told you I'd help, Buck, but I didn't want to travel with you."

"Yes, you gave me that impression." His smile was friendly. "It only made me take matters into my own hands."

Amanda looked at him soberly. "So I see. What did you have to do, buy stock in every airline flying to Bangkok?"

Buck laughed. "No, Kelly is a very clever young lady when it comes to unorthodox situations."

"Sounds like you're always putting her to the test."

"No, Amanda, I assure you this is my first attempt at air piracy."

She couldn't help smiling at the friendly blue eyes and handsome face. "Actually, it is more like a kidnapping."

The flight attendant arrived to take drink orders, offering a choice of champagne or tropical drinks. "Well," Buck said as the woman left, "at least I don't like to see my victims suffer."

Amanda's face grew serious. "I know you expect me to be appreciative, Buck, and in a way I am, but I have to tell you I don't like being manipulated like this. I feel resentful. You completely ignored my wishes."

"I suppose I did and I'm sorry about that, but you left me little choice. You see, I saw this trip to Bangkok as an excellent opportunity to take care of my project. I'm convinced your help will be essential. I want to track down that child, Amanda."

Again the mysterious business about the girl. Amanda had an uneasy feeling that she couldn't completely trust Buck. In a way, she felt he wanted to use her and even his abundant charm was cause for alarm. "I've already said I'd help, but I don't see why we have to travel together."

Buck shrugged, letting Amanda speculate on the answer to her own question.

"Well, I want you to know that I've got responsibilities and a number of things I have to accomplish on this trip. I'll help you, Buck, but there are limits to what I can do."

The flight crew began preparations for takeoff, and Buck covered Amanda's hand with his own. "You know what I like about you, Amanda? You can be beautiful and logical." He poked his tongue into his cheek, grinning.

She gave him a sideward glance before easing back in her seat, realizing there wasn't much she could do about his audacious act now.

After they were airborne and headed out over the Pacific, the champagne arrived, and Buck toasted her. *"Salut,"* he said with his most endearing smile.

She touched his glass and watched the corners of his eyes crinkle with delight. "Buck, if you're such a busy man, how is it you can fly off to Bangkok like this on a lark?"

He smiled at her question. "First of all, I've had a week to prepare for it. Second, I haven't done anything for me in years. Third, I've known for a long time that if an executive can't leave his shop out of fear that it will fall apart, he's not doing his job—I decided it's time I find out. Fourth, I figured at thirty thousand feet, it'd be a little harder for you to run away from me like you did at the party."

"I didn't run away from you," Amanda replied casually. She sipped her champagne.

"Look, if I offended you, I'm sorry. Consider it a by-product of my misguided, but good, intentions." He paused and his voice mellowed. "Can we be friends?"

Amanda noticed his cologne as he leaned closer and moved his glass toward hers. She let him touch her glass. "Sure," she replied, battling her physical awareness of him. "You realize, though, that friendship is a mutual proposition."

"Meaning?"

"I'm not a plaything."

Buck smiled appreciatively. "I'll keep that in mind, Amanda."

Between the champagne and their agreed-upon truce, Amanda relaxed and they soon fell into lighthearted banter. Eventually, the conversation turned to more serious subjects. They talked about their pasts, though not about Southeast Asia. Buck entertained her with stories about the newspaper business but maintained humility by gently poking fun at himself as well. He asked lots of questions of Amanda, seemed every bit as interested in her life experiences—which were modest beside his—and delighted in stories about her work as much as in telling her about his encounters with the president and other celebrities.

After a third glass of champagne, Buck's genial company had Amanda feeling at ease and happy. She was progressively aware of the physical man and knew the mood easily could have become seductive if they'd been in more conducive surroundings. But they weren't, and Amanda could luxuriate in comfortable companionability instead.

Flying west as they were, the aircraft chased the sun and the afternoon seemed to linger in a suspended state. Time between lunch and dinner was a continuum of intimate patter, bonhomie and laughter. Buck became a friend—the kind only the peculiar isolation of travel can produce.

He had just finished telling Amanda about the trauma of taking over the *Tribune* after the death of his father when he fell silent. "Tell me about your family, Amanda."

"Now there's only my mother," she replied sadly. "She lives in San Diego. We're close, but I don't see her as much as I'd like. But she has a full life and so do I. We're happy."

"Your father died?"

"Yes, he'd had heart trouble for years. He was a doctor and took good care of himself, but he really started failing after my brother was killed in Vietnam."

"I'm sorry, Amanda."

"It was awfully rough on Daddy. Chris was twelve years older than I and was a doctor, too, a Navy surgeon. He was killed during the Tet Offensive in Da Nang. My father was never the same. Mother held up better, but then she lost daddy, too. Now I'm all she's got."

"You must have been a kid when you lost your brother."

"I was still in grade school when Chris was killed and had just started college when we lost my father."

"I guess you didn't know your brother well then, with such an age difference."

"No, but he was a hero to me anyway. He used to write from Vietnam and tell me about his experiences with the children there. He had very nearly gone into pediatrics. He loved children."

"Was your brother the reason you chose to work with war orphans?"

"It was a big factor, yes. I guess I wanted to validate my brother's sacrifice. After my first trip to Thailand, I knew it was something I wanted to make a career of." There was a film of moisture in Amanda's eyes. "I still read Chris's letters sometimes. It was a difficult time for my family and for the country. For all of us.''

Buck had grown silent. He, too, had retreated into some nostalgic corner of his past. He had not yet talked with Amanda about his years in Southeast Asia nor about the mysterious Amerasian child he was seeking. Amanda wondered if that was where his mind was, whether he would keep the untold story in his heart or whether he would take her into his confidence.

She leaned back in her seat, feeling alone with her thoughts, but aware of Buck's brooding silence. Looking past him out the window, she saw pink-and-mauve tinged clouds drifting by. Back in Los Angeles, night had long since fallen, but far out over the Pacific, the plane was only now losing its race with the sun. The talk of her brother and father had added to the sadness of the dying day, and Amanda felt her mood slowly turning melancholy.

"Amanda," Buck said, rolling his head toward her, "if you're going to help me with my project, I'd better fill you in on the details. Perhaps you'll have some ideas on what we might do."

"Okay...."

Their eyes met, and he seemed to be asking himself if it was all right to confide in her. He sighed and began his story.

"The girl I'm looking for is the daughter of a woman named Dameree. I knew her when I lived in Bangkok fifteen years ago."

"Dameree? What a beautiful name."

"Yes, and she was a lovely woman."

"Was she Thai?"

"The name's Thai and she's a Thai national, but ethnically she's Chinese. I didn't know it, though, for a long time. She was ashamed of her Chinese origins."

"Why is that?" Amanda asked with surprise. "I thought the Chinese were proud."

"Dameree was an unusual case. She was orphaned when she was a baby, and her aunt sold her to a Thai family."

"Sold her!"

"Yes, but it's not as bad as it sounds. It's more like adoption. She became part of her new family and was accepted virtually as though she had been born into it. She considered it to be her family and was a devoted daughter. Actually, she was so dedicated to her adoptive family that she tried to sever all connection with her Chinese past, a certain resentment at being abandoned, I suppose."

"But she had a happy life?"

"I couldn't answer that, really. Happiness is not always easily translated between cultures. Her Thai family was respectable but essentially poverty-stricken. The father was ill, and the family lived on a small government pension of some sort. Dameree was the oldest child in the family so it fell on her to work and support the others. There's a tremendous sense of obligation to family in Thailand and most of the Orient as you probably know. Dameree worked to help support the family, then later to educate her brothers and sisters. She spent little on herself and took everything home."

"She sounds like a saint."

Buck laughed. "That's the irony, Amanda, she made her money working in the most disreputable profession."

"She was a prostitute?"

"No, but almost. She was a massage girl."

"A massage girl?"

"Yes, I met her in one of Bangkok's old-line bathhouses. In spite of what you might think, it was a legitimate place for many years, very much in the tradition of the Japanese bathhouses. They were very strict and traditional, no locks on the massage room doors, and if any of the girls provided services to customers beyond what was proper, they were booted out."

"That hardly sounds disreputable."

"Well, being a massage girl, even without hooking on the side, is considered servile work. It can be fairly lucrative once a girl builds up a regular clientele, but it's not something a woman brags about doing. Most of the masseuses, I understand, were up-country peasant girls, isolated in Bangkok from their families and not too concerned about the stigma. Dameree's family never knew that she was a massage girl. They thought she worked in a shop or something."

Amanda watched Buck, sensing the nostalgia he felt and wondering about his relationship with this massage girl named Dameree. The story obviously moved him.

"It was a difficult life," he continued. "Dameree worked twelve hours a day, from noon to midnight, six days a week. She made fifty cents for each massage, which took an hour, and sometimes she wouldn't have a client for hours on end. I became one of her first regulars. I started going in once or twice a week, and then more frequently when I was in town.

"You see, the bathhouses in Thailand were traditionally places of social gathering. A man's massage girl became his friend, his confidante, and Thais would drop by the bathhouse just to talk and have a cool drink with their favorite girl."

"But it never went beyond friendship?" Amanda asked skeptically.

"No, sometimes sex or romance entered the relationship. At Dameree's 'company,' as she called it, a girl might start going out with a customer, but in the early days before the buildup in Vietnam, they had to be discreet."

"But that changed?"

"Yes, with thousands of servicemen going to Bangkok on R and R, the demand for more than just a massage became great. After a while, the bathhouses almost become synonymous with brothels. Some of the places were always a little loose, but prostitution soon became virtually mandatory."

"What happened to Dameree?"

"When the policy at her place changed, she left. At first, she tried getting other kinds of work, but she lacked the experience necessary for a job that would pay the money she had been earning. She turned to friends and former customers for help, including me." A nostalgic look came over Buck's face. "It was sad, really. Dameree was a victim of society. She had been living on the fringe, but her values and morals kept her from doing the easy thing."

"You mean prostitution?"

"Yes, prostitution. Thousands of other girls in her situation succumbed."

"But she never did?"

"No, not really. Although I found out later that she had occasionally 'gone out' with men in her days as a massage girl."

Amanda wanted to ask Buck if Dameree had "gone out" with him, what their relationship had been exactly, but she didn't. She felt the need to be more circumspect.

"So if Dameree didn't become a prostitute, what did she do?"

"She came to me at a critical juncture in her life. Somehow, her family found out what she had been doing—apparently when the money stopped. She couldn't explain why having lost a job in one shop, she couldn't get one in another. The truth was there was no longer work for a legitimate massage girl. Anyway, she had to leave home, and I offered her my place. The war in Vietnam was at a critical stage, and we had lost our correspondent in Saigon. I was there more than I was in Thailand.

"Dameree became almost a housekeeper in that she took care of the place for me. For a while, I was only there three or four days every two weeks. Then when I settled down to a regular schedule and was home more, Dameree just stayed. Eventually, we shared the house. That lasted for the better part of a year."

Amanda chafed at Buck's circumspect account. What did he mean they "shared the house"? Were they lovers? "Then what happened?" she asked, trying to mask her growing curiosity.

"I was in Vietnam covering the U.S. withdrawal when I was involved in a helicopter crash up in I Corps. I was badly injured and was taken eventually to Cam Ranh Bay, then Tokyo. A few months passed before I was in good enough shape to even think about Bangkok. From the hospital in Tokyo, I dictated a letter to Dameree. I didn't get a response and wrote again. By then I had recuperated enough to be moved back to the States, and after I'd been home a while, I finally heard from her." Buck stopped talking though Amanda could see that his mind continued working.

"And?" she prompted anxiously.

"Dameree told me she was about to have a baby, and she realized that my accident and return to the States was an omen. She knew she couldn't count on me for the rest of her life, particularly now that she was to have a child. She said the time had come to part and that she and the baby would make their own life."

"What did you do?" Amanda asked, now thoroughly caught up in Buck's story.

"I wrote immediately saying that I would be coming back as soon as I had recovered. I was in physiotherapy by then and knew it'd be a number of months before I could go back. Dameree didn't respond to my letter. In fact, I never heard from her again."

"She just disappeared?"

"I had been keeping track of her indirectly even from the time I was in the hospital in Tokyo. There was the Thai who worked for me in Bangkok, Kupnol Sustri. I had him take care of my affairs, including looking after Dameree. My letters to her were routed through him and he confirmed that she was still in my house. He passed on the money I sent to enable Dameree to keep the house and live.

"She stayed until the baby was born, six months after I left Bangkok. Dameree had never responded to my letters, but Kupnol told me that the child was a girl and Amerasian. I sent a thousand dollars to her after the baby was born, hoping she would stay until I could get back, but she refused the money and returned it to me through Kupnol. Right after that, she disappeared. I had Kupnol search for her, but he wasn't able to find her."

"So that was the end of the story?"

"No. I returned to Bangkok about ten months after the accident. I had suffered a severe spinal injury, and the bones in my right arm and both legs had been badly crushed. They were able to put me back together almost as good as new, but it took quite a while, including plastic surgery for several years afterward.

"Anyway, when I finally got back to Bangkok, Dameree's trail had grown cold. I spent six weeks looking for her, spread enough money around to uncover anyone, but to no avail. I decided finally that if she was alive and still in Thailand, she knew I was looking for her and was hiding. She didn't want to be found."

"But why?"

"I don't know."

"So you gave up?"

"I didn't know what else to do. I went back to Los Angeles, took a job on the editorial staff of the paper and, within a few years, I got married and settled down."

"You forgot about Dameree until the articles last summer piqued your interest again?"

"Well, a lot of time passed. I had my life, my career. Eventually, Bangkok faded into the past. I decided I'd made a good effort to find Dameree and that either she couldn't or wouldn't see me again. What the articles did was focus my attention on the child instead of Dameree. I had always thought of them as a unit. It occurred to me that they may have separated. Having an Amerasian child, I came to realize, was not without its problems for a woman over there.

"That's what prompted me to go to Bangkok last summer. I wanted to try looking for the child under the assumption that Dameree might have covered her own trail but not necessarily the girl's. It's a different approach, and it might pay off yet. I've had Sustri working on it and, well, at least he put me on to you. So some good has come of it." Buck smiled and took Amanda in with one long, languorous look.

Amanda's awareness of Buck Michaels the man was suddenly rekindled by that single look. The unexpected gesture coming at the end of his long story pleased her, but she couldn't help thinking of it as a diversion.

"If nothing else comes of the exercise, it will have been worthwhile," he said, staring at her in much the same way he had before he'd kissed her on the boat.

Amanda decided the best antidote to this new twist in the conversation was to ignore him and remain business-like. "I'm beginning to understand the urgency of finding the girl. I admit your story has caught my imagination. I suppose that was your intent."

"I'm not sure what you mean," Buck said, "but I figure if we're going to be working together on this, you have to know the history."

"Yes, you're right," she replied. "I'm glad you told me about Dameree."

Buck seemed to accept her response and tilted his seat back, sighing deeply. They had talked for hours, and Amanda sensed that his story about the Thai woman had taken a little out of him emotionally, and he, like she, needed quiet—some time alone with his thoughts.

Night had fallen though the last traces of daylight seemed to cling interminably to the western horizon. Amanda closed her eyes, knowing that at home she would be in bed by now, but her body gave no indication of an intent to sleep.

The long and pleasant hours of conversation she had shared with Buck Michaels drifted through her mind. She had genuinely enjoyed his company, but her thoughts kept turning to the mysterious woman, Dameree. Buck had told her much, but he had left out the most intriguing point of all—whether he and the woman had been lovers and whether the child was his.

Amanda couldn't imagine how it could not be his child considering the tremendous interest, even obsession, he had in finding the girl. But then, there could be much more to the story than he had told. Nevertheless, it seemed that if Buck knew that the child was another man's, he would have said so.

Feeling curiously uneasy, Amanda rolled her head and looked at her companion. He was reclining beside her, his eyes closed, his expression composed and serene. She studied the nicely formed contours of his face, the straight, well-shaped nose, the slightly stubborn curve of his lower lip, the masculine lines of his chin and jaw. Even in relaxation, there was the faintest self-satisfied curl at the corner of his mouth as though he were aware that she was admiring him.

Just at that moment, Buck opened his eyes and caught her looking at him. "What were you thinking just then?" he asked.

"To be honest, I was wondering about you—what makes you tick. That sort of thing."

"Any conclusions?"

"Not really. Well, maybe some questions..."

"Like what?"

Amanda looked at him, pondering her response. "Why, after all these years, have you suddenly begun a search?"

"I don't know if it's so sudden. There was that series of articles at the paper that got me thinking and my trip to Asia a while back but—"

"That's all recent, Buck. Surely you had the same, or an even greater sense of urgency at the beginning."

"Yes, you're probably right," Buck reflected. "But now I suppose I'm at a stage in my life where I have to know—before it's too late, before the child's gone for good." He looked at Amanda thoughtfully. "Even though I tried to find them twelve years ago and spent a lot of time and money in the process, I was able to rationalize my failure. I guess I'm not willing to do that anymore."

"Is she yours, Buck? Is the child yours?"

His smile was a little sad. "The irony is, I don't know. Dameree never told me and didn't answer when I wrote and asked. The uncertainty of that bothers me as much as the fate of the child."

Amanda touched Buck's arm. "I'm beginning to understand."

He nodded.

"Is it painful?"

"I would say more frustrating than anything."

"But she obviously has become very important to you."

"Yes, I guess she has."

"Do you have other children?"

"No. God, no. Carolyn had no interest in children. She was a totally selfish woman. It's a good thing we didn't, too."

"Why? Because of the divorce?"

"Yeah. The poor things would have been just more 'possessions' to fight over."

Amanda thought for a moment. "How long have you been divorced?"

"About six years."

"Do you miss being married?"

"Miss being married?" He was surprised at the question. "No. Why do you ask?"

"I don't know, it sounds to me like you're looking for some permanence in your life. Maybe the family you never had."

Buck leaned back, staring straight ahead. "Maybe." Then he turned his head toward Amanda and shrugged.

They exchanged tentative smiles, and Buck fell silent, letting his eyes close.

Amanda watched him for a moment longer before leaning back and closing her own eyes. The animosity she had felt because of his arrogance and brashness seemed to fade in the face of the tenderness she had just seen. There was apparently another side to Buck Michaels— one that moved her.

He now seemed less pernicious and off-putting than he had at first, perhaps because she had come to terms with him. But Amanda had no illusions. It was flattering that she could turn his head, but she also understood how little it meant. The key to dealing with him, she knew, would be keeping Buck in perspective and—as required—keeping him at bay.

For some reason, his kiss on the boat came to mind, the sweetly delicate way his lips had touched hers. Although she had not permitted herself to enjoy it at the time, the man did have a way about him. But his charm wasn't accidental—he was obviously well practiced and clearly not her type.

A soft moan, the sound of incipient sleep, emitted from Buck's throat, and Amanda knew he would soon be lost to his dreams. The lights had been lowered, and the pervading mood in the cabin was languorous. She felt a gradual state of relaxation overcoming her and knew it would not be long until she, too, was asleep.

Minutes later, Amanda was vaguely aware of a flight attendant putting a blanket over her and of Buck stirring beside her as he helped cover them both. She was giving herself up to the warmth and comfort she felt in her half sleep and only half resisted when Buck Michaels gathered her toward him until her head fell deliciously and comfortably on his shoulder.

If it was a dream, it was a dream she would let herself enjoy, safely protected from him by her slumber.

CHAPTER FOUR

By THE TIME their limousine reached the outskirts of Bangkok, it was after eleven at night, but Amanda's body, like the city of Los Angeles, considered it to be eight in the morning. As they whisked along the highway, pedestrians in white shirts, cyclists and slow-moving *samlors* loomed up, then disappeared behind them in the dark.

Though the limousine was air-conditioned, Amanda had a sense of the heavy tropical air from the few minutes they had spent outside at the airport. The sights beyond the windows of the vehicle also evoked the familiar smells and sounds of Thailand. She greeted the city through bleary eyes burning with fatigue.

"I hope you don't mind," Buck said, reaching over to cover Amanda's hand, "but I've made arrangements for you at my hotel."

She looked at him in surprise. "Buck, I've got reservations at the Manohra on Suriwong Road. I always stay there. I've prepaid two days."

"We can call and cancel in the morning."

"What if I prefer the Manohra?"

"Don't you like the Oriental?"

"You're missing the point, Buck. I have my own plans, and I intend to follow through with them."

"But why, Amanda? It'd be much more convenient if we stayed at the same hotel. It wasn't easy getting these accommodations at the last minute, and besides, it's already arranged.''

She bristled. ''Well, then, you can unarrange it.''

''I'm doing no such thing.''

''I won't be bullied,'' she snapped.

''Look, Amanda, I'm simply trying to be accommodating . . . and practical,'' he replied calmly.

''Don't you see that you've totally disregarded my wishes—*again*?''

''Not maliciously.''

''That doesn't matter. The point is, you can't just run around doing as you please, walking all over people, stuffing things down their throats.''

Irritation crossed his face. ''A lot of people wouldn't mind being 'walked over' like this, having the Oriental Hotel in Bangkok 'stuffed down their throats.' ''

''Well, I'm not a lot of people, and I do mind!''

They rode for a while in angry silence. Given Amanda's state of mind and her fatigue, even friendly Bangkok looked strangely hostile now. Soon they pulled up in front of the Oriental. Buck climbed out, leaving the door open for Amanda to follow, but she stayed in the limousine, wondering how much resistance he would offer to her continuing on to the Manohra.

There was a lot of commotion outside the limousine. Amanda had never seen so many people in white uniforms rushing to accommodate just one man. Buck was speaking to the driver who had gotten out and walked around to the curb. Several bills passed between them, and the driver returned to the limousine. Now the doorman was listening to Buck. Their backs were to her, but by the nodding and smiling, she assumed more *baht* were being dispensed.

A few minutes later, Buck returned to the limousine, leaned over and looked in at Amanda. "Aren't you coming?"

"No, Buck. I told you, I'm staying at the Manohra."

He had his hands on his knees and was peering through the window. She would have found the situation funny if she weren't so angry.

"I don't think this limo goes there, Amanda."

She could see that Buck's money was already at work. "I'll take a cab, then."

"I have a feeling these taxis are all reserved," he said in an apologetic tone.

"I'll bet they are!" Amanda slid out of the limousine, and Buck took her hand, helping her. She looked around. "Where's my suitcase?"

"I think it's inside."

Her hands were on her hips, her eyes flashing.

"Please, Amanda, at least come in and we'll talk about it over a cup of tea."

She glanced around, but all the staff had discreetly withdrawn save the doorman, and he was averting his eyes. Taking her hand luggage, she marched into the hotel without giving Buck so much as a look.

Amanda sank into a cushioned wicker chair in the lobby, and Buck sat down across from her. He leaned forward, speaking in a low tone. "Look, Amanda, I'm sorry. My intentions were good, and…frankly, I thought you'd be pleased."

She felt her anger softening at his contrition. "If you'd handled it differently, I might have been."

"I didn't and I apologize." His smile was imploring. "Give me another chance. Let's start over. Okay?"

Amanda sighed, feeling both exhaustion and hunger.

"I can see now why you're upset. I didn't really consider that it would be a problem for you, but I understand that it is. Maybe I'm a little spoiled, Amanda. I'm used to having my way. It's a natural reaction for me to 'arrange' things, but I promise I'll try to do better." There was a slight grin on his face. "I can't guarantee anything, of course, but I'll try."

Buck's sincerity was disarming and, in any case, she didn't have the will to fight him anymore. Because her look told him so, he got up and walked over to the registration desk.

Amanda felt uneasy and disoriented as she looked around the elegant lobby. It was actually a very generous thing for Buck to do, but she wished he had done it with a little more consideration and without the arrogant presumption that seemed to have become a pattern in their relationship.

A hostess in a floor-length skirt and silk blouse walked through the otherwise deserted lobby, smiled a gracious welcome to Amanda and proceeded with her business. Overhead, great bell-like chandeliers adorned with delicately carved golden ornaments hung amid the tops of towering tropical plants. The room was elegant and comfortable at the same time.

After finishing at the registration desk, Buck returned to Amanda and sat down again. "Look, in keeping with my promise to be considerate of your wishes, I'd better explain a little more about the arrangements I've made."

Amanda eyed him warily.

"You see," he continued, "they have these wonderful suites here in the oldest part of the hotel called the Authors' Residence."

"Suites?"

"Before you get alarmed, let me assure you there are separate bedrooms. It's just that there are only four of these suites—they're normally booked up months in advance. I love them, and there was a last-minute cancellation when Kelly was making reservations."

Amanda started to speak, but Buck, anticipating her question, quickly added, "I've already checked, there aren't any other rooms available. The place is overbooked."

Amanda rolled her eyes.

"At least come and look."

A moment later, a bellhop in a starched white uniform led them through the lobby and into a remarkable older structure, the central room of which was several stories high with clumps of bamboo clustered in each corner, reaching junglelike to the skylight.

As they walked across the white marble floors, Buck turned to Amanda. "This is the Authors' Residence. The four suites are named for authors that have been guests. Conrad, Coward, Maugham and Michener, I believe. We'll be in the Noel Coward Suite."

They were ushered through giant double doors into a magnificent salon of emerald and peacock hues. The walls above the wainscoting were covered in an intricate pattern of Thai silk, and the furniture consisted mostly of ornately carved Oriental pieces. There was an antique breakfront. Gilded chairs and fresh flowers were everywhere.

When the attendant completed turning on lights and seeing to other details, he handed Buck the keys and withdrew.

"Our bags should be here in a few minutes so if you'd like to freshen up, I'll treat you to some of the best curry this side of India."

Amanda looked around the room in disbelief. She could see why Buck was so adamant that she stay at the Oriental. But why this arrangement? She wondered whether the intimacy of a private suite was for a purpose beyond simple convenience. If so, she had no intention of accommodating him.

Buck seemed to sense Amanda's reluctance. "Come on," he said, taking her hand. "Let's choose rooms." He led her to one of the tall doors, pulled it open and they both peered in. "Ah. Here we have a jade-green four-poster, glass curio case, blue plush velvet chairs." He closed the door, and they walked across the salon. He opened the twin doors. "Bigger room," he said, looking in. "More blue than the other. Two beds instead of one."

Buck was still squeezing her fingers as Amanda craned her neck in the doorway. "I think I'll take the smaller room."

"Yes, excellent choice. The color suits you, Amanda." He looked at her. "May I call the Manohra now?"

She smiled, unable to resist his effort at diplomacy.

Buck's look became heavy with awareness of her. His grip tightened so as to ensure she wouldn't escape, but there was a knock at the door, and she pulled free. It was the porter. Their luggage had arrived. Amanda quickly retreated to the jade room that she sensed would be her place of refuge.

Several minutes later, they were walking across the river terrace outside the hotel in the heavy tropical air. Though it was nearly midnight, a few people were sitting here and there, watching the lights of passing boats on the dark waters of the Chao Phraya River. In the daytime, the river was a congested highway, a principal artery of commerce, but at night, it was yin and lunar, a repository of the city's soul.

"The Verandah Restaurant closes at midnight," Buck said, "so we'll have to hurry. I hope they'll wait for us if we're late. I called from the room to say we were coming."

They arrived with several minutes to spare. A handsome young Thai, the maître d', was awaiting them at the door with the ubiquitous friendly smile that marked the staff at the Oriental. "Mr. Michaels, good evening." He bowed politely to Amanda. "Good evening, madame."

After the maître d' had locked the door behind them, they were shown to a table overlooking the river. A few late diners were just finishing their meals.

"I hope you don't mind," Buck said, "but I ordered for us on the phone. I didn't want to miss the curry."

She could see he had grown gun-shy after their spat in the limousine, and she knew it was up to her to defuse the situation. Amanda smiled. "No, not at all. Curry would be nice. I must admit, though, it seems like we should be having breakfast, not dinner."

"I find the best way to handle the time change is to jump right into the schedule wherever you are. That's one reason I usually don't sleep much on the plane going west."

The white-jacketed waiter arrived with two chilled Singha beers and a smile. He bowed to the couple and left. Before long, the curries were served, and Amanda ate with greater appetite than she expected. The beers were replenished, and though they were virtually alone in the restaurant, they sat relaxed, watching the river and each other.

"I suppose we should try to get some sleep," Buck said after staring out over the water for a time. "Then maybe you'll be ready for breakfast."

They walked back across the river terrace, and to Amanda's surprise, Buck took her hand in his. It was an affectionate gesture, and she decided he intended it as his way of ensuring the peace. The closeness and easy familiarity they had shared on the plane swept over her again. In spite of everything, she had to admit she liked it.

In permitting him to hold her hand, Amanda knew she was acknowledging their friendship. She glanced at him, sensing an awareness, a seductive appeal . . . and she felt herself responding to the masculine aura of the man.

Buck kept close by the water's edge as they walked, and she could tell he was enjoying holding her hand and the pleasant freshness of the night air. But she worried a bit about what might happen when they returned to their rooms and the time came to say good-night. Ironically, she felt safer alone with him outside in the dark tropical night.

At the far end of the quay, they came to two long sleek craft gleaming white in the darkness. The ships were moored quiescently, in a sort of regal slumber. The impression was confirmed when Buck pointed out the names—the *Orchid Queen* and the *Oriental Queen*.

"These are the hotel cruise ships," he said. "We'll have to take a trip or two up the river before we go."

"They're beautiful, aren't they?"

As they strolled alongside the craft, a man who had been sitting on the deck in the shadows stood up, smiled the Thai smile of greeting and bowed.

"It's the night watchman," Buck said to Amanda. Then he addressed the man. *"Sawat dee khrap!"* Good evening.

The other grinned broadly and bowed again, more deeply than before. Buck called out several more phrases in Thai with some difficulty, but the night watchman's only response was to bow and offer more deferential smiles. "He doesn't want to understand," Buck said.

"What were you saying to him?"

"I was trying to ask if we could come aboard." Then Buck spoke to the man again, this time adding some emphatic sign language.

The guard responded with a few words and some sign language of his own. First he pointed to his wrist where one would wear a watch, though the man wore none. Then he put his face against his folded hands as a sign of sleep.

Buck chuckled. "He's saying I should be home in bed."

Amanda laughed softly. "Tell him it's only ten o'clock in the morning in California."

"What do you suppose the word for 'jet lag' is in Thai?"

"You're the expert, Buck."

"Well, I have a feeling if we're to get on this ship tonight it'll have to be a forced boarding."

"You *are* an experienced pirate as I recall," Amanda chided.

Buck tweaked her nose, and they walked on in the moonlight, waving farewell to the night watchman. At the end of the quay, there was an elevated grassy area under a large tree that hung over the edge of the river like a great canopy. They made their way up to it and stopped to stand under the shadowy boughs.

Amanda felt Buck's arm slip around her waist, and he gently pulled her against his side. Suddenly, she became cognizant of how completely alone they were. She had been aware of the man, even thinking about his touch, but now that she was experiencing it, she felt strangely unprepared.

She stiffened slightly, recalling Buck's insistence that she stay at the Oriental with him. He had arranged for them to share a suite. Was this an indication of what he had in mind?

Buck held her easily, almost more with affection than any sexual intent. He was watching the river flowing under the shadows of the tree, seemingly as aware of the setting as of her. Amanda felt the cool air lying heavy and moist around them, and she gradually relaxed, settling her body against his, welcoming the warmth of him. Buck tightened his embrace, and when she turned to him, his eyes foretold more than just friendly affection. She looked up into his face with fright and expectation, not realizing until this moment how thoroughly she desired his kiss. A second later, his mouth dropped down and covered hers, taking it hungrily, urgently.

Amanda tasted his kisses hesitantly for a moment, but then her desire welled, and the dammed-up craving for him burst. She kissed Buck Michaels with a shameless, feminine hunger all her own, offering him the recesses of her moist and eager mouth. She was relieved that he had finally taken her, grateful for his tight embrace, momentarily pleased with the pleasure and pain of being crushed in his arms.

Once the initial relief abated, Amanda felt her body stirring in a more primal fashion. Release gave way to arousal, and the tongue that sensuously probed her mouth began suggesting more profound invasions. Buck's hand slipped from Amanda's waist to the curve of her buttocks, and when his pelvis pressed tightly against hers, she knew his masculine desire had progressed beyond what she was prepared to accept. In the brief instant that followed, she found herself afraid of his desire. With an emphatic effort, she pulled her mouth free, then wedged her hands between them.

Despite the faintness of the filtered moonlight, when Buck finally ceased his advances, Amanda could see surprise and annoyance on his face.

"What's the matter, Amanda?"

"I shouldn't have let you kiss me."

"Why not?" he snapped.

"It's not what I wanted."

He scoffed. "You could have fooled me."

Amanda pulled free of him, feeling resentful, confused. She knew she couldn't blame Buck, but she felt anger nonetheless. "It's not your fault," she rejoined. "It's mine. The point is, I don't want you to get the wrong impression. In agreeing to stay here at the Oriental with you, I wasn't agreeing to anything else."

"Like what?"

Amanda turned away in anger, not liking the provocation.

"Like what?" he insisted.

She faced him squarely. "Like Jillian."

"What's that supposed to mean?"

"I'm not on this trip to be your playmate."

"I don't consider you a playmate, Amanda. Nor is Jillian, for that matter. Our relationship is casual now though at one time we were closer."

"She didn't act very *casual* at the party."

"I'm aware of her feelings, and I've been as honest with her as I can be."

Amanda suddenly felt embarrassed by the conversation and wished now that she had reacted a little more dispassionately. She turned from him again.

His heavy breathing behind her in the darkness told her of his frustration. She waited, expecting him to say something further, but he didn't. Amanda wondered whether she had been too heavy-handed or unkind. "Perhaps we'd better go in," she said softly.

"Yes," he said in a low tone. *"Mai pen rai."*

Amanda knew the expression. It was virtually the Thai national philosophy—it doesn't matter, what will be, will be. They returned to their rooms in a heavy silence.

THE NEXT MORNING, Amanda came out of her room and found Buck seated across the salon at a table by the window, bathed in sunlight. For a moment, she stood looking at him and he at her.

Ever since awakening, she had worried about their clash the previous night, but seeing him, she could only think of the stunning image he presented. His blue-gray epaulet shirt was open at the neck, exposing the dark matted hair of his chest. The sleeves were rolled up to the middle of his biceps and fastened there with a buttoned tab.

As she walked across the room toward him, feeling uncertain, his blue eyes followed her, taking in her short-sleeved, pink silk blouse, the straight, trim lines of her pleated white linen pants. She felt her slender neck flush under his gaze. It was exposed for the first time because she had pulled her hair up in a sleek chignon, a precaution against the tropical heat.

Finally, his eyes settled on her face as he rose to greet her. There was an unfathomable politeness to his smile, but he betrayed none of the rancor they both had felt the night before.

"I didn't know what you'd want to eat," he said, gesturing toward the table overflowing with an assortment of fruits, pastries and several covered chafing dishes, "so I ordered a little of everything."

Amanda smiled self-consciously, embarrassed because of what had happened between them. Her cheeks felt feverish as he came around the table to seat her. "I'm afraid I'm not much of a breakfast eater," she managed.

"There's plenty here to tempt you," he said, lifting the cover of each of the chafing dishes in turn. "Eggs Benedict, caviar blintzes..." Buck returned to his chair and looked at Amanda cheerfully. "Coffee?"

She decided he had chosen to forget their clash and was relieved. "Yes, please."

Buck took the coffeepot and poured a cup for Amanda. "What are your plans today?"

"I have to go to the Ministry of Foreign Affairs and initiate paperwork for the next group of children that will be sent back to the States."

"Knowing the Thai bureaucracy, that could take all day."

Amanda sipped her coffee, eyeing him, detecting no resentment whatsoever. "I'm afraid it could."

"I'm going to meet with my man Sustri," Buck said. "It might take me all day to get a straight story out of him."

"What do you mean?"

"Before I pursue this project any further, I've got to be sure that he's been playing it straight with me."

"You don't trust him?"

"To a degree, yes. But only to a degree." Buck took a plate and put a little of everything on it before handing it to Amanda. He didn't see the amusement on her face at his paternal gesture. "Why don't we plan on dinner together?" he said matter-of-factly.

"Buck, you needn't try to take care of my every need."

A wry grin passed over his face, and Amanda realized that he had censored a suggestive comment. She colored again, hoping he wouldn't notice.

"Reservations have been made for the Normandie Grill tonight at eight," he said, "assuming, of course, that's all right with you. If you've never eaten there, you shouldn't miss it. Best French cuisine in Southeast Asia, and some of the best I've had anywhere."

Amanda held back several comments before acknowledging his attempt at deference toward her. "I appreciate your consideration, Buck. I have no other plans. Eight tonight would be very nice, thank you."

He grinned. "Great." Then wetting the tip of his finger, he stroked the air as if to say, "One for me."

They both laughed.

"I'm looking forward to it," she said with a smile.

THE TAXI WEDGED ITS WAY through the narrow back streets, jockeying for position with dozens of *samlors*, the ubiquitous three-wheeled, covered motorcycles that congested the streets of Bangkok. Seated beside Buck, Amanda watched the hectic street life out the window of the old Datsun while Buck contented himself with watching her. She was a lovely creature. Each encounter they had had brought a new dimension to his desire for her. He couldn't think of Amanda without engendering the same curious mixture of want and frustration that had plagued him since the party.

Her beauty was obvious, but the creamy purity of her skin he found particularly attractive. In the oppressive tropical heat, a woman couldn't wear makeup, and Amanda's complexion was clear and silky. He longed to touch her cheek and kiss the long ivory arch of her neck. But that must wait; he had already ventured too far, too fast. The incident the previous night had proved that she had a mind of her own and couldn't be taken for granted. He liked that.

Studying Amanda, Buck felt the wrenching ache of desire for her, but he felt something else as well. In the short time he had known her, she had rattled emotions hidden deep within him, emotions that he had carefully guarded over the years, emotions that made a man crave more of a woman than her body. Ever since Carolyn, he had repressed the urge to know women that way, but Amanda Parr had educed it from him as easily and naturally as if she were his first love.

Just then, she turned toward Buck, her emerald eyes looking at him with brief curiosity before peering out again at the commotion in the street. He didn't mind that she saw him admiring her; it was honest admiration, and experience had taught him that it was the most eloquent statement a man could make to a woman. He sensed that underneath the facade of propriety, she was beginning to like his attentions. At first, she had seemed to enjoy their kiss by the river. She might again.

When their eyes met, Amanda smiled a little self-consciously, then spoke. "It's kind of you to drop me off, Buck, but I hope you trust me enough to find my own way home. The way you pamper me, I *will* become incompetent."

He laughed, but her pretty smile and perfect white teeth distracted him from his intended response. He let his fingers touch the cool smooth flesh at the back of her neck, but the caress was apparently too aggressive for her because distress flickered over her face, and she turned away.

Buck smiled to himself, knowing that eventually her reluctance would be overcome. It all boiled down to a matter of feminine pride. It always did. But he had his pride as well, everyone did, and it would be foolish and selfish of him not to respect hers.

The sad part, he thought, was that she was dismissing what he felt as a simple desire for conquest. Women had a way of interpreting every masculine overture as implicit aggression when the real objective was mutuality.

Maybe it was just as well, Buck decided. Without the mating dance, there would be no opportunity for shared evaluation. After all, his worst relationships had been those where all the mutuality a woman cared about was in his bed or in his wallet. Amanda Parr intrigued him because those things didn't appear to interest her particularly and, despite their clashes, she seemed to like him.

Buck took great pleasure in looking at Amanda, and he realized that, in a way, he had become a victim of her beauty. It had already propelled him to move more quickly and rashly than was prudent. Even now, the nakedness of her ear made him hunger to kiss it, to tease the delicate shell with his tongue, to whisper his honest desire.

Amanda was staring straight ahead, and her long lashes flickered nervously, telling him she was uncomfortable with his scrutiny. Buck decided the best way to handle the problem was to address it.

"Do you always feel uncomfortable when a man admires you, Amanda?"

She turned to him abruptly, her face registering both accusation and surprise. She started to respond, then paused, apparently uncertain of his intent and thus the appropriate response. Then, "You enjoy teasing women, don't you, Buck?"

"Teasing? Why is an honest observation teasing?"

"I get the feeling you enjoy making people feel uncomfortable."

"Not everyone," he said wryly. "Very few people, in fact. Actually I don't 'enjoy' it at all. It's my way of knowing about people and becoming known. I only do it with people I care about."

Her smile mocked him. "Am I supposed to be flattered?"

"Well, certainly not offended. I think you misunderstand me."

She turned away for a moment. "What is it you want me to understand?"

"Nothing very mysterious, Amanda. I do admire you. I find you a lovely woman. And I feel something is . . . I don't know . . . standing between us."

Her green eyes leveled on him fearlessly. "Could it be that we're not interested in the same things, Buck?"

He was a little shocked at the audacity of her remark. "Perhaps, but I don't think you know what I want."

A knowing smile crossed the woman's face, and Buck felt a spark of anger, but before he could express it, Amanda softened her response. "It's not my place to judge you or attribute motives, Buck. All I can do is make my position plain. You've been more than generous. I've accepted your hospitality—with some reluctance, I admit—but I regard our relationship as professional. I don't want to give you the wrong impression."

He couldn't repress his pique. "If you think there are any strings attached to what I've done for the Amerasian Children's Foundation, Amanda, you're wrong. I expect nothing from you but civility. But, by the same token, I'm not afraid to say what I think." He paused, feeling the anger draining out of him. "I happen to find you a very attractive woman. And, more importantly, I like you." A crooked grin crossed his face. "Or at least most things about you."

Amanda laughed a little self-consciously, not sure what to say.

Buck continued. "I won't elaborate on the last point, however, discretion being the better part of valor."

He could see she was at a loss so he reached over and took her hand, pulling it to his lips. "I'm not a man easily deterred, but I respect you enough to meet you on your own terms."

The taxi arrived at the government offices. They exchanged uncertain messages with their eyes, and Amanda opened the door, seeming anxious to escape. "Thanks for the ride, Buck. I'll see you at dinner tonight."

He watched her walk with purposeful but feminine strides to the main entry of the building, his eyes taking in her lithe, pleasantly curving figure. There was a mixture of confidence and vulnerability even in the way she walked, or so it seemed to Buck.

"Koi tee nee." Wait here, he said to the driver when he heard the man put the vehicle in gear. And Buck kept his eyes on Amanda until she disappeared inside the building. He knew he wanted her more than ever now.

CHAPTER FIVE

KUPNOL SUSTRI'S THAI SMILE had faded slightly under
Buck's questioning, but any hint of resentment or anger
remained well hidden. His cheeks were fat though the
man himself was not, thus giving a cherubic appearance
to an otherwise middle-aged demeanor.

"Believe me, Brother," Sustri said imploringly, "I am
in position where it is not easy for me. I gave my word to
the gentleman. He wants no more to talk of this matter."

"He may not, Kupnol, but I do. I'm not asking you to
break a trust. I just want you to tell him that the information he gave about the child is not enough. I can't find
her with it. I must have more."

"Buck, you are my friend. Everything I do to help you.
This you must know. I believe the gentleman cannot tell
more. Maybe there is not more."

"Only the smallest detail could make the difference.
The date Dameree took her to the orphanage, that may
be enough. And a name—perhaps he knows the name
Dameree used when she turned over the child."

"No, the name he does not know. I am sure of this. I
myself knew a name would be important so I asked it to
him several times. He would only say he does not know
it."

Buck and Kupnol looked up as the door to the street
opened, and the young Chinese girl who was Sustri's

secretary and assistant entered. She was carrying a tray with two bottles of Coke, two glasses and a small plate with several little cakes. She smiled and placed the refreshments on the corner of Sustri's battered desk, then withdrew to the adjoining alcove where she worked.

Kupnol Sustri reached over, poured some of the soft drink into each glass and placed one in front of Buck. He sat back with a sigh. His face was beseeching as he looked at his old boss.

"Look, Kupnol, we're never going to get anywhere unless I talk with Dameree's brother myself. I want you to go tell him I want a meeting."

"I cannot be sure I can find him."

Buck gave Sustri a skeptical look. "Come on, Kupnol, don't be so negative. He's probably right here in the Sampeng. He is a Chinese businessman, isn't he?"

"I believe he has a business, but I don't know it," the Thai replied a bit somberly.

"Well, I leave it to your inventive skills."

"But, even should I find him, it is not certain he will agree to meet with you."

"Tell him this, then. I have no interest in seeing Dameree. My only interest is in the child. If he meets with me and is cooperative, there'll be a five hundred dollar donation to his favorite charity, even if it is the education of his children."

Sustri smiled appreciatively at Buck's insight and subtlety.

"Oh, and if you succeed, there'll be a hundred for *your* favorite charity, Kupnol."

The Thai bowed his head politely. "Mr. Chin does not speak too good English, Buck. If he wished, I will offer to go with him as translator."

"That would be excellent," Buck replied. He drank from the glass in front of him. "I will go back to the hotel—I'm at the Oriental—and wait to hear from you. I'd like to get this done as soon as possible, Kupnol. If it's convenient for Mr. Chin, bring him to the hotel this afternoon or evening. Tell him time is of the essence. I must begin my search immediately."

A few minutes later, Buck stepped out into the small alley just off Yawaraj Road at the edge of the Sampeng District, the Chinese quarter. Although Sustri was not Chinese, many of his foreign clients had business in the Sampeng, and he found it convenient to be located nearby. Besides, the rents were affordable, and Sustri's business remained modest.

In spite of the heat, Buck decided to walk along the Yawaraj to the New Road, then south a mile or so to the Oriental Hotel. He felt the need to absorb a little of Bangkok's atmosphere, which at one time had been such a familiar part of his life. Buck glanced into the glittery shops and Chinese hotels. The jewelry stores seemed rather tranquil compared to nighttime when they would be ablaze with neon and electric lights and jammed with customers.

Taking an unharried stroll gave Buck a sense of freedom, for having a few idle hours had become uncommon in his life. Until he met with Dameree's brother, there was not a lot more he could do so there was no point in rushing back to the hotel.

Walking amid the bustle of the commercial street, Buck's thoughts turned to Amanda, and he surprised himself with the wave of emotion that passed through him. The image of her engendered a delicious craving, suggesting more affection than sexual desire, and made him want to touch her. The irresistible allure of the woman continued to plague him.

Buck searched his mind for something he might do to get their relationship free of the morass in which it had become bogged down. He stopped and looked in the window of a jewelry shop and contemplated the possibility of a gift but dismissed the idea. He was afraid that she would misinterpret the gesture as she had already shown she was prone to do.

Walking on, Buck considered a change of tactic toward Amanda, a temporary retreat, a show of indifference, a bit of reverse psychology. However, he disliked the fundamental dishonesty of the notion. If he felt affection and desire, then affection and desire would be what he'd show. After all, if she were going to reject him, it may as well be him and not an affectation that she was rejecting.

Passing near the gates to the temple at the Wat Pratuma Konga, Buck saw a street vendor selling a snack he used to enjoy in the old days. It had been years since he had even thought of the treat, and he wondered if his digestive tract had become too flabby for both the vendor's standards of sanitation and the concoction's mélange of flavors. Throwing caution to the winds, Buck bought a leaf wrap containing small cooked shrimp, shredded shallots, lime, ginger, hot chilies, coconut and ground peanuts. The mixture was topped with a kind of coconut syrup.

After making his purchase, Buck went up the street reimmersed in the Bangkok of old, taken back as only smells and tastes could do. Munching happily, he wondered whether Amanda would enjoy the leaf wrap as much as he did. He made a mental note to buy her one the first chance he had.

THE TAXI STOPPED at the main door of the Oriental, and Amanda Parr struggled out with her arms full of packages. The doorman, a boyish-looking young man wearing white gloves and the traditional Thai *jongkraben* pants, jumped to assist her.

Amanda paid the driver and entered the hotel, her packages handed from the doorman to a bellhop who followed her as a discreet and obedient servant. At the front desk, she was given a message that Buck was out on the terrace if she would care to join him for a drink. Pleased at the thought of him waiting for her, she proceeded to their suite with the bellhop in tow.

In her room, Amanda opened the largest package, which contained an emerald-green Chinese silk cheongsam, a formfitting dress with a mandarin collar, cap sleeves and a slit up one side of the skirt. On an impulse, she had decided to buy the traditional Oriental dress for dinner that night. In another package was a pair of delicate silk heels dyed to match the dress perfectly. She had also bought some silks and other fabrics, but the dress in particular excited her.

Amanda took the cheongsam to the mirror and held it in front of her, trying to see herself through Buck's eyes, trying to anticipate his reaction. She was gratified by the image in the mirror even though she was unsure why it was so important to her that she please him. In her heart, she knew that there was more than her feminine vanity at work.

After hanging the dress in a large rosewood armoire, Amanda freshened herself in the bath, added a touch of lip gloss, then went to find Buck Michaels.

Standing on the upper level of the terrace, she surveyed the small sea of tables until she spotted him in the far corner at the water's edge. He was facing upriver, a newspaper open before him, one foot propped casually on the chair across from him, a pair of sunglasses protecting his eyes against the glare of the late afternoon sun.

Amanda slowly approached at an angle from which he wouldn't see her without turning his head. His bush jacket was draped over the back of the chair, and his tanned arms and face gave him a rugged, handsome appearance that belied his sophistication. Buck Michaels was all male—physically, mentally, psychologically. Amanda had never known a man who seemed to represent such thorough counterpoint to every aspect of her femininity. At that instant, she understood why he was so compelling, yet frightening at the same time. No part of her was safe from him.

When her movement caught Buck's eye, he looked up and smiled broadly. The delight on his face was that of a fox having seen a hapless rabbit come charging into his den.

"Well," he said, rising to his feet, "I'm glad to see our Amanda safely home." He pulled out a chair for her. "How was your day?"

She slid into the chair and felt Buck's hands briefly touch her shoulders before he returned to his seat. The smile she gave him said she was happy to be back. "Fine," she replied. "I finished at the ministry more quickly than I expected so I pampered myself and did a little shopping."

"Oh? Find anything interesting?"

"I bought a dress for dinner tonight."

"Just for me?"

It was arrogant, but it pleased her. "Just for you."

Buck looked at her as though he wasn't quite sure to what he should attribute his good fortune. "Then we'll

have a special bottle of champagne this evening to celebrate.''

"What are we celebrating?'' Amanda asked coyly.

"Your consideration and my good fortune.''

She was pleased and let it show.

"Would you like a drink or would you care to go inside? They do a nice tea here in the afternoons.''

"Actually, the cab ride was warm. I wouldn't mind
going in.''

"Then tea it'll be.''

Several minutes later, they entered the leafy courtyard
of the Authors' Residence. The warm glow of sunlight
coming through the translucent roof gave the solarium a
bright yet mellow feeling. Buck sat down next to Amanda
on a white cane couch in the shadow of a scalloped par-
asol. His arm slipped behind her and, before she knew it,
he had kissed her softly on the cheek. He lingered near
her then so that his musky scent enveloped her, render-
ing her helpless to resist the masculine invasion.

Amanda was enjoying the soft warmth of his breath on
her neck when a figure approached, and they both looked
up into the smiling face of a young waitress.

"Tea, sir?'' the girl asked sweetly.

"Shall I tell her I've already found the honey?'' Buck
whispered into Amanda's ear.

"Don't you dare!'' she said aloud.

Amanda and the waitress exchanged embarrassed
looks, but Buck was still hovering close to her, evidently
enjoying her scent and the fun of teasing her. Amanda
shrugged to the girl. *"Farang.''* Foreigner, she said with
mock dismay, and the girl tittered, clasping her hand to
her mouth.

Buck, too, couldn't help laughing, and he turned to the
waitress and took a menu from her.

Amanda had won.

After Buck had ordered, four Thai men dressed identically in white linen suits and black ties walked through the room, then mounted a narrow staircase leading to a small balcony. The couple watched the men taking their seats by the railing.

"It's the string quartet," Buck said. "They play every afternoon during tea."

At first, the soft dissonance of violins and cello being tuned drifted down, then a moment later, the sweet euphony of a classical composition filled the room. For a time, Buck and Amanda listened, enjoying European culture as interpreted in a luxuriant Oriental setting. The piece was played with spirit though somewhat understatedly, enabling the listener to treat it as background music. Other guests were chatting quietly, and Buck and Amanda soon turned their attentions to each other, content with the ambience elicited by the musicians.

"So," Amanda said after the waitress had served their tea, "how did your meeting go?"

"It's hard to say. I'm not entirely certain, but I believe Kupnol's being straight with me. It's just that I've got a hunch that he knows more than he's telling."

"You mean he might know where the child is?"

"Oh, I doubt that. He's managed to track down Dameree's brother—that's where he got the information the girl may have been sent to the States through an orphanage."

"So what's the problem?"

"The information seems to me to be unnaturally vague, too sketchy. I think the brother knows more, or at least that's my hope. I've asked Kupnol to arrange a meeting."

Amanda sipped her tea and thought about the child and her mother, who had been Buck's lover in this very city fifteen years earlier. Had he loved her? Was he really searching for the girl foremost, or was it Dameree who still moved him?

"I was hoping I might hear from Kupnol this afternoon," Buck was saying, "but he may have had trouble convincing Dameree's brother to meet with me."

Amanda watched as he took a small canapé from the plate in front of him and popped it into his mouth distractedly. She remembered that evening at his office when Buck had eaten the nuts so compulsively. They had been talking about this mysterious child then as well. Buck seemed to notice Amanda's awareness of him, and he let his soft blue eyes rest on hers, causing her to wonder whether it was she or the child who moved him more.

"What will you do if the brother won't meet with you?" she asked.

"Since I've come all this way, I'll press it as far as I can. I'll go find *him*, if necessary. If that doesn't work, I'll see what I can dig up in the orphanages. That's where I was hoping for your help, Amanda."

"Tomorrow I begin my visits. You're welcome to come along if you wish."

"Thanks, I'd like to."

Buck and Amanda listened to the chamber music and finished their tea in relative silence, she feeling frustration for him and about him. It was difficult knowing just how to take the man—he seemed to be several men at the same time: patron, client, nemesis, friend, adversary, lover. In so many respects, he overwhelmed her.

"You know," Buck said after a while, "I finished with Kupnol fairly early and walked back to the hotel. I wanted to soak up a little of Bangkok and bring back some memories." By the timbre of his voice, Amanda sensed the emotion he felt. "I stopped and bought a leaf wrap from a market vendor like I used to do in the old days.... While I walked down the street eating it, the thought that went through my mind was how much I wanted to introduce you to that and other things about Bangkok that I cherish."

The sentiment and the gentle affection on Buck's face touched Amanda, and she reached over and covered his hand with hers. "That's very sweet," she whispered. "I just want you to know I'm glad we were able to make this trip together."

Under Amanda's grateful eyes, Buck popped another canapé into his mouth and winked at her. "I'm anxious to see this special dress of yours. Shall we go back to the suite and get cleaned up? I'm ready for a shower and maybe a catnap before dinner."

"I could use a nice long soak in the tub myself."

SAFELY IN HER ROOM with the door locked, Amanda removed her blouse, pants and bra, then in her bikini panties, padded over to the dresser where she took a black silk Oriental dressing gown from the drawer. Wrapping the cool, smooth fabric of the gown around her, she went to the bed and lay down. The thin film of silk provided just enough protection against the cooled air of the hotel. Running her finger absentmindedly over her skin at the open vee of her wrap, Amanda remembered the feel of Buck's fingers on the back of her neck that morning in the taxi.

At the time, the gesture had disconcerted her, but in retrospect, it was pleasantly and sensuously evocative. Each touch, each encounter with Buck Michaels was less troubling and more compelling than the one before.

Amanda had been moved by the languid look in his eyes and the sentimentality in his voice when he had told her how he wanted to share his Bangkok experiences with her. What had seemed at first to be nothing more than simple masculine desire for her appeared to be growing into genuine affection.

She worried that these promising signs were more her own wishful thinking than anything actually transpiring in Buck's mind, but the gravitational pull toward him was undeniable, and Amanda wondered if it would carry her to his bed. Staring at the ornate designs on the canopy above her, she contemplated whether Buck Michaels could possibly be developing serious feelings for her and whether she could risk admitting her feelings for him—even to herself.

Amanda thought of the implications of such feelings. The prospect of a serious relationship played at the edge of her mind, and she even pictured herself in his house on Balboa Island—not as Amanda Parr but as Amanda Michaels. His name sent a tiny surge of trepidation through her, but Amanda knew that Buck hadn't caused the sensation. It was her own fear.

She remembered his delight when she told him that she had bought a new dress for him. The boldness of the confession surprised even Amanda. Still, she was glad she had told him. It would add to the excitement, and she grew anxious for Buck to see her. Feeling a touch of euphoria, she got up from the carved Oriental four-poster and happily went off to indulge herself with a bath.

BUCK MICHAELS CAME OUT into the empty sitting room and cast an anxious eye toward Amanda's door. Although he had tried, he hadn't slept, and he was able to

drag out showering and dressing only so long. Buck knew
that he was too impatient for his own good.

Picturing Amanda sitting in a tub of frothy bubbles,
luxuriating herself, made him envy her, envy the womanly capacity for pampering. The image conjured up
Amanda's feminine aura, and Buck desired her as fully
and deeply as if she were there in his arms.

The woman was definitely having a strange effect on
him. Not only did he want her, he wanted to know her,
and just as importantly, he wanted her to know him. It
was a curious notion and one that hadn't struck him before, not even with his wife. Buck wondered if that might
not explain the clumsy way he had handled Amanda,
whether she had befuddled him because of the dormant
emotions that she had evoked.

He remembered her words, "Do you miss marriage?"
He hadn't—not until *she* had come into his life. But in
the short time he had known her, Amanda had made the
question a legitimate one again. Still, the notion was disconcerting. Buck had created so many defenses against
marriage and commitment that he didn't know if he
could ever seriously think in those terms again.

He walked to the window and peered out, his hands
thrust impatiently into his pockets. He had tossed the
jacket of his off-white linen suit over the back of the set-
tee when he came in, and he stood now in shirtsleeves, his
tailored pima cotton shirt the same pale blue as his eyes,
his necktie a midnight blue, the same dark tone as his
hair.

Again, Buck looked toward Amanda's door. He had
an urge to march over and knock. But what could he do?
Demand that she come out? His frustration seemed lu-
dicrous, but it was real. The woman was bedeviling him,
making him happy and angry at the same time.

He forced himself to calm down. Walking slowly around the room, he stopped to look at a first edition Noel Coward lying conspicuously on an end table. Buck opened the volume but quickly decided he wasn't in the mood for urbanity and wit. He closed the book, looked at Amanda's door and wondered if she could have fallen asleep.

Before Buck had managed to further exacerbate his frustration, the phone rang. He turned and looked at the offending instrument, unsure for the moment what there was in the outside world that could interest him. He picked up the receiver. It was Kupnol Sustri.

"Brother," he said in a breathless voice, "only now I have found Mr. Chin. We talked for a long time, and he agrees finally to come to you at the Oriental Hotel. He says to tell you, Buck, he has no useful information more than what I already told you."

"I expected as much, Kupnol. Tell Mr. Chin I appreciate his courtesy, and if he would indulge me, I'd like to meet him. Where are you?"

"I am nearby. Mr. Chin will come if you wish it."

Buck glanced at Amanda's mute and impeding door. "How soon could you be here?"

"Five minutes."

He looked at his watch. He knew that meant fifteen. "Okay, Kupnol, come right over. I'm in the Authors' Residence."

Buck had no sooner hung up than the heavy door to Amanda's bedchamber swung open and she appeared. Buck was stunned. So great was her beauty that he nearly gasped.

Her smile was radiant. The silk jacquard fabric of the cheongsam molded to her body, revealing its slender yet voluptuous lines. Buck took in the length of her several

times, and she spun around for him, delighted with his
delight. "Do you like it?"

"You look beautiful, Amanda. Absolutely gorgeous!"

She turned around again, wanting to bask once more
in his admiration. Buck walked toward her, his eyes on
the proud arch of her neck exposed under the loose roll
of her copper hair. Nearing her, he could see the sparkle
of diamond stud earrings and a large black Oriental comb
nestled in the luxuriant upsweep of her hair.

"Magnificent," he said, standing before her. "When
have East and West ever mingled so wonderfully?"

"I'm glad you like it," Amanda said happily.

Buck put his hands on her narrow waist, feeling more
her naked flesh under the silk than the fabric itself. She
looked up at him through her lashes, shyly. Jade, emerald, viridian, turquoise were everywhere—her eyes, the
garment, the room. Only the cream of her skin and the
rubescent copper of her hair were in counterpoise.

Amanda smiled slightly and he noticed her lips, the
glossy peach softness inviting his kiss. Buck smiled, too,
then lowered his head and kissed her, wrapping his arms
around her body, which arched against him as her arms
slipped about his neck.

She seemed so delicate then, a fragile reed of femininity, her heart beating against his shirt, a pulsing that reminded him of a baby bird in his hands. "Oh, God," he
whispered into Amanda's ear, "did I ever make a mis-
take."

She pulled back. "What?"

Buck kissed the questioning lower lip. "I just invited
Sustri and Mr. Chin, Dameree's brother, over here for a
meeting."

"Well, you wanted to meet with them. It's important, isn't it?"

"Not as important as this," he mumbled against her neck as he breathed in her fragrant scent. "Not as important as this."

There was a knock at the door, and Buck turned toward it with disbelieving eyes. He looked at his watch. "Damn, is nothing sacred anymore?"

"What is it?"

"You can't even count on Thai tardiness. I bet this is the first time Kupnol's been on time in his life."

Amanda laughed. "I'll wait in my room."

"No," Buck said, taking her hand. "Stay with me."

"Let me just straighten up a bit." She turned toward her door, but Buck wouldn't let go of her hand. "I'll be back in a few minutes." Another knock at the door. "Go ahead with your meeting, Buck."

He let her go reluctantly, watching her until she disappeared into her room. Then he opened the door.

"Good evening, good evening," Kupnol Sustri said. He stood smiling in the hallway.

Buck glanced at the short man in a white nylon shirt with Sustri. "Good evening, gentlemen. Please come in."

Kupnol introduced his companion, Chin, to Buck, and they went to the sitting area.

"May I offer you some refreshment?" Buck asked.

Kupnol exchanged a few words with Chin. "Mr. Chin would like whiskey if you have it. For me, just a soft drink or water, please, Buck."

He went to the cabinet against one wall, took out three glasses, poured Scotch in two of them and bottled water in the third. "Ice?" he called over his shoulder.

"Yes, please," Kupnol replied.

Buck took some cubes from the ice bucket, put a few
in each glass and returned to the men with the drinks on
a small tray. When they were seated, Buck turned to
Chin. "I appreciate you coming to see me, Mr. Chin. I
am honored by your consideration."

The other smiled and nodded politely.

"I'm sure Kupnol has filled you in on my purpose in
wanting to meet," Buck explained to the man, "but I
would like to make several points clear." He stopped,
waiting for Kupnol to translate, but Chin spoke.

"Please...sir," he said in halting English.
"My...I...understand, but it is the...speaking who is
not good."

Buck smiled. "I'll speak slowly, then." He glanced at
Sustri, then looked again at Chin. "Your sister Dameree
was my good friend. I tried to help her, and when she had
the child, I was concerned for it as well."

Chin nodded.

"I have not seen Dameree for many years. I do not
know if she is alive or dead. If she is alive, I know that
she has her own life, and I respect that. My purpose is not
to see her or to interfere. I have my life, too."

Chin turned to Kupnol and several brief words passed
between them. The Chinese turned to Buck. "I—I understand," he said in a small, halting voice.

"I am no longer the young man I was when I knew
Dameree," Buck continued. "I was always concerned for
the child's welfare but—"

Chin stopped Buck with his hand while Kupnol translated a word. He nodded again.

"But as a man of some years, now it has become important that I know that the girl is okay. I am worried
that the child might have separated from Dameree or...be
wanting."

Chin spoke to Sustri for a moment. Then the Thai turned to Buck. "Mr. Chin says that he understands your purpose. He says that his family was not rich, and many years ago, his sister had difficulty and took the girl to an orphanage that sends Thai babies to America. Mr. Chin says his sister believed that because the baby was also American, her home was also there. America is rich country, and this girl would have this instead of a poor life in our country."

Buck studied the Chinese. "Are you sure the child was sent to the States?"

"I know only . . . this child of my sister was sended to the . . ."

"Orphanage," Kupnol said, completing Chin's sentence.

"Which orphanage?" Buck asked.

"The orphanage at the Christian Mission," Chin replied.

Kupnol nodded.

"In Bangkok?"

"Yes," Kupnol said.

"Do you know when, Mr. Chin? What year was the child taken to the orphanage?"

"Perhaps ten ago. I do not know it. I am sorry."

Buck was feeling very frustrated. Although it was difficult to tell, Chin seemed sincere enough, but Buck was reluctant to ask the obvious question—could Chin find out? Obviously, Dameree would know the answers to his questions, but if he were to suggest this and if Dameree were alive and still avoiding him, the suggestion could be misconstrued as interest in Dameree herself. Buck knew he had to find a way to put Chin at ease—and perhaps Dameree as well.

Just then, the door to Amanda's room opened, and she came into the sitting room. The men turned as she entered, then rose to their feet in unison. From the corner of his eye, Buck saw Kupnol looking at him questioningly. An idea hit him.

"Amanda, darling," Buck said, extending a hand to her. "Come and meet my friends."

She walked with slow, elegant strides to the men, smiling.

"Darling," he said to her startled eyes, "I'd like you to meet Mr. Chin..."

Chin bowed with formal politeness.

"And this is Kupnol Sustri, my friend and former associate. Gentlemen," Buck addressed them, "may I present my wife, Amanda."

Buck's arm was around Amanda's waist, and he pulled her to him, kissing her quickly on the cheek to cover the shock that started spreading over her face. "Please," he whispered in her ear.

Then Buck turned with a ceremonious gesture to the men. "We were married recently," he said with a grin.

"*Very* recently," he heard Amanda say under her breath.

"Oh, Buck! A wife!" Kupnol exclaimed. He pressed his hands together in front of his face and made a deep *wai*, the traditional Thai sign of respect and greeting. "Mrs. Michaels, I am deeply honored."

Chin, too, was smiling broadly and bowing respectfully.

"Buck," Kupnol was saying, "I thought you were a divorced man, still alone."

"Not any longer," Buck replied. He felt Amanda squirm anxiously under his hand, and her beautiful mouth, though smiling still, showed strain. Buck had an impulse to kiss her. The game amused him, an effect he hadn't expected. He looked at his guests. "Please sit down, gentlemen." Then to Amanda, "Can I get you a drink, dear?"

"No, thank you, *dear*." The tone of her voice revealed enough for Buck, but not the others, to get her point. He was enjoying himself.

"So," he said to Chin, "you can see that, as a married man, my intentions in this matter are most honorable. My wife," he added, touching Amanda's hand, "is also anxious that the child be well cared for."

"I understand, Mr. Michaels," the Chinese replied.

"It would certainly be easier for me if you were able to provide a bit more information. But I understand that you are removed somewhat from the matter." Buck leaned forward. "Perhaps you would be kind enough to check with other members of your family. The date, the name used for the girl when she was taken to the orphanage, any such information would be most useful to me."

Chin was smiling slightly at Buck but betrayed no indication of his thoughts. Finally, he spoke. "Mr. Michaels, I will make inquiry, but I cannot...promise something."

"I understand." Buck watched as Chin drained the Scotch from his glass. "Should you be able to help me, Mr. Chin, then we can complete the arrangement I discussed with Mr. Sustri."

Chin nodded slightly before turning to Kupnol and speaking to him.

The men rose to their feet, and Kupnol said, "We have taken your time, Brother. We should leave you now."

Buck shook hands with each man. "Thank you for coming. I appreciate your time."

Sustri made a slight *wai* to Amanda as Chin bowed. The Thai grinned at her happily. "You are so beautiful, Mrs. Michaels. My friend Buck is very lucky."

"Thank you," she said and watched with polite restraint as Buck showed them out.

When he had closed the door, he turned his back to it and smiled across the room at Amanda. She was eyeing him with a mixture of anger and amusement. As he walked toward her, one hand went to her hip, and her attitude became a little defiant.

Buck ignored the hints of hostility and displeasure she was throwing out. He took her by the waist. "You know what, Mrs. Michaels? You're far and away the best wife I've ever had."

Amanda couldn't help it when her stern look crumbled into a smile. She fell against him, burying her face in his neck. "Preston Michaels, you're a devil."

Buck threw back his head and laughed, enjoying what he had done and the feel of Amanda Parr's slender arms around his waist.

CHAPTER SIX

SHE WATCHED HIM staring out at the lights of Bangkok spread before them like a blanket of stars in the moonlight. Buck Michaels had begun to fascinate her, and that made him dangerous, very dangerous. But the danger was sweet and inviting, the sort a woman could not easily ignore. Amanda was having trouble fighting her awareness of him, and it was beginning to worry her. What's worse, she liked him—more than was safe.

Buck's arm was casually on the back of his chair, his wineglass in his hand, his face serene and reflective as he looked out the window of the restaurant perched atop the hotel tower. She knew he was aware that she was watching him. It was just like that morning in the taxi, except she was now the observer and he the object of observation.

Buck turned to her, a pleasant, provocative smile on his lips. "Strange how a city can affect you, isn't it?"

Amanda could see he was keeping a careful distance between them—enough to titillate but not to disconcert her. "You like Bangkok, don't you, Buck?"

He sipped his wine. "A great deal, yes." He looked at the ruby liquid in his glass. "How about you?"

"Oh, yes, it's so exotic, so..."

"Romantic?"

She nodded.

Amanda could feel his restraint more strongly than if he had been blatant. "You enjoyed that little deception—telling those men that I was your wife—didn't you?"

He grinned at her. "Who wouldn't?"

"Well," she countered, "having a wife for a day is a man's fantasy, not a woman's."

"You didn't enjoy it then, I take it."

"It isn't a matter of enjoying it or not," she replied coyly. "I realized what you were doing. You wanted them to feel comfortable about your motives with regard to Dameree."

"True, but that didn't prevent *me* from enjoying the notion."

"You're entitled to your fantasies and I to mine."

"And I suppose it would be impolite of me to ask you about yours?"

"Buck, you've gotten surprisingly considerate. When I met you, you didn't seem to care one bit about my preferences."

"Must be the effect you have on me." He sipped his wine.

Amanda found the thought intriguing and the fact that he would voice it even more so.

"Well, this is your night, Amanda. What would you like to do?"

"It's your town. Maybe you should decide."

"A willing accomplice?"

"Within limits."

Buck grinned, letting his eyes drift down her cheongsam just as he had half a dozen times before. Amanda knew he was considering her "limits" within the context of his own desires, but his refusal to comment on it made the effect of the thought all the stronger.

"Are you up to some of the color that brings people to Bangkok from all over the world?"

"What sort of color?"

" 'Lurid' is probably as good a description as any."

"Sounds like you're suggesting a den of iniquity."

"That may be a little strong, but let's say it's the Bangkok that Japanese businessmen take special tours to see."

"I think I get the picture."

"If it doesn't appeal, that's fine, but I thought it's not the sort of thing you'd be out doing when you're alone in Bangkok. This way you can go with a modicum of propriety."

"In other words, it's a place that a wife might go with her husband?"

Buck laughed. "Maybe a new wife." He turned and signaled the waiter.

They were soon in a taxi making their way along New Petchburi Road where the street was teeming with the press of vehicles and humanity. The lights, noises and smells were evidence of the richly vibrant life that lay dormant in the heat of the day.

Amanda and Buck, like much of the rest of the population, were headed to the steamy district where business was the commerce of night. She felt excitement and the allure of the forbidden, and Buck Michaels was the spice that made the experience personally provocative.

Although his thigh pressed against hers in the close quarters of the cab's back seat, he remained discreetly remote, attentive but unaggressive. The result, which he doubtlessly intended, was that she felt drawn to him and the safety he represented.

The club he had selected was off a small but well-lit alley, guarded at the street by an old woman selling

flowers and at the entry by a doorman in a white uniform with large brass buttons. Inside and down a flight
of stairs was a cabaret-type room, crowded, smoky and
very dark, with an American-style bar running along one
wall. A small jazz ensemble was playing, and two dancers—a man and a woman—were on a tiny stage in the
corner. Nearly naked, both were writhing with sensuous
undulations, halfway between a dance and a sexual act.

Amanda stood close beside Buck as they waited to be
seated. She glanced at the dancers, but what caught her
attention even more were the patrons, mostly men, who
seemed caught up completely in the performance.

One man sitting at the bar was totally transfixed. He
sat immobile and stony faced, a cigarette hanging from
his lips, his eyes narrowed and frozen on the dancers.
Amanda shivered, and Buck turned to smile at her pretty
face, now touched vaguely with alarm.

"I picked one of the tamer places," he whispered into
her ear. "Didn't want to shock you."

Amanda rolled her eyes, and the captain came to show
them to a table just at the edge of the stage. Most of the
other patrons were only momentarily distracted by the
arrival of the tall, attractive American couple, but
Amanda felt self-conscious nonetheless, particularly
when several men nearby continued to look at her with
seeming admiration. She felt almost as though she were
the next act and that they half expected her to mount the
stage.

Amanda scrunched down in her chair as close to Buck
as she could, taking his arm with her hand. The dancers
had begun moving into the final gyrations of their love
act, their near-naked bodies only a few feet from
Amanda and Buck. The woman, who was quite pretty,
moved gracefully yet most suggestively. Although she

was Thai and very slender, her breasts were quite large, unnaturally so.

She was on her knees and bent backward so that her long black hair was fanned out on the floor behind her. The man, also Thai though large and muscular for his race, was above her, his body moist from the exertion of the dance. As he hovered over his partner's undulating body, his chest grazed her erect breasts.

At first, Amanda watched with a degree of embarrassment, feeling very much as though she had walked in on a couple in their bedroom, but after a time, she became less self-conscious and lost somewhat in the event. The waiter was at Buck's side, but Amanda hardly paid any attention when her escort inquired about her drink preference. Several moments later, a small liqueur glass of greenish liquid was placed in front of her.

"What's this?" she whispered to Buck.

"Absinthe," he replied. "It's as much sin as I thought you could handle as a neophyte."

She bristled slightly. "What makes you think I'm a neophyte?"

He pinched her cheek. "Wishful thinking, perhaps."

Amanda took the glass and touched it to her lips. When Buck wasn't looking, she tasted the film of liquid with the tip of her tongue. She leaned over and whispered in his ear. "Isn't this supposed to be an aphrodisiac?"

"That's what I've heard."

Amanda pushed the glass away from her a bit and looked again at the dancers.

He leaned toward her. "I never feel I need it, either," Buck said dryly.

She gave him a look, but he didn't notice. A moment later, he took her hand, rubbing the back of it with his thumb. With the dancers moving to a heated frenzy of simulated passion, Amanda began feeling acutely aware of Buck's touch and the currents within her that were evoked. She caught herself starting to reach for the absinthe and pulled her hand back.

The erotic act on stage came to an end, and Buck turned to Amanda. "It's rather warm in here. Would you like something cool to drink? A beer or soft drink?"

"A beer sounds good, actually," she replied, eyeing the forbidden liqueur on the table before her.

Buck took a sip of his own absinthe, then saw Amanda looking at him with eyes containing both dismay and disapproval. He grinned. "I think it takes a few thousand glasses before you start going insane."

The waiter responded to his call.

"Two San Miguels, please."

The next act was a belly dancer, reputed to be imported from the Middle East, but to Amanda she looked to hail from nearer shores, perhaps Indonesia or Malaysia. Regardless, she was quite good until her routine began straying from the traditional movements to more sexual improvisations. Buck seemed as disappointed as Amanda, and when the belly dancer was followed by two erotic female dancers, he assented to her request to leave. Both of them had grown tired of the eroticism.

After walking around the quarter for a while and browsing among the wares of the street vendors, they grabbed a taxi and headed back to the hotel. It was still fairly early and the evening was a mild one so they decided to stop the cab and walk the last half mile or so to the Oriental.

They strolled along the New Road, but before they had gone a block, the street and surrounding district suddenly fell into total darkness.

"Ah, looks like a power failure," Buck said, taking Amanda's arm.

There was a rising din of voices. People on the street as well as those coming out of surrounding buildings and houses were chattering with excitement. The major thoroughfare became like a country highway with only the passing vehicles casting light onto the darkened pavement. Buck and Amanda moved cautiously along the sidewalk under the light of the full moon.

Soon people began appearing with flashlights and lamps. A small boy with a lantern approached, and Buck hired him to walk them to the hotel. Now able to clearly see where they were going, they hurried through the throng of curious faces. The effect was like walking through the jungle with a flashlight and finding it teeming with life normally unseen in the obscurity.

They arrived at the Oriental, and Buck gave the boy several *baht*, much to the child's delight. Waiting at the darkened entry was a small band of bellmen, each carrying a candelabrum, ready to escort arriving guests into the darkened interior of the building. The lobby was lit by numerous candles, giving the elegant chamber an air that was more akin to that of a temple than a resting place for travelers. They went in procession to the Authors' Residence—first the uniformed bellman followed by Amanda and Buck.

As they walked along, the candlelight bent the shadows, revealing beyond each turn in their route another unlit passage or chamber. Finally, they arrived at the door to their suite. The man escorted them inside and placed the candelabrum on a table. Then, taking a small flashlight from his pocket, he bid them good-night and left.

Amanda moved to the sitting area and found a bottle of champagne in an ice bucket with a white cloth draped over it. "Look at this."

Buck was beside her. "Must be a gift from the management, a sort of apology for the inconvenience."

"How nice." She turned and looked at him for the first time since their return. The flickering candlelight played on his face, accentuating its masculine contours. The glimmer in his eyes betrayed an ardor that made Amanda wish for an instant that they weren't alone. But then he spoke, his soothing tones reassuring, decorous.

"May I offer you a glass?" Buck slipped off his suit jacket and tossed it over the back of the couch as Amanda sat down. Sitting beside her, he opened the champagne, pouring a little of the frothy liquid into each of the flutes on the table. They touched glasses, then both leaned back and sipped their wine.

For a while, they sat silently in the aura of the candelabrum amid a room draped in long, quivering shadows. Noticing Buck studying her, Amanda felt as tremulous as the light playing on their faces. She sipped the champagne nervously.

There was kindness on his face as he reached over and touched her cheek with the back of his fingers, drawing them slowly across her skin. Amanda smiled almost in reflex at the affection, acutely aware as his wandering hand found its way to the nape of her neck. She trembled noticeably.

Buck, smiling, eased closer to her, then kissed her softly on the temple. His mouth lingered there, spreading the warmth of his breath over the side of her face. She turned to him with uncertain eyes, and he gently covered her waiting lips with his own.

His kiss was tender, restrained, leaving Amanda feeling unsure about the pent-up desires that he had masked with reserve. She tasted his sweetness, enjoyed the gentle caress of his lips and the cautious explorations of his tongue.

Buck's thumb firmly traced the line of her jaw, hinting at his latent passion. Then his mouth pulled free of hers, and he drew a long breath, his cheek pressed hard against hers. Amanda felt his fingers tighten on her arm and sensed the force of his desire emerging from its self-imposed dormancy.

The stirrings inside her own body were a warning, and Amanda immediately realized that she must need it. Grasping his hand and pushing it away from her, she scooted to the edge of the couch, then stood and began nervously pacing. Eventually, she gravitated to the window and the bright moonlight that filtered through the curtains of the room.

She did not look at Buck, but she was aware of him sitting silently behind her, waiting for her emotions to play themselves out. Finally, Amanda turned back toward him. His eyes, gleaming in the half-light, drew her. But she resisted still.

"Must I come to you?" he asked.

Amanda couldn't say yes, but Buck saw the invitation on her face and walked slowly to where she waited. He looked down at her, his expression serious and hungry. He could tell that she was losing her will to resist.

For a moment, he savored the silvery glow of the moonlight on her skin, then he took her in his arms, crushing her against him. Teeth that had been passive nibbled her lips. Amanda felt herself respond with a ravenous passion of her own. Anxiously, she clutched him, eagerly accepting the tongue that foraged her mouth and the fingers that pressed through the silk of her cheong-sam to her skin.

As his desire heightened, Buck's fingers slid to the zipper at the back of her dress and, in one sweeping motion, opened it to the waist. Amanda trembled with uncertainty as his hands pushed aside the fabric and began coursing her skin. He caressed the flesh of her back and shoulders, all the while holding her tightly against his body.

The thin strap of her bra impeded Buck's affections so he unsnapped it, drawing the palms of his large hands up and down her naked back. Slowly, he rubbed away the rigid hesitancy of her body, and Amanda let go, melting within the circle of his arms as her breasts were crushed against his chest.

She craved him as much as she feared his advances, yielding to his mouth, permitting him to probe deeply into her own with his tongue. So inflamed was she by his erotic touch, Amanda was only vaguely aware when Buck pulled the cheongsam off her shoulders, then down off her arms so that the dress and bra fell to her waist, exposing the proud arch of her breasts to the moonlight.

With a low sigh of desire welling from his throat, Buck bent over and kissed the bud of each breast softly with moistened lips. He held her arms tightly, making Amanda feel helpless against the deliciously arousing titillation of his tongue.

Tremors coursed her body as his mouth caressed her hardening nipples. Amanda closed her eyes and let her head roll backward, loving the sensations he had provoked, surrendering to them.

"Oh, Buck," she murmured only half consciously.

He stopped kissing her breasts and lifted his head. When the flood of sensations finally ebbed, Amanda opened her eyes and found him looking at her with eager desire. Again he kissed her, drinking deeply of her, his strong hands welded still to her arms. After they had kissed for a long time, Buck looked at her in a way that told Amanda he wanted more.

"Amanda," he purred into her ear, "I've never wanted a woman the way I want you now."

Buck's tone was tender, even loving, but Amanda heard what he was implying even more than she heard what he said—never had he wanted a woman more. She knew that was meant as a compliment, a favorable comparison, but the notion of being compared at all was troubling. It reminded her of what she had foolishly been trying to forget all evening—who Buck was, the kind of man he was. She stiffened, aware that she was half naked in his arms.

He kissed her affectionately on the forehead. "What's the matter, don't you like the fact that I want you?"

"Yes," she replied vacantly. "I mean no. I—I mean I'm flattered...." She looked up at him gravely. "Don't you see it doesn't matter, Buck? I can't make love with you."

"Can't?" His voice was gentle.

"I mean I don't want to...not now."

After a moment's hesitation, Buck kissed her again on the forehead, then gathered her into his arms, almost protectively. "I'm sorry if I rushed you, Amanda. You're quite a challenge to a man's willpower, you know."

Amanda laid her head against his shoulder, appreciative that he wasn't pressing her. "I don't mean to be."

"Well, you are. You're irresistible."

"It's the champagne and the candlelight."

"What is it you want," Buck teased, "assurance or compliments?"

Amanda pulled back a little indignantly. "What makes you think it's either?"

"Sorry, I'm just trying to please..."

Amanda turned away, pulling up her dress and bra, embarrassed at the circumstances. She felt Buck's fingers fumbling at her back. He was trying to fasten her bra.

"That's okay," she said and reached back, taking the ends of the strap from his fingers. After she had fastened it again, Buck's hands were on her shoulders.

"Here, let me help you with your zipper."

The next thing Amanda felt was his lips on the back of her neck. Their warm moistness sent jolts down her spine. "That's not helping," she protested.

"I'm enjoying it."

"I think that's how things went astray earlier."

Buck turned her around to him. "You aren't telling me you haven't enjoyed this?"

She lowered her eyes. "Enjoyment is not the issue."

"What are you trying to tell me then, Amanda? I keep hearing it's good, but it's not good."

"You're a very charming, attractive man, Buck. I'm a woman. That affects me. But it doesn't mean I'll succumb to it."

He smiled. "I have the strangest feeling that you're accusing me of something, but I'm not sure what. You aren't attributing bad motives to my feelings for you?"

"It's not a question of motives. I just don't want to be your plaything—"

"Amanda! We've been over this ground before...."

"Okay, let me be more direct, then. I'm not interested in a roll in the hay."

"You mean you're not interested without assurances, don't you?"

"What's that supposed to mean?"

Buck's expression hardened. "Well, isn't that the thing to say? 'I'm not a girl that does this sort of thing without love, commitment, etcetera.'"

"Strange how your sarcasm makes the idea seem so unworthy."

"I wasn't being sarcastic. I—I'm just not used to thinking in those terms."

"Evidently not."

"Come on, Amanda, is it so bad to feel attraction and to express it?"

"No, Buck, it's not bad. You're free to live as you wish. But I'm not obligated to cooperate."

He sighed with exasperation. "No, that's true." He took her hand. "Look, I meant no offense. None. Believe me."

The sincerity in his eyes was so intense that Amanda lowered her head. His hands glided upward to her shoulders as she toyed with the button on his shirt. "I believe you."

Buck lifted her chin with his finger, then touched her lips with his own. "What kind of commitment is it you're looking for?" he murmured.

Amanda smiled under the caress of his lips. "You sound like a man checking the price of a fancy car he's coveting."

"It was a serious question, Miss Smartypants."

She looked at him for a long moment. "It's not a pledge or a promise, if that's what you're worried about."

"Then what?"

"It's a feeling, Buck. A feeling of being on the same wavelength and wanting the same thing. Of knowing the other person feels the same way you do."

"How do *you* feel?"

She smiled mischievously. "Tired."

He laughed. "You see! We are on the same wavelength. I'm tired, too. Shall we go to bed?"

"To our own beds, yes." Amanda grinned.

"Precisely what I had in mind." He kissed her softly on the lips. "Amazing how much we think alike, isn't it?"

She breathed in his wonderful masculine scent, realizing how much she was coming to like him.

THE NEXT MORNING when Amanda came into the salon, Buck was already drinking a cup of coffee. His clean, virile image struck her just as it always did when she first saw him.

His eyes swept over her sunny-yellow Thai silk blouse and white linen wraparound skirt. He smiled.

"You look lovely."

"Thank you."

"Shall I order breakfast, or would you rather go out on the terrace to eat?" he asked.

"Maybe I should just have a coffee, Buck. I'm due at the ministry in half an hour so I really don't have time to eat."

He poured her a cup. "I guess I'll have breakfast out on the terrace later, then."

Amanda sat down beside him. "What are your plans today?"

"I want to go to that Christian Mission Orphanage that Chin mentioned last night."

"I was planning to visit there this afternoon. Would you like to go with me?"

"Yes, that'd be perfect. Will you be back for lunch?"

"I should be, yes."

"Good. We'll have lunch together, then go to the orphanage." Buck looked at Amanda contemplatively. "Have any plans for this evening?"

"Not unless the king and queen invite me over for dinner."

"I guess I can live with being second choice, if you'd care to join me."

She looked at the soft blue eyes that she now thought of as friendly. "I'd love to." Amanda was really glad Buck had mellowed. He had been less proprietary lately and even quite understanding the previous night. She wondered what it meant.

They drank their coffee in silence for a few moments, then Amanda glanced at her watch.

"I wish you didn't have to go," he said softly.

The wistfulness of his tone touched her. She reached over and put her hand on his. Their eyes met. "Thanks for being so understanding last night, Buck."

He looked pleased with her comment but said nothing.

Amanda slid a little closer and kissed him on the cheek. "I do appreciate it." His eyes were questioning, and his expression made him seem all the more endearing. She knew if she stayed there longer, near him, something would happen. She rose to her feet, and taking her briefcase and purse from the table, went to the door. There she stopped and looked back at Buck, who seemed to be in a quiet turmoil of his own. "See you at lunch," she said and left the suite.

Buck stared at the door for a long time after she had gone. His first thought was that she had changed, that her resistance was beginning to dissolve, that she was warming to him. Then it occurred to him that it may not have been Amanda who was changing so much as it was he.

He thought about the conversation they had had the previous night after she had thwarted him, and realized that what he was beginning to feel for her was not just the usual attraction. Amanda Parr was having a different sort of effect on him.

Buck wanted her as much as ever, but the compulsion to possess her was tempered now with a caring and concern that he found strange. He felt a bizarre need to protect her, and he wanted very badly that she desire his protection.

Buck Michaels languished for a while in the melancholy of Amanda's absence. He missed her. After idling away his time thinking about her a bit longer, he finally gathered his resolve and decided to call his office in Los Angeles before everyone had gone for the day. He quickly got through to Kelly, who gave him an update on everything that had been happening at the *Tribune*.

"So how's everything going with Miss Parr, Boss?" Kelly asked after they finished with their business.

"Oh, fine, fine," he replied in a noncommittal tone.

"That's all?"

"Well, this is business, not a pleasure trip, Kell. Besides, you know how these social service types are—early to bed and all that."

"But who with, that's the question."

"Kelly!" Normally, his secretary's teasing on the subject of women didn't bother him, and Buck was surprised at how protective he felt of Amanda.

"Sorry, I should have known all you two would do is write each other thank-you notes." She laughed, not having caught his genuine tone of disapproval. "I take it you *are* coming back someday."

"Yes, I should have things wrapped up here soon." He promised to call the next day and hung up, suddenly feeling very hungry.

CHAPTER SEVEN

BUCK PAMPERED HIMSELF with a leisurely breakfast on the terrace, watching the boat traffic on the Chao Phraya River. When the table was cleared, he sent one of the busboys to the hotel shop for a copy of the Asian edition of the *Wall Street Journal*. He would have liked to see a copy of his own paper, the *Los Angeles Tribune*, but they were scarce in Bangkok and would be five days or a week old in any case.

After reading most of the paper, out of the corner of his eye Buck noticed someone approaching. Looking up, he saw a Chinese man in a business suit standing at his table.

"Mr. Michaels," he said in a low voice, "may I speak with you?"

Buck studied the sober-faced stranger for a moment, sensing that his purpose wasn't friendly. "Do I know you?" he asked.

"No, but that is unimportant, Mr. Michaels."

"To you, perhaps, but I like to know who I'm speaking with, unless of course you're only interested in chatting about the weather."

The interloper seemed unamused by Buck's sarcasm. "I want to speak with you about the girl you're looking for. I think you would be wise to hear what I have to say."

The statement came as a surprise. Buck gestured toward the chair opposite him. "Sit down."

The man bowed slightly and took a seat. "Let me be blunt, Mr. Michaels. Your search for the child has proved embarrassing for a certain gentleman—"

"What gentleman? Who?"

"At the moment, that is not of concern. What is important is that the gentleman would like for you to discontinue your inquiries. You see, Mr. Michaels, this man has important connections in government circles. He is very influential and is not someone you should cause to be unhappy."

"How would my search for an Amerasian child make anyone unhappy?"

"That is unimportant. Your interest apparently is in finding the child so let me make it easy for you and tell you that she is no longer in Thailand. She is in your country, America. There is no need to search further for her here."

"How can I be sure?"

"I have no reason to deceive you. My purpose is to make it easier for you, Mr. Michaels."

"Why should I trust you? You won't tell me who you are or why you want me to abandon my search."

The man let irritation show on his face, drawing his mouth into a hard line.

"Are *you* this mysterious gentleman?" Buck asked, showing his own impatience.

"No, I am sent by him."

"Why doesn't the man come to me himself, if I am such a problem for him?"

"Mr. Michaels, you ask many questions, but you do not understand that I am here because of the courtesy of my patron. Please take my advice and return to Los Angeles or content yourself with seeing the many wonderful sights of our country.''

"What is your patron afraid of?"

"You are very insistent, Mr. Michaels." He looked at Buck placidly, his eyes flat, without expression. "I will tell you this but no more. The gentleman wishes to protect his wife against the memories that your search for the child could produce."

"His wife?" All of a sudden, Buck understood. "Are you referring to Dameree?"

"I have said all that I will say, Mr. Michaels, except that it is in your interest to heed my warning."

"And if I don't?"

"I think your own wife cares a great deal about the work that she does in our country. It would be most unfortunate if the government decided that her efforts were no longer desirable. I am sure that Mrs. Michaels would be most unhappy." His eyes grew cold. "Please take my advice, Mr. Michaels, for your wife's sake if not for your own."

Buck felt the anger rising inside him. It was all he could do to keep from lashing back at this unknown adversary across from him, but he knew that would be pointless. The man was no more than an agent. Apparently, word had gotten to Dameree or someone close to her through Chin. But the fact that Amanda had been brought into it disturbed Buck most. "Do your patron and his wife understand that my purpose is simply to find the girl and confirm her welfare?"

"My patron's sole concern is that you abandon your efforts and leave the country before there is trouble."

"Will you give me information that will help me find the child in the States?"

"I have no such information. Only that she is gone from Thailand."

"But someone must know something. Surely Dameree—"

The man stood abruptly, scraping his chair along the stone of the terrace. "I am sorry, Mr. Michaels, but there is nothing more I can say. For your wife's sake, drop this matter and return to your own country." He bowed slightly and walked briskly away.

Buck watched him walk across the terrace, then disappear into the hotel. He was seething with anger and frustration. Bringing Amanda into it was simple blackmail, a cheap trick but an effective one. Whoever was behind it knew what they were doing, of that much he was sure.

Buck had felt that Amanda was the key to his search for the girl all along, but she was now proving to be his Achilles' heel as well. After thinking about it for a while, he realized that he wouldn't be able to shield her from what had happened. He had no choice but to tell her everything. After all, it was Amanda's work and her career that were now at risk. It wasn't something that Buck relished, but it was rapidly becoming obvious that there was no alternative.

BY THE TIME Amanda returned to the hotel that afternoon, she was anxious to see Buck, anxious to see if the favorable trend in their relationship would continue. During the long wait at the ministry, she had thought of little else than Buck Michaels. He was beginning to take on a whole new image in her mind, and she was starting to doubt her convictions about the kind of man he was. Buck made her feel special now, and he seemed sincere.

How could she have been so wrong about him before? Or was she?

Amanda was pleased to find him waiting in the suite when she arrived, but her happy smile faded at the sight of the somber look on his face. "How was your morning?" she asked tentatively.

"Interesting. And eventful, as a matter of fact."

"Oh?"

"An anonymous gentleman called on me while I was on the terrace having breakfast."

Amanda was affected more by the gravity in Buck's voice than by what he had said. "What about?"

He beckoned her over to the sitting area, then related the gist of the conversation he had had with the mysterious man.

"Buck, that's terrible," Amanda said after he finished his story. "How could anyone be so upset about your looking for a child?" She understood his consternation now. "Do you think it's Dameree? Do you think she's trying to scare you away?"

"I don't know. I suppose it's possible."

"But why?"

"I haven't the vaguest idea." He thought. "The fellow kept referring to the 'gentleman,' as though it were the man and not the wife who was concerned. But I can't imagine who the wife would be if it isn't Dameree."

"Maybe it's another woman—someone who got the child from Dameree—an adoptive mother, perhaps."

"Yes, I suppose that's possible, too."

"What are you going to do, Buck?"

He looked at her with resignation. "I think it may be more your decision than mine, Amanda."

"You think the threat is serious?"

"It's certainly possible. I tend to think idle threats are less common in Eastern cultures than in our own."

"But do you really believe that the government of Thailand would shut me down just to satisfy someone's vindictive purposes?"

"Stranger things than that have happened. It depends entirely on the kind of influence this person has."

"If any."

"Considering the risks, Amanda, I don't think you should take it lightly."

"Well, he may have threatened you, but he didn't threaten me. There's nothing to prevent *me* from looking for Dameree's child."

"Don't forget, they think we're married. Your actions may be equated with mine."

Amanda smiled. "I didn't turn out to be such a fortunate wife after all, did I?"

Buck squeezed her hand. "If they succeed in thwarting me, it won't be because of you. It will be because someone clearly doesn't want me to find either the child or Dameree...or both of them."

Amanda could see that the influence of this child in their relationship was going to be significant. The girl had, in a sense, brought them together, but she also hung over them like the sword of Damocles. "Look, Buck," she said, feeling decisive action was called for, "I realize that this business may have consequences for me and for the foundation, but I refuse to be blackmailed. This threat you received may justify caution but not surrender."

"What do you mean?"

"I'm going to find out what I can today at the Christian Mission Orphanage, and as far as I am concerned,

you can come along. If that offends somebody in high
places, then so be it."

Buck grinned. "You know what, lady? I like your
spunk." He pulled her to him and kissed her affectionately.

His touch weakened her, and she melted into his arms.
For the first time, Amanda felt she was a part of his
struggle. There was a closeness between them that only
two people sharing the same goal can feel. Buck kissed
her again, and Amanda wished that she had the power to
find this girl that obsessed him so.

THE CHILDREN WERE PLAYING in the shade of a *bho* tree,
avoiding the heat of the afternoon sun, as Amanda and
Buck watched from a window in the reception room. The
courtyard, enclosed by high walls, contained little else
apart from the tree, a patch of dusty ground and some
wooden benches placed against the building. The benches
and the few square yards of cement under the overhang
of the porch roof was all the play area the children had
during the summer monsoons. But now that they were
moving into the dry season, the whole courtyard was
available though the area under the tree was clearly the
preferred locale.

"They look to be mostly Thai children," Buck said as
they watched the play.

"They are," Amanda replied. "There are only two
Amerasian children in residence at the moment. Two
boys. One about eight, the other four or five." She studied the group. "There's the older boy," she said, pointing. "You see the tall one with the lighter hair?"

Buck nodded. "Have they been here long? Why is it
they haven't been sent to the States before now?"

"These two are fairly new at the orphanage. Probably because they were just recently brought in or were picked up in the streets."

"Why weren't they brought in as babies?"

"It's hard to say. It isn't always apparent to the mothers how difficult life will be for their racially mixed children until they're older. Then, too, the children are sometimes on their own before they are brought here. Frequently, the mothers are prostitutes and not the most responsible sort of persons to begin with."

He shook his head. "I hate to think that my...Dameree's child was here, Amanda."

Buck's slip and the timbre of his voice told her how deep his feelings were. "They're actually well taken care of, compared to the life some of the poor little things have on the outside."

But Buck's mind was off somewhere. "You don't suppose Dameree could have abandoned her in the streets, do you?"

"I don't know, Buck, but everything seems to point to the fact that she was sent to the States through an orphanage—this one probably. And chances are she was put in a good home."

He was staring out the window. "She's practically a young woman by now, Amanda. Imagine." When he turned to her, his eyes revealed pain. "I've already lost her childhood," he said sadly.

"Buck," she said, touching his arm, "your purpose isn't to recover her, it's to verify that she is in the States and all right. Don't let this obsession get out of hand. Keep perspective, or it will only be harder on you."

He smiled weakly. "You're right, of course. I know what you're saying." He squeezed her hand. "Don't worry about me."

But she did.

There was a general commotion out in the courtyard, and Buck and Amanda turned to see the children all clamoring around the trunk of the tree, pointing excitedly up into the boughs.

Buck chuckled. "Looks like they've found themselves a pet."

"What?" Amanda said, trying not to sound too alarmed. There was a special lilt in Buck's "pet" that she knew meant "mouse," "snake," "spider," or the like.

"It's a lizard. See it on the trunk of the tree? A big, blue-and-green one."

Amanda saw it and felt her stomach clinch. "God, it looks like a dragon."

"I'm sure it's harmless."

Several of the larger boys had decided to go after the creature and were climbing on one another's shoulders to try to reach it. There was much shouting and laughter. Amanda herself couldn't help laughing at the children's antics. Finally, the lizard retreated high up into the foliage out of sight, and the hunt was abandoned.

Amanda and Buck watched awhile longer as the children returned to their games and groups. She noticed that the older Amerasian boy kept pretty well to himself and wondered whether it was a result of being new at the orphanage or a consequence of the life experiences he had had prior to his arrival.

"That Amerasian boy doesn't seem very well accepted," Buck said, having noticed as well.

"Yes, I was just thinking about that myself. It may be because he's new."

"The little one seems to be getting on well enough."

"It's easier for the younger ones." Amanda saw genuine concern on Buck's face.

"Do you suppose it would be all right if I went out and talked with him for a while?" he asked.

"Sure. I expect Mrs. Pakorn will be free soon, but it may be best if I spoke with her alone first anyway. I'll ask her about Dameree's child."

Amanda watched as Buck went out, sauntering across the courtyard toward the tree. Play stopped as the children took their measure of the tall American approaching them. He tousled the hair of several of the youngsters, and the general apprehension soon abated. After brief exchanges with some of the older children, he eventually approached the Amerasian boy, who Amanda could see looking up at Buck with wide, skeptical eyes.

Several minutes later, Buck seemed to have gained the child's trust, and a conversation of sorts was underway. Amanda smiled, admiring Buck for his interest in the boy and his manner with him. Then a door opened behind her, and Mrs. Pakorn, the director of the orphanage, came walking into the reception area.

"Miss Parr, so good to see you again." The somewhat plump woman bowed slightly in greeting. She glanced out the window where Amanda had been looking. "Oh, a gentleman."

"Yes, that's Mr. Michaels. He came with me, Mrs. Pakorn."

"*Mr.* Michaels? I thought it was *Mrs.* Michaels who is with your agency."

Amanda looked at the woman, perplexed.

"A letter was hand delivered for Mrs. Michaels of the Amerasian Children's Foundation this morning. I thought it was certainly an associate of yours, Miss Parr, but I am surprised to find a gentleman instead. Does he have a wife, perhaps?"

"Oh!" Amanda said with a laugh. "I understand now. I think the letter is intended for me."

Now Mrs. Pakorn was surprised.

Amanda instantly decided that the letter must somehow be connected with Mr. Chin, Kupnol Sustri or Buck's visitor that morning. On an impulse, she decided to extend the charade Buck had begun the previous night. "You see, Mrs. Pakorn, Buck and I were recently married."

The woman clasped her hands together, beaming. "How wonderful. A new bride! Congratulations, Miss Parr...I mean, Mrs. Michaels. What a great surprise."

Amanda felt a little embarrassed at Mrs. Pakorn's effusiveness. She glanced out the window at Buck, who was still occupied with the boy. "My husband seems content with the children. Perhaps we could talk and I could see the letter."

"Certainly, Mrs. Michaels, certainly. Please come into my office."

Amanda followed the director into the adjoining room, a spartan little chamber with an old worn wooden desk, several chairs and a small bookcase. The religious pictures on the walls and a small vase of flowers added a touch of color to the otherwise drab surroundings.

The women sat on opposite sides of the desk, and Mrs. Pakorn handed Amanda a sealed envelope with ceremonial politeness.

"Would you mind if I read it now?" Amanda asked, barely able to contain her curiosity.

"Please, Mrs. Michaels."

Amanda smiled politely, thinking how being thought of as Buck's wife was beginning to appeal to her. She glanced at the front of the envelope, which was simply addressed "Mrs. Michaels, Amerasian Children's Foundation, U.S.A.'' The hand was careful and distinctly feminine. She tore open the envelope and read.

My dear Mrs. Michaels,
I write to you this letter hoping that as a woman like me you will understand. I am happy for your marriage to Buck and say to you congratulations. Please understand that I pray for you the best.

I know that Buck now looks for my daughter, which is very sad for me. I hoped before that he would forget this, but I see that it is not so. I want to help Buck, but for me this is not easy because of my husband who very much protects me. He does not even know that I know you and Buck are in the country looking for my daughter. So you see, I must be very careful.

I cannot see Buck to tell him the things he wants to know. But since you are his wife and a woman I can talk to, I ask to you if you will meet with me to answer Buck's questions. If you agree, it must be a very important secret so that my husband is not unhappy with me. Please do not tell this to Buck also.

If you say yes to this offer, I will meet you in the ancient city of Ayudhya tomorrow morning. It is on the river not far from Bangkok and a safe and quiet place to meet together. A girl will call you in your hotel for your answer.

Please, Mrs. Michaels, for the sake of your husband, let us keep this secret.

Your friend,
Dameree

Amanda folded the letter, replaced it in the envelope and looked up into the smiling face of Mrs. Pakorn. She returned the woman's smile and glanced anxiously toward the door.

"Would you like for Mr. Michaels to join us?" the director asked.

"No, but I should be going soon. Perhaps we can spend some time later in the week discussing the two boys. My main purpose today was to see the boys and ask that you send their files to the ministry as soon as possible." She smiled weakly. "You know how long it takes them to prepare the necessary documentation."

The woman nodded. "Yes, and I know your time is valuable. But be assured, Mrs. Michaels, we will do our best here to speed things along."

"You are always most helpful. Thank you."

The other acknowledged Amanda's courtesy with a polite nod of her head. "May I see you to the door, then?"

As the women exited the office, Buck was approaching from the courtyard. "Oh, there you are, darling," Amanda exclaimed. "I'd like you to meet the director of the Christian Mission Orphanage." Amanda took Buck's arm. "Mrs. Pakorn, may I introduce my husband, Buck Michaels. Buck, this is Mrs. Pakorn, the person responsible for all the wonderful assistance we get in Thailand."

Buck, surprised, took the hand the woman extended to him. "How do you do?" He looked at Amanda, his eyes questioning.

She couldn't help grinning, pleased at seeing the tables turned. She shrugged coquettishly.

"I understand congratulations are in order, Mr. Michaels. I only learned of your recent marriage today."

Buck nodded. "Thank you, Mrs. Pakorn. Amanda is such a delightful addition to my life, I've already forgotten what it was like to be single."

Amanda felt her cheeks color.

"She's a lovely young woman," the orphanage director said, "and we enjoy working with her so much. I certainly hope you'll let her continue to come to Thailand on behalf of the foundation."

Buck patted Amanda's hand. "I know it means a great deal to her, but it's not easy to let her go. I promise, though, to give it the utmost consideration."

Amanda discreetly pinched Buck as hard as she could, but he didn't flinch.

"I trust you ladies had a satisfactory meeting," he said sweetly.

"Oh, indeed, Mr. Michaels."

"Are you ready to go then, dear?" Buck asked, grinning at Amanda.

They went out into the hot sun and were fortunate to find a taxi waiting nearby. When they had climbed into the back seat, the laughter Buck had been suppressing came spilling out. Much to the driver's surprise, Amanda punched Buck in the side, but it didn't deter him. Tears of mirth began streaming down his cheeks, and Amanda had to give the driver instructions.

When the cab pulled away, Buck put his arm around Amanda's shoulders and pulled her against him, still consumed with laughter. She glanced at him with feigned disgust, but she knew right then that Buck Michaels was a man she could easily come to love.

"So tell me," he said after having sufficiently recovered to talk, "what was all that about? Did the idea of marriage appeal to you so much that you couldn't resist another deception?"

Amanda gave him a dirty look, but in truth, she was in a quandary. She wasn't quite sure what to tell Buck. Her instinct was to tell him about Dameree's letter, but she couldn't be totally sure of his reaction. Although she felt an obligation to him, she also felt a certain responsibility to Dameree—because of the trust the woman had placed in her, if for no other reason.

After the threatening visit he had received that morning, Amanda decided that to involve Buck might put him in a difficult situation. She thought it better that he not know about the letter, at least for now. Instead, she would obtain the information he wanted, acting on his behalf.

"I'm serious," Buck said, still grinning. "Why did you tell Mrs. Pakorn we were married?"

"Apparently someone had been checking up on me at the orphanage, Buck. Mrs. Pakorn asked me who 'Mrs. Michaels' was because someone had made some inquiries about a person affiliated with the Amerasian Children's Foundation by that name."

"Who made the inquiries?"

"I don't know, but I assumed it must have something to do with Mr. Chin or your friend this morning. So rather than upset the applecart, I decided to play along and told her we were recently married."

Buck's expression became grave and Amanda felt dreadful. She hated lying, but now it was too late. Besides, what else could she do?

"Were you able to find out anything about the girl?" he asked.

Amanda lied again. "The case didn't sound familiar to Mrs. Pakorn, but that's not surprising. It was a long time ago. She's agreed to check her files."

Buck nodded, his expression one of resignation. Finally, a smile broke through the gloom on his face. "Well, look at it this way, Amanda—if word gets back to your organization in Los Angeles and back to the *Tribune*, we may have to get married just to salvage our honor."

"Oh, that sounds like a marvelous reason to get married."

Buck took Amanda's hand. "Just think of the fun we'd have coming up with a better reason."

"Thanks, but becoming 'Mrs. Michaels' was something I did for charitable reasons. I like being Amanda Parr just fine."

He was grinning again, and Amanda felt another little twinge of guilt as though what she had just said was somehow disingenuous. She looked out the window of the cab into the bright sun of steamy Bangkok, realizing that Buck Michaels was beginning to color her every thought.

CHAPTER EIGHT

IT WAS A HOT DAY, unseasonably warm, and by the time they returned to the Oriental, Amanda was flushed from the heat and her hair wet with perspiration. Climbing out of the cab, she dabbed her upper lip with her handkerchief and stepped briskly into the lobby where the cool air was a welcome relief. She was glad to be back, but she still had to come up with a story for Buck about her plans for the next day before the phone call came to confirm her appointment with Dameree.

"I don't know about you," Buck said, "but I could use a cold beer."

"It sounds wonderful, but I think I'll have a shower first."

"Why don't I have room service bring us several chilled Singhas. That way we can do both."

When they had entered the suite, Amanda tossed her purse and briefcase on a chair and turned to Buck, feeling like a wrung-out mop.

"You look bushed," he said sympathetically.

Just then, the phone rang and Buck went to answer it.

"Hello." He waited. "Hello," he said again, then looked at the receiver quizzically. "That's funny. No one there." He hung up.

Amanda wondered if that had been Dameree's friend. Perhaps hearing a man's voice had frightened her off.

"I'm expecting a call, Buck. It might have been for me."
She dropped down on the couch.

"If so, they were too shy to ask for you."

"I'm in the middle of a rather sensitive case involving
an Amerasian child, as a matter of fact. The call I'm
expecting is to confirm a meeting I have tomorrow
morning in Ayudhya."

"Ayudhya? What a strange place to meet."

"I've never been there. What's so strange about it?"

"It's as much a shrine and an archaeological site as a
town. Ayudhya was the ancient capital of Siam."

"But it's near Bangkok, isn't it?"

"Thirty or forty miles, I'd say."

"Hmm." Amanda hadn't thought about transportation. "How do I get there? Is there a bus or something?"

"It's on the river so the boats run up there. What
time's your meeting?"

"I don't know, it has to be confirmed. But in the
morning sometime."

"Then your best bet is probably the train, Amanda.
The boats are slow. It's actually a pleasant trip, though."
Buck dropped down beside her on the couch. "If you
have no objection, I could go along and we could make
a day of it. Maybe catch one of the hotel ships for the ride
back to Bangkok."

Amanda was already regretting her deceit. She could
see there might be no end to her web of lies. "Well...it
may be better if I went alone, Buck." She could see the
disappointment on his face.

"Is it *that* sensitive? I realize that there's no need for
me to be involved in your meeting, but there couldn't be
any harm in us traveling together to Ayudhya, could
there?"

Amanda anguished.

"I can go to the museum while you conduct your business."

She saw no graceful way out. "Well, perhaps. But this is very sensitive, Buck. My credibility is at stake."

His mouth twisted into a smile. "Believe it or not, even journalists can be discreet."

When Buck looked at her with eyes that foretold his desire, Amanda suddenly felt the need for a shower. She jumped to her feet. "I'm going in to get cleaned up," she announced.

"Don't you want to wait for your beer?"

"No, save me one," she said over her shoulder and was gone.

AMANDA WAS JUST GETTING OUT of the shower when there was a knock at her door. "Yes?" she called out, grabbing a towel.

It was Buck. "Amanda, there's a telephone call for you."

"Oh, God," she mumbled, taking a quick look in the mirror. "Could you ask them to hold on a minute, Buck?" She quickly dried herself, ran a comb through her wet hair and slipped on her short silk dressing gown, tying it securely at her waist. Heading for the door, she hoped Buck would have the decency to withdraw or at least ignore her.

Unfortunately, he was sitting on the couch, right next to the phone. As she approached, he looked up, surprised and delighted with what he saw. Instant desire filled his gaze, and Amanda regretted that she hadn't declined to take the call. She picked up the receiver. "Hello?"

"Mrs. Michaels?" It was the voice of a young woman.

"Yes."

"I am calling for the lady in Ayudhya. You know?"

"Yes, I was expecting your call." Buck was just inches away and Amanda turned to him, feeling naked under his gaze.

"My lady wishes to know if you can meet with her tomorrow morning?"

"Yes, I'd planned on it."

"Very well, Mrs. Michaels, if you would—" The line suddenly went dead.

Amanda looked at the receiver, then at Buck. "The phone went dead."

"Maybe the switchboard cut you off. Hang up, she'll probably call back."

Amanda put down the receiver. Buck reached over and took her hand.

"Here, sit down by me and wait for your call."

There was a touch of lechery in his voice, and Amanda felt very vulnerable though not afraid. His fingers were caressing hers as she sat on the edge of the couch, her knees welded together under Buck's admiring scrutiny. He took a few strands of her wet hair between his thumb and forefinger.

"I like the color of your hair."

"I'm a mess, Buck," she said, wiping away the mascara she felt certain was under her eyes. "I just got out of the shower."

"Yes, I was noticing that. I like the way you smell, too." He leaned close to her and took a deep breath. His fingertips touched her cheek.

Amanda looked anxiously at the telephone, thinking she'd best retreat to her room before things got out of hand. But before she had gained her feet, the instrument sounded again. She took the receiver. "Hello." Buck's arm was around her waist.

"Mrs. Michaels, I am sorry for the telephone. The line was cut."

"Yes, I'm sorry, too." Amanda squirmed under Buck's touch, liking his attentions but feeling vulnerable. "You were going to tell me the time and place of our meeting."

"Can you come to Ayudhya at ten in the morning?"

"I think so, yes."

"There is a train at seven from Bangkok."

"Okay." Buck was kneading her skin under the silk of her gown.

"Do you know the Panan Cherng Temple, Mrs. Michaels?"

"No, but I'm sure I can find it." Buck's lips were on the side of her neck, sending tremors through her.

"Please go to the garden of the temple at ten o'clock and wait at the foot of the Buddha. I will meet you there, Mrs. Michaels."

Buck's hand was at the opening of Amanda's gown, lightly caressing her skin. "At ten o'clock, then. Oh, how will I know you?"

"I will find you, please don't worry. You are a tall lady with red hair. Is it not true?"

Amanda was so distracted by Buck that she missed what the girl had said. "Pardon me?" She poked Buck with her elbow and stood up quickly before he could grab her again.

"I said you are a tall lady with red hair, so I can find you easily."

"Oh, yes, fine." She was glaring at Buck, who found the whole thing very amusing.

"See you tomorrow then, Mrs. Michaels."

Amanda hung up, and her hands settled on her hips. "That was very inconsiderate, Buck Michaels."

"It was inconsiderate, yes, but so much fun." He stood up and wrapped his arms around her. "Droit de seigneur, Mrs. Michaels."

"If that means what I think it means, Mr. Michaels, we're headed for a quick divorce."

"Surely bestowing my name entitles me to certain prerogatives."

Amanda raised her chin proudly. "None."

Buck leaned over and kissed her so softly on the neck it felt like a feather.

She shivered.

"I guess I'll have to entice you to compassion." His tongue lightly traced a trail across her throat.

Every muscle in her body tensed. Waves of desire swept over her. Never had this happened so quickly. She looked into his eyes questioningly.

Buck cupped her face in his hands and lowered his mouth to hers. Then he kissed her. Suddenly, Amanda wanted him to take her—she wanted him now, more than she had ever wanted any man.

After a moment, the kiss ended, Buck released her and they stood facing each other just inches apart. His hands were at her waist, toying with the tie of her gown. It came unfastened and slithered to the floor at her feet. She was looking down at his hands now, each of which held an edge of her gown. They were both aware how little was between her and total nudity.

Amanda's hands lightly touched his as if to keep them from going too far astray, but he proceeded anyway, gently. His fingers first touched the skin of her abdomen, then glided around her waist under the silk that hung loosely from her shoulders. She felt his warm breath on her face and the primal stirrings within her that he had evoked.

Buck's mouth hovered near hers, but he didn't touch her lips. Only his steamy vapors caressed her, coaxing her desire to a deep, urgent craving. When his hands slid up her sides, then cupped her breasts, Amanda thought she would die. She wanted so badly that he kiss her, hold her, but he didn't. He simply rubbed her nipples with his thumbs, slow, light strokes that brought them to instant erection.

Then Buck leaned down and kissed Amanda's breasts, taking each rosy bud into his mouth until it pulsed with excitement. When she moaned in pleasure, he stood upright and kissed her quivering lips, smothering the sounds that told him of her desire. He pushed her gown from her shoulders until it fell behind her on the floor, leaving her naked before him, her breasts still tingling from the moist residue of his kiss.

Without hesitating a moment longer, Buck gathered Amanda against him so that his protective embrace shielded her from the desire in his eyes. He stroked her hair.

"I want you," he whispered.

Amanda knew this was the moment that he, as a gentleman, owed her. It was her moment of decision. But all she could think of was how she wanted to be held by him, how right it seemed to want him and be wanted by him. Amanda's words of doubt and denial were there in her head, but they waned before the magnitude of what she felt. She knew the time had come. And Buck did, too.

Lifting her into his arms, he carried her to her room, setting her gently on the bed, which had been turned down. Amanda slithered between the sheets, feeling the imperative of his unspoken command. She could see anxious admiration on his face as his eyes brushed down, then up her body.

Buck did not release her from his gaze as he unbuttoned his shirt and pulled it from his trousers. He was soon stripped to the waist, his tanned skin almost a cocoa brown in the filtered light of late afternoon.

He slipped off his shoes and unfastened his trousers, all the while watching her with resolute masculine eyes that made no secret of his desire. Amanda felt trepidation at the sight of his unfamiliar body and its promise of intimacy. She looked for reassurance in his face as he removed the rest of his clothes without turning from her. Then, when he crept onto the bed, her heart began hammering inside her, dreading yet craving his naked touch.

He touched her damp hair, lifting strands and tresses as though they were fine gilt threads woven around her head. "You're lovely," he whispered as his fingers trailed over her shoulders and across her chest.

Amanda quivered with pleasure under his touch, knowing his naked masculinity was just inches from her side. Her heart was beating with fear, but she was no more capable of flight than a bird charmed by a snake.

Buck put his arm around her waist and inched closer. She virtually felt the heat of him, he was so near.

Inclining his head so that his mouth hovered just inches from hers, Buck let his breath graze along her cheek to the soft shell of her ear. His lips touched her just a second before his moist, warm tongue penetrated her recesses, causing her to moan at the sensation. He swept the perimeter of her ear once more before dragging his tongue along the flesh of her neck.

"Oh, Buck," she murmured, "you're torturing me."

His hand went to the curve of her hip, and he pulled her toward him so that they were both on their sides, facing each other, close together but still apart. "Torture? I would have hoped pleasure," he mumbled into her lips. His hot breath caressed her like a tropical breeze.

Amanda's mouth lifted to prolong the contact, but he withdrew beyond her reach. She writhed, hating the distance between them, wanting to provoke him and somehow take revenge for his torture. Ignoring the insolent smile on his face, Amanda arched her breasts so that they nearly touched his chest. Buck emitted a throaty groan, then moved toward her, but she withdrew, keeping the narrow band of space between them.

Tiring of the game he had initiated, Buck took her by the waist and pulled her against his hard muscular body. She felt the silky mat of his chest against her breasts, the powerful arm that pressed her to him, his thighs and pelvis, his turgid masculinity now throbbing against her.

Buck's mouth covered hers, capturing and claiming her rather than entreating her as before. Anxiously, he pulled her naked body against his.

Fear swept over Amanda as she realized she had only her will to protect her. She had not looked at him fully, being both too shy and afraid. But she felt him hard and large against her thigh, as intriguing to her as he was threatening.

Buck began kissing her neck and shoulders, nibbling gingerly at her soft flesh, tantalizing her with light sweeps of his tongue. Amanda fell back against the pillow, exposing herself to his hand that began roaming the length of her torso, pausing to cup each breast and caress the nipples to erection before moving down over the smooth porcelain of her stomach.

His fingers roamed errantly over her skin with a feathery touch that sent tremors through her. They toyed at the copper fringe of her private place, already pulsing, dewy with desire. When he ran his hand over the top of her thigh, then up the inside of it, her legs spontaneously opened to accept his touch.

The throbbing moistness of her femininity invited him immediately to caress her. His manipulations sent jolts of pleasure from her toes to her fingertips, from her breasts outward to the goosey flesh of her back and sides. Amanda gasped at the sensations sparked by his touch.

Not content with the incipient pleasure he had given, Buck fell upon her breast, taking it into his mouth and sucking the bud, all the while stroking the fiery point of ecstasy between her legs. The combination was almost too much for Amanda to bear, and her body lurched in an uncontrollable spasm.

"Oh," she moaned. "Oh, God."

Buck quickened the rhythm of his ministrations, boosting her to higher and higher levels of excitement. The pleasure was so overwhelming now that she could do no more than writhe in concert with his touch, her hips rocking to meet the movement of his finger, her stomach and legs quivering with spasms of physical joy.

The sensation Amanda felt was so wonderful that she wanted it to go on forever, to be lost in it as she had become lost in her desire for Buck. It all seemed incredible to her—the irresistible attraction she felt, the mesmerizing effect of his caresses, the uncontrollable excitement that he provoked. She wanted him, craving him more intimately, needing to know that it was their spirits as well as their bodies that were united.

For all her yearning to touch his soul, Amanda felt her body inexorably moving toward climax. The moans and shallow gasping breaths welling from her throat must have told Buck so because all at once he stopped. But the sensations lingered on, and when she felt him shifting his body over her, she realized that he intended to take her.

The reality of total union frightened Amanda though waves of pleasure still washed over her. Her eyes rounded in the glow of the afternoon sun and implored him to make it right, to share her feelings, not just her desires. Buck paused, and for a breathless moment, he seemed to look beneath the mask of her passion to the woman who craved him. She waited. He gently brushed her hair from her face, and Amanda knew that he understood.

She kissed Buck deeply then and slipped her arms around his neck, opening her legs so that he could settle between them. The coveted jewel of her femininity lay waiting for him.

Then in an excruciatingly wonderful instant, he entered her. Amanda gasped and her body quivered. He paused, and sensing the profundity of the moment, kissed her lightly before slowly pressing farther into her.

The feeling was incredible, but his sexual adagio too cruel for her to endure. Without willing it, her pelvis arched, forcing even deeper penetration. Buck gasped with pleasure at her initiative, then, unable to hold back any longer, fell hard upon her.

Amanda was vaulted almost instantly to the heights of womanly excitement. She craved the explosion of his climax. But even as she craved it, her body found the thread of its own autonomous frenzy. The delirium wrought first by his finger returned, and her body began heaving toward an ultimate conflagration. The explosion loomed suddenly before her. She cried out.

"Oh, Buck! Now!"

Her pleading exclamation sent him to the brink, and he exploded inside her, his loins purged. The fire storm of sensation lasted only half a minute, but in the end, he was spent, reduced to a mere shadow of the Herculean engine he had been.

Amanda herself collapsed, her legs falling to the bed, her lungs barely able to breathe under his weight. Yet she endured, the conquering female prevailing through accomplished submission.

Feeling him powerless inside her, she marveled at the spasms of sensation that continued to radiate from her core. Buck had given her an experience like she had never known. The desire that had plagued her for days had been satisfied, replaced by the awe of what they had shared.

Slowly, Buck was recovering, the deadweight of his body coming to life. He stirred, sighed his contentment, then rolled onto his side next to her. His soft blue eyes settled lovingly on hers, his moistened neck and shoulders gleamed in the light, and he touched her face with his fingertips.

"Oh, Buck, I didn't know it could be like this."

He kissed her on the temple and gathered her close against him. Another sigh of pleasure coming from deep within him told her he was on the verge of sleep. Amanda didn't care. Her body still pulsed with the ebbing fervor of her fulfillment. She knew she would never be the same.

"WHO WOULD HAVE THOUGHT we shared a passion for eating in bed?" Buck felt genuine awe though the notion was trivial enough. He reached for the remaining prawn on Amanda's plate, but she slapped his hand before he could snatch it away.

"Some things I'll share with you, Buck Michaels, but not my last prawn. Not when I'm as hungry as I am anyway."

He touched her thigh just below the point where her gown stopped, letting his fingers creep under the edge of the silk. "I did like what we shared earlier," he drawled, as his eyes savored skin the color of fresh cream. "In fact, I loved it."

Buck meant the words, but he knew they fell short of the feelings he had for Amanda just then—their depth amazed even him. Sex was a remarkable invention, and he seemed never to tire of it though most of his partners had worn after a time. But the strange thing about Amanda Parr was that she made him want more of her. Not physically, not sexually—he wanted more of the woman. It was a new feeling.

"What are you thinking, Buck?"

He had been looking at her and had forgotten himself. "What do you suppose?"

"You're probably hating me for not sharing my prawn."

"No, as a matter of fact, my thoughts about you just then were rather charitable."

"How so?"

He smiled. "You're asking what I was thinking?"

"Not if you don't want to tell me. You just looked a million miles away."

"No, I was right here in this room." He paused. "Well, in one sense I was here, in another sense I may have been somewhere else—somewhere in my past, I guess."

"Thinking of other ladies?"

The question may have been serious, but Buck saw whimsy on Amanda's face, and he was glad. "You might say I was comparing, yes."

"Oh, God. Just what a woman wants to hear."

"I was thinking how different I feel with you."

Amanda looked genuinely surprised. "What do you mean?"

"I don't know exactly. I just know that it seems . . . different."

Her grin became wry. "Maybe it's because you finally found someone who likes to eat in bed as much as you do."

"I'm being serious, Amanda."

"I'm sorry."

"I've thought about some of the things you've said to me over the past few days. I've thought about my life. . . ."

Her look was both quizzical and uncertain.

Buck had to stop and laugh at the sound of his own words. "What I'm trying to say is that I've thought about what you said the other night, that what mattered to you was not so much formal commitment as it was a feeling about the other person."

"Yes. . . ."

"Well, I want you to know, I didn't consider what we shared this afternoon to be a roll in the hay."

He could see by the expression on her face that she was moved by his comment, and he was glad.

"Thank you, Buck." She touched his hand. "I appreciate you saying that." Her face suddenly became impish. "But you still can't have my prawn!"

Buck reached for the disputed prize, but Amanda grabbed it just in time, getting it between her teeth as he was upon her. He captured her wrists before she could escape, and they fell back onto the bed, Buck over her, Amanda looking up with wide, frightened eyes, the large shrimp still between her teeth.

He laughed at the sight. "Well, don't you look lady-like."

She tried to respond, but with the fish in her mouth, all she could do was mumble incoherently.

Buck laughed again. "What was that, my little pet? Did you say you were willing to part with that prawn?"

Amanda's eyes rounded again. More mumbling, the word "no" somehow getting through.

He lowered his face near hers. "Did I hear you say you'd share, perhaps?"

She rolled her head back and forth on the pillow emphatically as if to say she wouldn't.

"Must I take what I want, then?"

There was disbelief in Amanda's eyes as Buck slowly took a large bite of the prawn just above the tail.

"Mmm, not bad," he said over her mumbled protest. The next bite took him to her lips.

Her resistance turned to passive fascination with what he was doing. Then Buck took the tail of the shrimp between his teeth, enabling Amanda to finish the bite that had been halfway in her mouth. Leaning to the side, he dropped the tail onto the tray at the edge of the bed and waited for her to finish chewing.

"You thief!" she exclaimed when she had finally swallowed.

Buck leaned down and kissed the corner of her mouth, then let his tongue skitter along the edge of her lip. "Not bad at all," he said, enjoying the taste of her. He fell heavily upon her then, kissing her deeply as he released her wrists. Amanda's hands slipped around his neck, and Buck knew they would have each other again—as beautifully and as sweetly as before.

CHAPTER NINE

BUCK STAYED WITH AMANDA, soon falling into slumber after their last kiss, his arm across her. She liked the closeness, the warmth of his body, the peaceful companionability that followed their intimacy, but he was still a stranger to her, and Amanda found it hard to fall asleep though her body craved it.

The flame of the candle Buck had lit for their dinner dwindled to a pinpoint of light before it finally died, leaving them in total darkness. Amanda was completely alone with her thoughts and her concerns about this new development in their relationship. She tried not to worry about the calamities that might befall her, thinking instead about the possible joys that lay ahead. She marveled at the twists of fate that brought her to this bed and hoped it wouldn't be an event she'd one day rue.

In the hours that followed, Amanda relived every minute of the short period of time she had known Buck Michaels. She thought about the seductive days and hours leading up to their ultimate encounter. She thought about their conversations, the times they had teased each other, laughed together, sparred and quarreled.

Amanda also thought about the mission that had brought Buck to Thailand, the girl and the woman, Dameree, whom she was to meet the next morning. She wondered what she would be like—her lover's lover from years past.

Amanda's mind began drifting into fanciful imaginings of Dameree, picturing her as the dancer they had seen at the club—an exotic beauty, dark, mysterious, delicately feminine. The woman would actually be much nearer Buck's age than her own though Amanda imagined her still as a young massage girl. After a while, the exotic visions, in combination with fatigue, dragged her into an ethereal but restless sleep.

Hours later, she was being buffeted by phantasmagoric images of Dameree and herself dancing in a lush tropical garden when she felt a hand on her bare shoulder. She blinked awake in the early morning light to find Buck looking down at her with a sleepy smile on his face.

"Are you all right?" he asked with a mixture of bemusement and concern.

Amanda was still struggling to bring the reality before her into perspective when Buck pulled strands of her hair away from her mouth, then leaned down and kissed her on the cheek.

"You must have been having one hell of a dream," he said. "I've never heard such moaning."

Amanda blinked, just now beginning to realize what was happening. Buck pressed against her, and memories of their lovemaking the night before came spilling into her consciousness. "I was asleep," she mumbled.

"So I gathered," he said with a laugh. "No bad dreams, I trust."

She yawned. "I was dreaming about Dameree, as a matter of fact. We were dancing in the jungle."

Buck laughed. "You don't even know Dameree. How can you dream about her?"

"Imagination, of course."

"Well, that's understandable, I suppose." He reflected. "I don't know if I'd recognize her myself. It's been about thirteen years since I've seen her.'' Buck fell silent, musing.

Amanda saw the faraway look on his face and wondered what he would think if he knew that her meeting that morning was in fact with Dameree. She glanced toward the window that was only now letting in the first signs of daylight. "What time is it, anyway?"

"Five-fifteen."

"Oh, God."

"We've got a seven o'clock train to catch, remember?"

Amanda started to throw back the covers, then realized that she was completely naked. She felt suddenly shy.

"You have to go now," she announced. "I have to get ready."

Buck grinned and rolled to the edge of the bed. Getting to his feet, he immodestly stood there, gathering his clothes. Amanda was glad it was he and not she who had to get up.

Brazenly stealing glances at him, she marveled at his well-proportioned physique and handsomely tanned body. But he didn't make it easy for her to do so. He was paying as much attention to her as she was to him. As Buck slipped on his shorts, Amanda found it more convenient to look the other way. She tried hard to appear indifferent.

After he had fastened his trousers, he picked up his remaining things, kissed her lightly on the lips and left the room. As he closed the door, Amanda sighed deeply.

He had been a perfect lover—gentle, considerate, affectionate. He was also full of an exquisite fire that made their lovemaking like no other. He had become much more integral to her life than the man in her frivolous daydreams at the beginning. Since they had undertaken the quest for the child, a bond had been forged between them.

But despite her hopeful expectations, Amanda remained cautious—there were so many uncertainties. How would his feelings for her survive the test of time?

WHEN AMANDA CAME OUT into the sitting room, it was a few minutes before six and Buck was waiting. He had ordered coffee and pastries, and upon seeing her, poured them each a cup of coffee. He glanced at her taupe safari dress approvingly.

"You look wonderful," he said, and kissed her on the cheek. "Thought we could have a quick bite in the room to save time. It's either that or resort to begging bowls."

"Begging bowls?"

"Yeah, haven't you seen the monks?"

"Buck, what are you talking about?"

He glanced at his watch. "You aren't a morning person, are you?"

She looked at him quizzically.

"If you're willing to take a few quick gulps of coffee and bring your pastry with you, I'll show you one of the most interesting sights in Bangkok."

Minutes later, they were out in front of the hotel. The omnipresent doorman and two sleepy cabbies were the only people around. Buck held the door to a taxi open as Amanda jumped in. He gave the driver instructions, and they swept out the hotel driveway and into the streets that were beginning to fill with people and vehicles. Five minutes later, they stopped in a small square in front of one of the city's many Buddhist temples.

Amanda looked out the window to see a long procession of monks with their saffron robes and shaved heads exiting the temple grounds. Like an army of ants, they filed out into the streets and *sois* of the surrounding district.

"What are they doing?"

"They're going out to collect their food for the day. See the bowls they're carrying? Those are their begging bowls. They collect food in them every morning at six."

"They have to beg?"

"It's not really begging. It's all part of the system here. The religious orders are supported by the community. Every family takes on the duty of contributing to the sustenance of the monks." Buck pointed. "You see the women by their doors? They wait for the monks every morning to make their contributions to their daily ration."

Amanda watched as an elderly monk stopped at the door of a nearby house. A young woman standing in the doorway with a large bowl placed a spoonful of food in the monk's bowl. No words were exchanged. After making her contribution, the woman made a deep *wai*, and dropped to her knees for a brief prayer before the monk silently moved on.

"You see," Buck explained, "the woman gains merit by her charitable act. She accomplishes her own religious objectives, and the monk obtains food to sustain himself for the day."

Amanda watched in amazement as another monk approached the same house. The ritual was repeated.

"What do they do for dinner?"

"Nothing. The monks only eat in the morning. They never take nourishment after eleven. The rest of the day supposedly is devoted to study and meditation."

"My God, with a life like that, how come there are so many of them?"

Buck laughed. "Virtually every male Thai spends at least a little time during his life as a monk or novice. It's practically one's patriotic duty."

"I had no idea it was that rigorous. I've seen them in the temples, of course, but—"

"You just have never gotten up this early to see how the other half lives?"

Amanda gently poked Buck in the ribs. After watching the spectacle for several more minutes, Buck spoke to the driver again, and they headed off toward the train station.

They found the old European-style structure very crowded. Amanda immediately noticed a certain energy about the place though the movement of the people seemed more like milling about than hurrying. There were a few other foreigners, but most of the people seemed to be up-country peasants though there was a smattering of workmen, priests and more affluent-looking people in Western clothing.

Buck bought their tickets, and they went to the platform where the train was scheduled to depart in ten minutes though there was no train in sight. Nevertheless, a sizable crowd was gathered waiting. People were looking at the American couple with curiosity, and Amanda felt herself moving closer to Buck, not out of fear but in response to the strangeness of their surroundings. She took his arm and remembered the way she felt encircled by him the night before.

About five minutes after the scheduled time of departure, the train arrived and everybody pushed and jostled their way on board. Buck and Amanda took a seat on the left side of the train so that they could see the river as they traveled north yet avoid the sun that was beating down through the windows on the other side.

Not long after their hurried departure, the train had gained the outskirts of the city and was rolling through the low, flat farmland along the Chao Phraya. On the sun side, the louvered shades were down, blocking out the punishing rays but still permitting the refreshing breezes to enter the car. The window beside Amanda and Buck was open, the sweet country air wafting in and caressing them as they watched the river and its people.

Amanda felt a certain thrill at their adventure. When she turned from the window, she found Buck looking at her, his mouth bent at the corners in amusement. He squeezed her fingers affectionately. In response, Amanda pressed his large hand between hers and looked into his eyes, feeling excited, carefree and happy.

Their eyes were locked in silent communication, a mute dialogue of awareness. She sensed Buck was reliving their intimacy—just as she was—when he touched her lips, first with his finger, then lightly with his smiling mouth. Amanda sighed and turned again to the richly verdant Thai countryside.

They had been gliding along the tracks for an hour and a half when Buck looked at his watch and announced they were not far from Ayudhya. "Who are you meeting with that's so secret?" he asked, taking wisps of her red hair between his fingers.

"It concerns a very sensitive case I'm working on." Amanda knew she sounded evasive, but she was unwilling to spin greater tales of deceit. She already felt disloyal to Buck because of her conspiracy with Dameree.

Amanda glanced at him nervously when he didn't comment further. She could tell he was thinking about her response. The urge to confess everything came over her, but she resisted again, telling herself that she was doing it for him.

Buck watched Amanda out of the corner of his eye—
he could tell that she was uncomfortable. There was
something fishy about this trip. It had seemed strange
from the first time she had mentioned it, coming on the
heels of the "Mrs. Michaels" charade at the orphanage
and the call she had received at the hotel shortly after.
Something told him it had to do with the mysterious visitor he had had at breakfast that morning. But what
would cause her to take on a meeting herself? Why hadn't
she confided in him?

Buck worried that somehow Amanda thought she was
sparing him or protecting him, though against what he
couldn't imagine. There was no reason he could see to
fear violence of any kind, but there were too many
strange twists in the adventure they had undertaken to
leave anything to chance. Even an unpleasant confron-
tation was something to be avoided.

Before long, they arrived in Ayudhya. Amanda had
thought about Dameree off and on during the trip, but
now that her meeting with her was imminent, she began
to feel nervous. She tried to act casual, but she sensed in
Buck awareness of her duplicity.

The town was very much as Buck had described it, a
small, quiet provincial community full of ancient ruins.
It was hard for Amanda to believe that, centuries earlier, more than a million people had lived there.

Outside the station, they found a *samlor*, and Buck
negotiated the fare for a trip first to the museum, then on
to the quay where Amanda had told him she wanted to be
taken. They climbed into the cramped cab of the vehicle, their bodies pressed close together.

"Hard to believe families of five or six ride in these
things, isn't it?" he asked as he slipped his arm around
her.

"I don't think they were made for people our size."

Despite the heat and discomfort of the situation, Amanda enjoyed the feel of Buck's leg against hers. She smiled at him when he squeezed her thigh just above the knee.

"Are you sure you don't want me to come along with you, at least to the place where you'll be meeting?"

"No, I'll be fine, really." She managed a smile intended to reassure him but knew it fell short. Amanda prayed this would go smoothly. She didn't want it to develop into a problem between them.

At the museum, Buck got out and paid the driver. "You don't have to give him anything else," he said, leaning over and looking into the cab at her. There was concern in his eyes. "Think you can find your way back here all right?"

Amanda had to laugh. "Buck, you treat me like an incompetent child. I can take care of myself. How do you suppose I got by on my previous trips to Bangkok?"

His expression became remorseful and he shrugged.

Amanda reached over and touched his hand. "I don't mean to sound ungrateful, and I do appreciate your concern."

Buck nodded. "See you at the entrance to the museum at twelve, then?"

"Okay, but if I'm a little late, don't worry."

He grimaced and stepped back, waving the driver on. "See you later," he called after her.

As Buck watched the *samlor* move down the street, he felt torn. He tried to convince himself to let her go, but his instincts told him to follow her. Knowing he had to act quickly, Buck stepped to a nearby taxi stand under the shade of a large tree. He roused the dozing driver of a battered old *samlor*, told him to follow the vehicle moving down the street and handed him a fifty *baht* note. The man came to life instantly, but Buck had an anxious moment when the engine failed to turn over on the first few tries. Finally, the driver got the little vehicle going, and they sped off in pursuit.

Fortunately, there was little traffic in the sleepy town, and they soon caught up to Amanda's *samlor*. Buck had to caution the driver not to get too close. Moments later, they were approaching the river, and Buck told him to stop.

A hundred feet ahead, Amanda's vehicle stopped, too, and Buck watched as she got out. A smile crossed his lips when he saw her hand the driver a bill—undoubtedly a tip—and he realized that she was right, he was being overly protective and paternalistic. *Why?* he wondered. He had always endeavored to be considerate to women, but he'd never received complaints before. Was it Amanda? Or was it that he treated her differently? He *felt* differently about her, that was for sure.

Amanda headed toward a nearby dock. Buck got out of his *samlor* and followed her, staying in the sparse crowds as much as possible, keeping his distance. He watched her walk along the quay, stopping to talk to people, probably trying to find someone who spoke English. Heads turned after her, and in spite of the rather delicate game he was playing, Buck found himself admiring the woman's shapely legs and the curve of her hips.

Finally, Amanda found someone she could communicate with, and Buck watched a scrawny boatman point farther up the dock, giving directions with elaborate sign language. Then, as she moved along, Buck followed, staying close to the crowds clustered near the street vendors.

When Amanda stopped at a sampan ferry point, Buck realized that she intended to cross the river. He knew that if he waited to cross after her, she would have disappeared by the time he got there so he decided to look for someone who might take him over at the same time. Stepping to the water's edge of the broad quay, Buck looked up and down the dock for a motor launch of some kind.

He spotted several men in an old boat half full of baskets of produce. He pulled two one hundred *baht* bills from his wallet and waved them at the men. *"Dai prod! Dai prod!"* he called, trying to get their attention. And with the money, he did.

THE OLD BOATMAN LOOKED UP at Amanda with a toothy grin and helped her step down into the sampan. His weathered skin and sinewy body indicated strength as well as age. The planking was wet, and she nearly slipped as she made her way toward the varnished wooden seat the boatman had gestured for her to take.

Amanda had expected it to be cool under the low, corrugated iron roof of the craft, but the metal had been warmed by the late morning sun and radiated heat like an oven.

She centered herself on the slippery seat as the boatman prepared to cast off. He moved agilely in his bare feet along the narrow gunwale and the plank from which he maneuvered the craft with a single oar. Amanda pressed a handkerchief against her moist face and looked around with curiosity as they started across the river.

There were a number of larger powerboats on the water and their wakes caused the sampan to bob up and down like a cork. As the boat rolled underneath her, Amanda slid on the slippery seat from one gunwale to the other. She looked up at the boatman, who gave her a toothy grin and exclaimed something in Thai that she didn't understand. Amanda chuckled to herself.

On the far shore, they landed at a small dock wedged amid houseboats and floating shops. Amanda asked the boatman the way to the Panan Cherng Temple, then headed off in the direction he pointed. A short distance up the road, she came to the gates to the wat where the temple was located.

Entering, she found a quiet garden though there were a number of people about. Some were resting in the shade of the large trees, others were engaged in the commerce of the temple—buying fortunes from a priest, sticking gold leaf on the statue of Buddha, bartering for religious souvenirs.

Amanda looked at her watch. She was ten minutes early but decided to wander toward the enormous bronze Buddha that looked to be fifty or sixty feet high. She heard the word *farang* whispered after her several times and realized how much she stood out. Still, there was a serenity about the place that left her feeling comfortable despite her unique appearance and her nervousness at meeting Dameree.

Amanda stood under a tree near the Buddha watching some young men shaking fortune-telling sticks out of bamboo holders. Although they seemed serious enough about what they were doing, they also appeared to be having a good time, chattering quietly as they read what their fates would be on the small slips of paper the priests handed them.

After a few minutes, Amanda strolled over to the base of the Buddha and waited as the girl had instructed her to do. She looked up at the bronze statue towering above her and felt a sense of awe. She wondered if Dameree had intentionally selected this place to meet as a psychological gambit.

"Mrs. Michaels?" came a soft voice behind her.

Amanda turned around to find a thin young woman in a white blouse and black skirt smiling up at her shyly. "Yes, I'm Amanda Michaels."

The girl bowed slightly. "Please come with me," she said softly, then turned and walked farther into the garden.

The grounds of the wat were quite large, and the farther they went from the temple, the fewer people there were. At the back of the garden, they came to a vine-covered wall with a large wooden gate. Amanda's guide knocked, and a moment later, the door swung open and a young man in a white jacket buttoned to the neck appeared.

Several words were exchanged between them, and the man stepped back to permit them to enter a small, private garden, cool and completely shaded with lush tropical plants. As Amanda stepped into the retreat, she saw a lovely woman in her late thirties standing against a backdrop of deep-green ferns. Her hands were clasped at her breast, and she wore a red silk panung, an exotically feminine garment wrapped tightly around the hips and falling in a loose drape to the feet.

As Amanda and the girl approached, a slight smile crossed the woman's lips. She *wai*ed gracefully, then extended her hand. "Thank you, Mrs. Michaels, for coming here to see me." Dameree smiled more broadly now, and as Amanda took her hand, she was struck by the fragile delicacy of it.

"I'm very pleased to meet you, Dameree."

The woman nodded graciously, dismissed the young woman who had accompanied Amanda to the garden, and gestured for the American to sit in one of the cushioned chairs nearby.

"You are very beautiful, as I expected, Mrs. Michaels."

"Thank you. You are most kind, but please, call me Amanda."

Dameree nodded. The young man was standing in the background, and the Thai woman glanced at him, then at her. "Can I offer to you some tea?"

"That would be very nice, thank you." Amanda studied the delicately beautiful woman as she spoke with the man. Her skin was milky white and as smooth as porcelain. Her eyes were black yet gentle. It was hard to believe this woman was the massage girl Buck had described.

Dameree's nails were very long and glossy scarlet, yet the effect suggested more a reedy flower than anything sinister. She wore several gold necklaces, rings with various precious stones and her black, luxuriant hair was twisted at the back of her head. Amanda thought of her own green cheongsam and her attempt to imitate the Oriental look and felt suddenly inadequate.

Having dispatched the young man, Dameree turned back to Amanda. "Please, how is your husband, Buck? Is he saddened by the child?"

"Yes," Amanda replied, feeling like a fraud. "He feels very frustrated not being able to verify her whereabouts."

Dameree looked perplexed. "'Whereabouts'?"

"I'm sorry. Buck is upset because he cannot find where the child is, Dameree."

"Yes, I know he has many questions. It is why I have asked you to come. My husband would not want me to speak to Buck, but I thought it would be good to talk to you, his wife. You have not said to him we meet...."

"No, you asked me not to so I didn't."

"Thank you, Amanda."

The young man returned with a pot of tea and two cups on a tray. There was also a miniature bowl with a lotus blossom floating in it. Amanda wondered if that touch was Dameree's.

The tea was placed on a low table between them, and the man withdrew at Dameree's signal. She took the pot in her graceful hands and poured tea into each of the cups, handing one to Amanda.

Dameree looked into her eyes, sadly. "I know he would like to know where is this child, Amanda. I am very sad to say I do not know it myself."

"Did you send her to the States? That's the information we've received so far."

"Many years ago, my husband's sister took the baby to the Christian Mission Orphanage in Bangkok to send her to your country, Amanda. I have not seen my baby since that time. She is a girl now. She is in America, I hope very much."

"Is there anything you can tell me that will help us identify and find your child?"

"Yes, I will tell you what is possible, but I must ask of you a kindness."

"Certainly, if I can...."

"You see, my dear Amanda, even though I send this baby away and she is no longer in my head, she is always in my heart. I have two fine sons with my husband, and they are my true children, but my heart cries to know that this first baby is well. I ask of you to give me news of my daughter, perhaps a letter one time each year? If you will do this, I will tell you what I can."

"Of course I will be happy to keep you informed of what I learn, but even with your help, it is not certain that we will find her. And then there are the obligations to the child and her adoptive parents. I have told Buck the same thing—I cannot break a trust."

"I understand this, Amanda. You are an honorable lady."

Amanda thought of her deception and winced inwardly. "I'd just like to help you and Buck if I can."

Both women sipped their tea.

"Please tell me about your daughter, Dameree."

Behind the cool, feminine veneer, Amanda saw emotion fill the woman's face. She was trying to steel herself for a painful conversation. It was apparent how difficult this meeting was and what a sacrifice it had been for Dameree to ask for it.

A sheen of tears appeared in the lovely woman's eyes, and Amanda saw her lip quiver. "I don't know what to say to you."

Amanda felt her own eyes misting with the emotional words of this heartbroken mother. It was the first time since she had begun working with Amerasian children that she had ever spoken directly with the natural mother of a child. "Why did you decide to give up your baby?" she asked as gently as she could.

Dameree looked at Amanda for a moment and seemed to understand that it was a part of the story that must be told. She lowered her eyes.

"For many months, I did not want to give up my baby, Amanda, but at the end, I had no other choice. You see, I was very poor and my family it was suffering. When the baby was only some months old, I met a man who I loved very much. He was Chinese, very rich, and I became his mistress. He loved me very much, too, but I did not tell him about my baby. I still lived in the house of Buck, and I made a story to deceive him.

"One day, my lover said to me he was very sad because he loved me, and if I was Chinese, he would marry me, but his family could not have the wife of a son if she is not also Chinese. This I was very happy to hear because at my birth, Amanda, I am Chinese, not Thai like second family. When I told the truth to my lover, he was very happy. Then he and his father met my family Chin, my birth family. The marriage was arranged."

"But he didn't know about your baby?"

"No, he did not know. To be a good wife, I knew I must tell him the truth about my daughter and so I showed her to him. He was not angry with me, but because the baby is also American and not pure Chinese, he said his family would be very upset. He knew my feelings as a mother, Amanda, but he wanted to marry me so much. I cried for many nights. Then I agreed when he says to me I should send the baby to the country of her father. This was twelve years ago. Now my daughter is nearly a young woman."

"It must have been a very difficult decision for you."

"Yes... most difficult." Dameree dabbed her eyes again.

Amanda watched the woman, sharing her pain, sympathizing with the burden she had carried all these years. Amanda thought of Buck and his sadness, which paralleled Dameree's. It seemed apparent that he was the father of the child though Dameree had not admitted it. For Buck's sake, Amanda knew that she could not leave without finding out.

"I thought that a day would come when I must know about my daughter's life," Dameree continued, "so when I sent the baby to the orphanage, I wrote also a note saying her name. I hoped that if I wanted to find her sometime in the future, I could follow her by it.''

"What is her name, Dameree?"

"Lotus Moon," she said in a half whisper.

"How lovely."

"Thank you," Dameree said, wiping the corners of her eyes with her handkerchief. "It was the name of my grandmother. Of course it was the Chinese name, but I sent to the orphanage the English words so that the people could understand it in America."

"I hope we can find Lotus Moon through the records."

"Let me tell you this, Amanda. I know that the records are not always good, and some people are not to be trusted. Because of this, I put a small tattoo on the left ankle of my baby. It is a lotus blossom and a crescent moon. This way, I will always know her." Dameree plucked the flower from the small bowl on the table. She spun it in her fingers. "Tonight also is the crescent moon. It is a good omen."

Each of them looked into the other's eyes with understanding.

"I know this has been hard for you," Amanda said softly, "but Buck will be grateful."

"Yes, he is a good man, a kind man. Please tell him the things I have told you and explain why it is I cannot see him. I think my husband has made trouble for Buck, and of this I am very sorry. He also is a good husband, and he wants to protect me and see that I am happy. He is a man, he does not understand that in a mother's heart a child never dies. I forgive him this. I hope you and Buck will forgive him also."

"Certainly, Dameree. The important thing is that we find the child to ensure that she is well. That is Buck's

purpose. I know he will appreciate what you have done."
Amanda looked at her watch. "It is late. Perhaps I should go now."

Dameree nodded. They both rose. "You will remember your promise, dear Amanda. Please write to me with news of my daughter."

"Yes, I will, Dameree."

Then the woman took a slip of paper from a fold in her panung. "Here is the address of my brother. Always please to write to me there so that my husband does not worry for me."

Amanda nodded, then spontaneously the women embraced.

"Should you ever see Lotus Moon, please send to her my love."

Amanda nodded, fighting back the well of emotion that suddenly overtook her. They walked slowly to the garden gate. She knew she had to ask Dameree whether Buck was the child's father, but she hadn't thought of a delicate way to bring it up...perhaps as they were saying their goodbyes. "Thank you for asking me to come and visit you, Dameree."

"You are very kind," she replied, taking Amanda's hand. "I am happy for you and Buck. I wish for you the best."

They briefly embraced again, and Amanda pulled open the large wooden door, formulating the ultimate question in her mind. Turning to Dameree, she was surprised to see dismay slowly spreading across the woman's face. Amanda abruptly spun around. Standing not ten feet from them and leaning against a tree was Buck Michaels.

CHAPTER TEN

AS SHE STARED INCREDULOUSLY, Amanda heard Dameree gasp. She glanced at the woman whose hand was over her mouth. Angrily Amanda swung her eyes back to Buck. "What are you doing here?"

Dameree let out a little cry of anguish. She brushed past Amanda and started to run across the grounds of the wat. Buck quickly intercepted her, grasping the woman by the arm. "Wait. Please wait, Dameree."

Amanda's face was red with anger and humiliation as Buck looked at her imploringly. He turned again to Dameree.

"I'm sorry, but I have to speak with you. Just a few words, please."

Dameree's head was bowed, her lip pressed between her teeth. "I have told your wife everything, Buck," she whispered, refusing to look at him.

"Is she mine, Dameree? Did you tell Amanda whether she is mine?" He looked at Amanda questioningly, his face twisted in torment. She lowered her eyes, feeling anguish for all of them.

Dameree emitted a little sob, nodding her head. "Yes," she murmured, "she is our daughter."

Buck's hand dropped from her arm. He was staring blankly at her face as though he were unable to comprehend the truth he had known all along.

Dameree looked up at him. For a moment, Amanda could see the pain Buck and his former lover shared. They were disparate souls separated by the passing years, thrown together for a brief instant of shared anguish— the parents of a lost child. They continued looking at each other, and Amanda felt her heart go out to them both. Nothing further was said so Dameree silently turned and left the garden.

AMANDA STARED OUT THE WINDOW of the *Orchid Queen*, her eyes passing over the reel of scenery drifting by without actually seeing it. The afternoon was languorous and Buck's mood melancholy as he sat across from her, lost in thought. There was nothing to do but comfort him.

They had walked in silence to the dock where the hotel ship called, she putting her arm around his waist and hugging him to cheer him up. He was appreciative and seemed to have recovered after that, but in the quiet of the ship's lounge he had drifted back into a bluer mood.

"Come on," she said, trying to cheer him again, "let me buy you another beer."

He smiled, lamely, but seemed to be making an effort. "Okay, another beer."

Their eyes met. "I'd have thought you'd be happy with the information Dameree gave us, Buck. At least we know that your daughter isn't abandoned in the streets of Bangkok."

"Yeah, that's true." His smile was more genuine now. "Sorry if I'm being a downer for you. Even though I expected it, I'm not doing very well with the reality of having a thirteen-year-old daughter I've never met."

"I can understand that. And it had to be traumatic for you seeing Dameree after all these years, too."

"I felt more badly about that than anything. I knew she didn't want to see me, but I *had* to ask. I *had* to know."

"I understand, and I'm sure she does, too. It's over now. No permanent damage was done."

"Yes, Amanda, but think how much of the girl's life I've missed. My own daughter and I've never even seen her."

She took his hand. "Buck, your purpose is not to see Lotus Moon, it's to verify that she's all right, remember? Don't get obsessed with what you've missed. That was fated long ago. Please be careful not to get caught up emotionally in the wrong objectives."

He nodded, but Amanda could see the qualification in his assent.

"Look, I promise to do my best when we get home to verify her well-being. Tell yourself that's all you'll need."

"You're right, Amanda, I know."

She looked into his cerulean eyes, trying to coax back the man who had been so taken with her the night before. After a moment, Buck began responding to the smile on her lips. His hand tightened over hers, and Amanda felt him returning to her again.

BY THE TIME the *Orchid Queen* docked at the Oriental Hotel, it was late afternoon, too early to eat, but neither of them felt like staying in their suite. Amanda could see that Buck was restless.

"Let's go out somewhere. Someplace where we can stroll," she said. "Is there a nice park you like?"

"There's Lumpini Park. Have you ever been there?"

"No. Where is it?"

"On the east side of town off Rama IV Road. It's only a few minutes by taxi. Would you like to go?"

"Sure."

A short time later, they were at the entrance to the park. Buck took her hand as they wandered along the meandering paths, staying out of the heat of the sun as much as they could. Amanda felt a closeness between them, yet she could tell he was still troubled.

Finally, they sat on a bench at the edge of a large open field where a group of men and boys were gathered, obviously in the midst of preparation for some sort of activity.

"What are they doing, Buck?"

"Looks like they're getting ready for kite flying. They're probably practicing for the big festival in the spring. Kite fighting is virtually the national sport."

"I've heard about it, but I've never seen it. How do they fight?"

Buck smiled. "It's very erotic, actually. The fights are between male and female kites."

Amanda glanced toward the field again, her mouth curling wryly. "Dare I ask how you tell them apart?"

Buck laughed. "Well, you don't have to turn them on their backs like a puppy or a kitten."

She poked him gently in the ribs.

"You see that star-shaped kite the man in the blue shirt is holding? That's a male kite."

"Looks rather hostile."

Buck grinned. "The female doesn't look so intimidating, but she can be rather insidious."

She looked up at him. "Are you referring to kites or people?"

"Uh..."

Amanda elbowed him again.

"Let me see if I can spot a female for you.... There," Buck said, pointing, "you see that squarish kite, the white one?"

"Yes."

"That's a female."

"Rather plain, I'd say."

"Wait till you see her move."

She glanced up at Buck, and he slipped his arm around her shoulders. The kite enthusiasts were beginning to put their crafts aloft.

"How do they fight, Buck?"

"The Thais call it 'the love poem of the gods,' or something like that. It's the male-female principle acted out in the skies."

"Is that what you mean by erotic?"

"Well, look at that little female. See her wiggle? Her movements are frivolous and alluring compared to the male's. Look at the big red one. See how sweeping and majestic his movements are?"

"Maybe that's because men made them and fly them, Buck. A woman's interpretation might be very different."

He squeezed her shoulder. "But the Thais are a little more subtle than you give them credit for. You haven't seen the male and female kites fight yet. The ritual is much more true to life than you would think." Buck ran his fingertips lightly along her neck, and she shivered under the pleasure of his touch.

"I don't know whether I dare ask what you mean by 'true to life.' "

"The best way to describe it is an aerial interpretation of male and female life forces, the yin and yang. You see, Amanda, the sport consists of the female trying to position herself above the male and come down over him, wrapping her trailing tails around him and forcing him to the ground.''

"Yeah, Buck, just like life."

"Well, you have to admit—"

Amanda turned to him, feeling a little indignant. "I have to admit what? That Buddha or Confucius or whoever was responsible for these myths was a man?"

Buck laughed. "I would have thought the idea of a female trying to dominate the male would appeal to you. Better than subjugation, isn't it?"

"Does it appeal to *you*?"

His fingers trailed along the back of her neck. "Well, I have a yen for the yin in you."

Amanda groaned. "You may be majestic, Buck Michaels, but your puns are terrible."

His eyes twinkled.

"I hate to bring this lofty experience down to earth, Mr. Yang," she said happily, "but I'm getting hungry."

Buck leaned over and kissed her softly on the lips. "The question is, hungry for what?"

Amanda smiled at him coyly. "After last night, not shrimp—that's for sure!"

AS THEY ENTERED THE LOBBY of the hotel, the desk clerk called to Buck. "Mr. Michaels! Sir, I have a telex for you."

Buck went over to the desk and was handed an envelope that he tore open and read while Amanda waited. His face grew somber.

"Bad news?" she asked with concern.

"I'm afraid so. There's a crisis at the paper. One of my key editors has resigned, and there's been a problem with our bankers. My financial people are all upset. I'd better get back to Los Angeles."

Amanda felt her heart drop. "When will you leave?"

"I'd probably better go tomorrow. I think there's a late morning flight."

Looking at Buck's worried face, Amanda thought about that first time she had seen him working at his desk, his glasses perched on the end of his nose, his thoughts wrapped up in the papers in front of him. She realized suddenly that the man in that office was the real Buck Michaels, and that this man who teased her, laughed with her and loved her was a man on vacation—a man who, for a while, had had a different set of priorities.

Buck looked up from the telex he had read over again and, seeing her long face, brushed her cheek with his fingers. "I am sorry, Amanda. I was looking forward to several relaxing days now that we've traced Lotus Moon." He smiled. "Will you be able to fly back with me tomorrow?"

"No, I'm afraid not. I've got at least three or four more days' work to do." She wondered whether he was being polite, whether he really did want her to return with him.

"Well, that's not so long." He folded the telex and put it in his pocket. "Come on," he said, taking her arm. "Let's go have a nice dinner."

He didn't say it, but Amanda heard "last meal" in his voice, and she suddenly felt very sad—like someone rudely awakened from a sweet dream. These idyllic days with Buck Michaels had been pure escape for her. Thinking of him in Los Angeles dealing with his concerns at work suggested a very different reality from what they had shared.

After freshening up in their rooms, they went to the Verandah Restaurant where they had eaten the night they arrived. As before, they ordered curry, but Amanda ate with less appetite than the first time. Buck seemed preoccupied, sitting quietly for long periods of time.

"You're worried about the *Tribune*, aren't you?"

He looked up at her guiltily, as a man who had been discovered. "I'm sorry, Amanda, I'm being a bore."

"No, of course not. I understand. It must be hard for you." She paused. "Are you sorry you came?"

"No, not in the least." He took her hand. "This has been a wonderful trip for me...."

She was sure she heard qualification in his voice.

"Being with you has been an incredible experience, and if it weren't for you, I'd never have tracked down Lotus Moon. That's a wonderful gift."

Amanda decided he was just making polite conversation. She wondered what he *really* felt. Then she thought of the male kites in the park trying to evade the tails of the female kites. Maybe Buck was right. Maybe kite fighting was true to life after all.

"Even though the trip is ending prematurely," he said, rubbing her hand with his thumb, "a lot of good has come out of it. I think we ought to celebrate—have a going-away party."

Amanda couldn't help the sad look she gave him.

"Come on," he said more brightly. "Cheer up. We'll have a welcome-home party when you get back to Los Angeles."

She made a conscious effort to lighten her mood, forcing a more cheerful expression. "Okay, but I'll hold you to it."

A devilish look came over Buck's face, and he pulled her hand to his lips. "How about celebrating tonight with a bottle of champagne?"

BUCK WATCHED HER standing in front of the mirrored door of the armoire as though she were questioning the sadness on her own face. She was still wearing the pale-yellow sundress she had changed into for dinner though she had removed her shoes. Moved by her beauty, Buck put down his champagne flute and went to stand behind her.

She looked at him in the mirror, smiling slightly as he slipped his arms around her waist and kissed the side of her neck.

"How can anyone so beautiful look so sad?" he murmured.

Her eyes engaged his frankly. "It's been a bittersweet day, Buck."

"You mean about Dameree?"

"Yes, that and your leaving."

His arms tightened, and he pressed her more firmly against the front of him. He kissed her neck once more. "It'll only be a few days, then we'll be together again."

"Will we?"

Buck looked at her reflection in the mirror, surprised. "Unless you plan to go home via China and defect or something...."

"Are you just saying that, or do you mean it?"

"See each other? Of course we will. Don't you want to see me?"

"It's not what either of us wants *now* that matters."

"What do you mean, Amanda?"

"I've had a wonderful time with you here in Bangkok, Buck. It's been like a fairy tale. But I've lived enough to know that life is not a fairy tale."

"You mean it's nearly midnight, and you're wondering what will happen when the clock strikes twelve?" He nibbled at her ear, delaying her response.

"Well, to be blunt, the Buck Michaels I've come to know here in Thailand is not the one I knew in Los Angeles."

He let his tongue slither across the back of her neck and felt a yearning for her in his loins. "You didn't know me very well in Los Angeles," he said to her reflection.

"That's not what I meant."

He pulled her body against his, feeling himself harden. "What did you mean?"

"I meant we both have full lives back home, with distinct priorities. I'm not sure that there's room for what we've had here in Bangkok."

Buck took the zipper at the back of her dress between his fingers and slowly pulled it to her waist. Then he lightly trailed his lips down her spine. "I can't speak for you, but I know what I've got room for."

"Buck, are you listening to what I'm saying? I'm being serious!"

"I've heard every word you've said. I just don't see any point in borrowing trouble. We have tonight, let's make the most of it."

She was silent, and the image in the mirror looked skeptical. Appearing to reflect on what he had said, she seemed to be wavering.

He kissed her lightly on the cheek. "Trust me, Amanda. Fairy tales sometimes have a way of coming true."

She reached behind her and touched his cheek with her hand. Buck kissed her fingers, then unfastened her bra, sliding his hands through the opening of her dress and around her torso. He cupped each breast in his hands, kneading the soft, ripe fullness of them. He had grown so hard that his clothing was constricting at his loins. As he kissed her throat, the soft murmur of her moan vibrated under his lips.

"Oh, Buck...."

"You weren't trying to tell me you'll be too busy to see me anymore?" he whispered into her ear, his hands working the soft flesh of her breasts.

Her head rolled back against him. "No..." she vaguely mumbled. "But I thought..."

Feeling assured, he lowered his mouth to hers and covered it, eagerly tasting its sweetness. She moaned again.

Buck looked at the woman in the mirror once more. She was lost in pleasure. He could see the rippling motion of his hands under her dress, and his desire for her became urgent. Amanda looked at him through half-open eyes.

"Oh Buck...."

He slid the dress off her shoulders, down over her hips and to the floor, where she stepped out of it. Amanda removed her bra and tossed it on a nearby chair. Buck threw the dress aside as well. Wearing only her bikini panties she turned to him, her arms in a modest attitude, partially covering her breasts.

He gathered her into his arms, holding her near-naked body hard against him. The woman in the mirror had her back to him now, but the view it afforded—the pleasant curve of her hips and buttocks—incited him even more. Buck chafed at his clothing, wanting to tear it from his body and take her, find his pleasure in her.

But as badly as he wanted her, as badly as his body craved hers, it was not just her body he wanted—it was the total woman, the woman who had touched him so deeply, so completely. Maybe Amanda was right—three or four days could be a hell of a long time.

"Come to the bed with me," he whispered. "I want to make love to you."

Moments later, Amanda lay naked, clutching the sheet up under her chin as Buck undressed. She felt strangely shy and didn't look at him until he walked to the side of the bed. He lifted the sheet and slid under it beside her. The warmth of his leg and hip against hers was welcome, and she wanted to be close to him, but she didn't want him to take her, not yet.

"Would you hold me for a while first, Buck?"

He kissed her on the temple. "Whatever you wish, my darling."

Being gathered into his arms, Amanda felt sadness overtake her again. She wanted him near, yet his touch only reminded her of their imminent separation. In her heart, she was afraid, afraid despite his assurances.

Buck seemed to sense her misgivings because he settled back on his pillow and stroked her head lightly. She felt like a child being consoled for some terrible loss. The affection was welcome, but it couldn't erase the imagined deprivation.

"Why don't we plan your welcome-home party," he said with a reassuring tone.

Amanda couldn't help wondering at the way his thoughts had been paralleling her own. "You don't have to handle me with kid gloves. I'm not a baby."

"No, you aren't. But a little tender loving care never hurt anybody."

"I should be consoling you, Buck. You were the one who had the rough day."

He was still stroking her hair. "Eh..."

"Come on, don't be brave. Tell the truth. What are you feeling now?"

"I'm wishing you'd hold your tongue long enough for me to kiss you."

"You don't feel upset . . . about anything?"

Buck kissed her on the forehead, then propped himself up on his elbow. He ran his fingers lightly over the exposed skin of her chest. "I'm a firm believer in the idea that what you think is how you feel. Right now, I'd rather think about how nice it is to be in bed with you."

Amanda touched his cheek, and Buck smiled down at her, turning his head to kiss her fingers.

"You're a very sweet man, Buck. In fact, Dameree said the same thing this morning."

"That I'm sweet?"

"Those weren't her exact words, I don't think, but it amounted to the same thing."

There was a touch of embarrassment on his face, but he said nothing. He leaned over and kissed her mouth, holding the caress longer than she expected. Amanda felt a spark of her earlier excitement. Finally, the kiss ended breathlessly.

Buck's hand slipped under the sheet, and he cupped her breast, his mouth falling against her ear. The excitement in his breathing aroused her, and her loins began to tingle. He kissed her again, his tongue penetrating her mouth. Eventually, his hand went to the exquisite place between her legs and, finding it moist with expectation, he lifted himself over her.

But Amanda, craving union with him, pulled Buck down to her. She clung to him, enjoying the feel of his hard strong body against her, and she wished with all her heart that she could have him like this always—warm and protective over her, gentle and loving.

He kissed her again sweetly. She opened her legs to receive him, gasping slightly as he penetrated her. Buck's lips were on her neck now, and she held his head against her own, so full of emotion that tears flooded her eyes.

Consumed as she was by his exquisite embrace, Amanda hardly noticed when the tears began rolling down her cheeks. She savored the physical pleasures of her body and listened to the sounds of Buck's passion, her lips silently asking the question, *But do you love me?*

CHAPTER ELEVEN

AMANDA ARRIVED BACK at the Oriental Hotel around noon the next day. The doorman in his *jongkraben* pants smiled a cheerful greeting, but she didn't feel cheerful in the least. She was alone.

Nodding at the man, she strode through the door he held open and went to the desk for her room key. "Any messages?" she asked, though she had no reason to expect any. Buck was on a plane somewhere over the Pacific, headed for home.

"No messages, Miss Parr."

Amanda turned, briefcase in hand, and headed for the Noel Coward Suite. She had told Buck that morning that she would switch hotels now that he was going, but he suggested she stay. "The room is paid up through the end of the week," he had said. "Why leave?"

Entering the suite she had shared with Buck, knowing he was already hundreds of miles away, Amanda felt an emptiness. Looking around the now familiar room, she saw his copy of the Asian edition of the *Wall Street Journal* and realized how much she missed him.

Amanda sat in a chair and removed the shoes that had been hurting her swollen feet. Walking in the heat that morning had been sheer torture. She had managed to complete the necessary formalities at the government ministry for transferring the next group of children and would be calling on Mrs. Pakorn that afternoon. The visit could prove to be an embarrassing one. Having to see her as "Mrs. Michaels" was not a prospect she looked forward to.

In the end, the deception had served to help both Buck and Dameree, but she would be dealing with Mrs. Pakorn for months and perhaps years to come. Amanda would have to find a way to tell her the truth though no acceptable justification for the lie came to mind.

Amanda walked to the side table and absentmindedly picked up the first edition Noel Coward, flipping through the pages without reading a word. It had been a wonderful week, one of the happiest of her life, one she'd never forget. Suddenly, she felt the need to express her gratitude to Buck and thought of writing him a note, a letter to tell him how she felt.

She went to the desk, looking for writing paper. To her surprise, she found a number of sheets of personalized stationery, some with "Amanda Parr" embossed at the top and some that said "Preston Michaels." Finding their names together brought up a surge of emotion. He had only been gone for a few hours, but it seemed much longer.

Amanda blinked away the tears that had filled her eyes and looked at her watch. It was nearly twelve-thirty, and she had told Buck to inform Kupnol Sustri that she would be on the terrace having lunch between twelve-thirty and one. Buck had wanted to give both him and Mr. Chin something, as promised, and asked Amanda if she would be the custodian until Kupnol came by to pick it up. Not wanting to miss the man, she hurried into her bath to freshen up.

A short time later, Amanda was sitting at a table on the terrace under a large white-and-black umbrella, sipping ice tea and watching the river traffic. One of the hotel cruise ships was departing from the quay, and she recalled the night they had arrived, Buck's conversation with the night watchman, and then yesterday the melancholy cruise back from Ayudhya. It had been an emotional week, and a fabulously exciting one, too.

But what of her future with Buck? Would there really be one, or were his reassuring words at their parting an attempt to smooth over a difficult situation? She thought of their deception—her role as Amanda Michaels. The name was bittersweet to her, suggesting both a yearning within that she hadn't fully addressed and a fear of waking up and discovering it had all been just a dream.

"Excuse me, Mrs. Michaels?"

Amanda turned in surprise, not fully appreciating the irony of the address until she recognized the cherubic face of Kupnol Sustri. "Oh, Mr. Sustri. Good afternoon." She gestured toward the chair opposite her. "Please sit down."

"I am sorry to disturb you, Mrs. Michaels, but Buck said I should come."

"That's quite all right. I was expecting you." She opened her purse and took out an envelope. "Buck wanted me to give you this."

He accepted the envelope Amanda handed him, bowing politely. "Thank you, Mrs. Michaels."

Amanda had the urge to blurt out the truth about her relationship with Buck, but she held back, realizing she didn't know what the consequences might be. Except for Mrs. Pakorn, all of the people who believed the phony story of their marriage were associated with Buck, not her. And the deception of Mrs. Pakorn had been Amanda's doing, not Buck's. The frustration she felt was mixed with a confusing array of emotions.

"I was very sorry that Buck must go so suddenly to Los Angeles, Mrs. Michaels. I was of the hope that you and he would be my guests for dinner some evening."

"That's very kind. I'm sure Buck would have enjoyed it very much." Amanda listened to her own words, marveling at how much like a wife she sounded.

"I hope there is no serious problem for Buck."

"It was urgent business at the paper. It's very hard for him to get away."

"Will you be returning soon to the States, Mrs. Michaels?"

"Yes, in a few days."

"Most unfortunate my good friend Buck must leave. As a new wife, you must be very sad."

"Yes, Mr. Sustri, I am."

"Your husband and I, we spend many, many months together when he lived here in Bangkok. He is my very good friend. You are a special lady to be the wife of Buck Michaels," he said graciously. "I could see it on his face that you are very special to him."

Amanda brightened. "Thank you."

"The first Mrs. Michaels I didn't know, but she could not be a lady half so good as you." He nodded respectfully. "The first one, she did not like children, I believe it. That is why, perhaps, he did not look for this girl of Dameree for all these many years. But a good lady like you, who would help her husband find the baby of him and another woman, is very special lady."

"Thank you for the compliment, Mr. Sustri, but when did you learn that Buck was the father of Dameree's child?"

"No one said it to me, but I thought always that it was so."

Amanda studied Sustri. She was curious about what Buck's old confidant might tell her about the past. She had heard Buck's version, and Dameree, too, had been very discreet. "Tell me, Mr. Sustri, you knew both Dameree and Buck. What was it like when he lived here in Bangkok?"

He smiled. "We have a saying here in Thailand. 'A man's tongue is sometimes longer than his memory.' I should not tell you things that are not my business, but because I have only good to say of Buck, perhaps it is all right."

"I know that they were lovers, of course, but there were other ladies, too, weren't there?"

"Ah, Mrs. Michaels, there were many. But I do not have to tell you of your husband's charms. And, of course, that was a long time ago."

"Why didn't Dameree answer Buck's letters after his accident when he was taken to the States?"

"Who can understand the mind of a woman but another? This I do not know except that the Oriental people are very...how you say...'fatal'?"

"Fatalistic?"

"Yes, fatalistic. I think Dameree knows that it was not her fate to marry Buck. She thought it best if she accept it as so."

"But Buck loved her and she loved him, surely."

"Love has many faces, Mrs. Michaels."

"Yes, I suppose."

"Now Buck loves you, this is true."

"How do you know?"

He turned his palms up and shrugged. "You are his wife!"

"That doesn't mean he loves me, it just means that it is politic for you to say that he does."

"Me, I am not a politician, Mrs. Michaels."

Amanda smiled to herself. "No, nor am I."

They laughed.

"So will you go to find this daughter of Buck and Dameree in your country?"

"Yes, Buck wants to ensure that she is all right. We hope she is with a good family, in a good home."

"Then she will not come to live with you and Buck?"

"No. That's not Buck's purpose." She looked at Sustri with curiosity. "Why? Did you think that was Buck's intent?"

"Months back when Buck was in Bangkok, I could see he wants very much to find this girl. Even when I could not find her, he insists for it. He was...how you say...'a dog and his bone'?"

"Like a dog with a bone."

"Yes, that's it."

"Buck *can* be persistent."

"He always knows what he wants, and he wants it yesterday." Sustri laughed. "Buck would not make a very good Thai."

Amanda wondered if the man's insight into Buck was cause for worry. His obsession with Lotus Moon did seem deep-seated. She sighed. There was already enough to worry about without taking that on as well. Of more immediate concern was whether her "husband" would even remember her when she returned home.

"Well, Mrs. Michaels, I have taken much of your time. I must leave you now." He stood. "Thank you again for this courtesy," he said, lifting the envelope. "Please to give my thank-yous to Buck and my best regards. And please, Mrs. Michaels, my best wishes to you in your new marriage."

"Thank you, Mr. Sustri." And Amanda smiled as best she could under the circumstances.

THE WEEK SEEMED to crawl by. Since Buck had gone, the days seemed hot, boring and empty. Everything was starting to annoy Amanda, even the good-natured Thais. The national philosophy—*mai pen rai*—became an anathema to her, and she longed to be home with Buck Michaels.

Friday finally came, just when it seemed as if it never would. Amanda had completed the work she had set out for herself and had managed to struggle through her sessions with Mrs. Pakorn still as "Mrs. Michaels," having decided to wait until her next trip to disclose the truth to the woman.

Her bag was packed, and she was waiting for the bellhop to come and take it for her. She looked around the sitting room that was filled with so many memories even though she had been there only a short time. There was the table where she and Buck had eaten, the couch where he had seduced her, the telephone. . . .

She remembered the call from Dameree's young agent and Buck's hands under her gown, arousing her. She remembered the champagne, Buck carrying her to the bed, him introducing her as his wife and how good it felt when Kupnol Sustri *wai*ed deeply and complimented Buck on her beauty.

Amanda swallowed the lump in her throat, knowing that her departure would cut off the remaining ties to that wonderful week with Buck. She was going home and would be near him but not near the man she had made love to in the exotic setting of Siam. She was going home to the man at the top of that office tower in Los An-

geles, the man she feared was still obsessed with Lotus
Moon.

WHEN AMANDA'S PLANE touched down at Los Angeles
International Airport, it was dark. The blue and green
lights along the runway and the placid hangars bathed in
muted white light made it seem cold outside the aircraft,
almost as though there ought to be snow on the ground.
It was home, and the airport looked familiar yet alien to
her at the same time.

Looking out the window, Amanda felt trepidation at
the thought of seeing Buck. What would he be like?
Would their reunion be uncomfortable? Would he even
be there? He had promised to meet her flight, but something could have come up. She knew that she was trying
to prepare herself for disappointment, but what she
wanted with all her heart was that things be the same as
they had been in Bangkok.

By the time the passengers began deplaning and
Amanda was walking through the jetway, she felt as
much reluctance as eagerness at the thought of seeing
Buck. She cleared customs quickly, then entered the
lobby. People were crowded everywhere, greeting arriving passengers, struggling with luggage, looking for
transportation.

Then she saw him. He was leaning against a pillar at
the back of the lobby. He had seen her and waved and
was moving toward her through the throng.

Amanda stopped, putting down her suitcase. She saw
his blue eyes and the smile on his wide mouth as he
weaved his way closer to her. He was wearing a gray tur-
tleneck sweater that gave him a casual, friendly look,
more handsome than she remembered.

Buck stopped in front of her. "Welcome home," he said with a happy smile, then kissed her. The familiar but forgotten scent of him filled her lungs, and she only opened her eyes when he pulled away. "How was your flight?"

She smiled wearily, happy to see him, to hear his voice. "Long."

Buck chuckled, picked up Amanda's suitcase with one hand and took her by the arm with the other. "I remember. It was four days ago and I'm just now recovering."

His touch felt so good. Only four days? It seemed like a lifetime. "It's good to see you, Buck."

He smiled down at her, then pulled her off to the side, out of the flow of people exiting the building. Dropping the bag, he took her face in his hands. "You look just fabulous, Amanda." He kissed her lightly on the lips. "I missed you," he said tenderly.

The words, the look on his face, chased away all her doubts. With a happy sigh, she pressed her face against his sweater, luxuriating in the protective embrace of his arms. "I missed you, too," she murmured.

"Well, if you can stay awake long enough to get to my car, I'll take you home—to my place, if that's okay. No sense going home to a cold, empty apartment, is there?"

Amanda looked up, too tired to consider his question, knowing only that she wanted to be with him. Buck took her weary smile as her reply, picked up the bag again and led her by the arm out the door.

ON THE DRIVE down the San Diego Freeway toward Newport Beach, Buck told her about the mess waiting for him at the *Tribune* when he got back and asked Amanda about the balance of her stay in Bangkok. She was so tired that the conversation was mostly unilateral. And although it felt good to be in Buck's company again, she was relieved when they finally drove across the bridge to Balboa Island.

Buck had left lights on in the house, and it seemed warm and hospitable to her when they entered. He led her directly to the master suite, which she hadn't seen the night of the party. It was easily as spectacular as the rest of the house. First, it was enormous—as big as Amanda's entire apartment. Then, like the rest of the place, it was wonderfully decorated. There were large plants and massive pieces of furniture in earth tones, very masculine in mood and cleanly elegant.

In the sitting room, two overstuffed chairs sat in front of the fireplace. Then, walking up several steps, she entered the bedroom. To one side was a king-size bed and to the other, a chaise lounge, more chairs and a desk. Opposite was a wall of glass overlooking the water; in the corner, a rowing machine.

"How lovely," Amanda said, dropping down on the chaise lounge.

Buck walked over to her and touched her face with his fingertips. "The guest room is the left side of my bed, if that's all right."

She looked up at him, relishing the thought of falling asleep in his arms.

"I know you're tired, but before I let you go to bed, I'm going to have you try something that ensures even sweeter sleep than exhaustion."

"What?"

"Come with me," he said, taking her by the hand.

Buck led her into the bath, which was enormous and more opulent than the rest of the suite. Everything was pure white except for the hardware, which was gold. Like the bedroom, the outside wall was glass, but rather than leading outdoors, it opened into a small solarium filled with ferns. In the center was a hot tub, roiling and steamy.

"Ten minutes in there," Buck said, "and you'll be ready for sleep, believe me." He put his arm around Amanda's shoulders and squeezed her.

"I must admit it looks wonderful, Buck."

"Go ahead and unpack whatever you need. Here's one of my bathrobes," he said, taking the garment from the large brass hook on the wall.

Amanda took the robe from him, and he leaned down and kissed her lightly on the lips.

"I've got another little treat for you, too. Is it all right if I come back in, say, five minutes?"

She nodded. "Sure."

Minutes later, after Amanda had just eased her naked and weary body into the hot, frothy water, Buck entered the bath, carrying a tray with two glasses of champagne. "A little something to wet your whistle," he said, kneeling and handing her a glass of the chilled wine.

"Thank you." Amanda glanced up at Buck as he seated himself on the small bench by the hot tub.

"Mind if I play lifeguard for a few minutes and enjoy my champagne?"

"No, of course not." Amanda sipped the amber liquid, savoring its dry, refreshing flavor. She smiled, aware of her growing desire for Buck engendered by the sensuous caress of the water.

Feeling all energy being drained from her by the hot, turbulent bubbles, Amanda took a large drink of wine, placed the glass on the deck behind her and let her head fall back against the edge of the tub. Only her face was above the surface.

Several moments later, Buck was kneeling beside her. He pressed a cold cloth against Amanda's forehead. "How do you feel, Amanda?"

She felt completely relaxed and surprisingly tipsy from the champagne. "Too weak to move," she murmured, half smiling at the handsome face above hers.

"Well, we don't want to overdo this. I think you'd better get out."

"Maybe I'll just sleep in here for a little while first."

"No, my dear, I'm afraid not. What's good for lobsters is not necessarily good for lovely young ladies. Come on, you'd better come out now."

Amanda struggled to sit up, and Buck took her hand, helping her climb out of the tub. As he put the large white terry robe around her steaming body, she began sagging, and he had to support her. They stepped into the bathroom, and Amanda looked at him through drooping eyes.

"I'm afraid you're a bit too well-done," he said. "I'll help you dry off."

Amanda felt herself being lowered to the stool next to the mirrored wall. She smiled at her own comical image, wondering how a few sips of champagne could possibly have put her in this state. Buck went to fetch a large stack of towels of various sizes.

First, he took a medium-sized towel and began rubbing her mist-dampened hair vigorously. When he had finished, the woman in the mirror was adorned with a dark-red halo of hair. Amanda laughed at the sight, and then her eyes met Buck's. Through her numbness, she remembered how happy she was to see him, and she rose to her feet and threw her arms around his neck.

He laughed and kissed her cheek. "Come on, let's get you dry and in bed." He slipped off the bathrobe so that she stood naked, facing the mirror.

Despite the haze that had enveloped her brain, Amanda knew that she ought to feel embarrassed or at least shy, but she didn't. It seemed perfectly natural for her to be like this before Buck, and she watched with detached amusement as he dried her off, running the large bath sheet over her shoulders, up under her arms, around the curve of her breasts, the small of her waist, and down her legs.

Then Buck grabbed the nightgown Amanda had taken from her bag and tossed on the vanity. He slipped it over her head and, cupping her face in his hands, kissed her once on the nose, then on the lower lip.

"Okay, now. Time for bed." He leaned down and picked her up in his arms.

A moment later, Amanda felt the welcome coolness of the sheets. Her head sank into the pillow, she remembered the warmth of Buck's lips on her temple, then there was silence evaporating into darkness, and nothing more.

AWAKENING THE NEXT MORNING, Amanda felt as though she were coming out of a drugged sleep. How many hours had passed, she had no idea, and it took her several moments to figure out just where she was. She looked around the room, and the memory of Buck came to her from the foggy recesses of her mind, but he was nowhere to be seen.

She sat up in bed and looked toward the bright, sunlit window. The blue water of the bay beyond was sparkling, and several sailboats traversed the shimmering seascape as silently as the soaring gulls overhead. Amanda climbed from the bed, her limbs stiff from her long sleep. She went to the window and stared out. There was no sign of Buck. She decided he must be somewhere in the house.

The tangled mess on her head that greeted her in the mirror was startling, and Amanda wondered what Buck must have thought when he saw her that morning upon awakening. She quickly climbed into the shower, washing her hair and slathering it with conditioner.

Buck's large hair dryer was lying on the counter so she used it. There was a bottle of hand lotion among the colognes and other toiletries she found on the vanity so she helped herself to that, too, deciding Buck wouldn't mind.

Buck's bathroom, she decided, was fabulous, and she knew if the house were hers, at least half of every day would be spent in it. How wasted this was on a man.

Returning to the bedroom to dress, Amanda still found no sign of Buck. What time was it, anyway? The clock on the bed stand said eleven forty-five. The day was half over!

She quickly dressed in her white linen slacks, a teal-blue, V-necked T-shirt and espadrilles. For the first time in days, she was able to wear her hair down. After a final look in the mirror, Amanda wandered out of the master suite and through the house, curious where Buck was.

The large atrium room, which she entered first, was deserted except for the brightly colored parrot who was chattering noisily in his cage. She went over and looked at him. "Polly want a cracker?" she cooed.

"Not on your life, sister. Not on your life!" the bird replied, and Amanda broke into hysterics.

"Hey, what's going on out here?" It was Buck at the doorway leading to the kitchen.

"Your parrot, Buck," she said, laughing. "He's a co-median."

"Not on your life!" it croaked again, and Amanda again broke up in laughter.

Buck stepped down to where Amanda was by the cage and took her hand. She smiled up at him, her face still full of amusement.

"Did you sleep well?" He kissed her.

"Fabulously. What did you put in the champagne? A sleeping potion?"

"No, there's something about the combination of fa-tigue, hot water and champagne. Does it every time."

They walked toward the kitchen. "Thank goodness there was a lifeguard on duty."

Buck squeezed her waist. "I just found you. Do you think I'd want to lose you already?"

The parrot screeched after them, "Not on your life, sister. Not on your life."

Laughing, they entered the large, sunny kitchen with adjoining eating area. "What'll it be," Buck asked, "breakfast or lunch?"

"What are you having?"

"Well, I had breakfast four hours ago, but I can fix you whatever you like. It's Saturday—short-order day, since the housekeeper's off."

Amanda sat down at the table as Buck stepped around the counter.

"I can do crepes or omelets, ham and eggs or oat-meal...."

"What's easiest?"

"Whatever you'd like is easiest," he replied with a grin.

"How about an omelet."

"Okay, m'lady, an omelet it is." Buck winked at her and turned to the refrigerator.

Amanda watched Buck working in silence, relishing each little look or smile he gave her as he moved about the kitchen. She realized that without doubt, his appearance in her life had been a monumental event. This reception was delightful, absolutely incredible. She felt like a queen, but what did it mean? What did Buck intend by it?

"So how have you felt since you've been home, Buck? Or have you been too busy catching up to think about it?"

"You mean about my daughter?"

His tone was cheerful and upbeat, but there was a possessiveness in it that Amanda found disconcerting. "Yes, Lotus Moon."

A thoughtful expression came over Buck's face. "You don't suppose she's still called that, wherever she is, do you?"

"It's hard to say, but I would guess not. Unless a child is pretty old when they're adopted, most parents give him or her an American name. It seems Lotus Moon was a baby when she was sent over so I would think she has a different name."

Buck was cracking eggs into a mixing bowl. "How long will it take us to find out?"

There was an earnestness and intensity in Buck's speech that reminded Amanda of Kupnol Sustri's comment that he could be like a dog with a bone. She hoped that he wouldn't permit his interest in the girl to get out of hand. "I'll check the files when I get to the office Monday morning."

"Great. I'm anxious to find out what's happened to her."

Amanda looked at him wearily, but he didn't seem to notice, bustling about the kitchen as he was. "You know, Buck, it's not for certain I'll be able to track her down, and even if I do, there's no guarantee I'll be able to get more than cursory information."

Buck stopped beating the eggs in the bowl and frowned at Amanda. "You mean there may only be cursory information in the file. But we... or at least I... could investigate the situation more thoroughly." He resumed beating the eggs.

"Perhaps, but probably not, Buck."

He stopped again. "Why not?"

"Like I told you when we first talked about it in your office, the rights and wishes of the adoptive parents must be honored. The Amerasian Children's Foundation is only a liaison or intermediary organization. The placing agency that was used may be totally unwilling to cooperate with me even, let alone you."

Buck stared at her, thinking. "Hmm. I hadn't anticipated that."

"As I said in Bangkok, it's best not to let yourself get emotionally involved."

His smile was polite but suggested an unrelenting frame of mind. Amanda could almost see the bone between his teeth.

"What do you like in your omelet, madame—mushrooms, cheese, onion, ham?"

She shrugged, looking at him guiltily. "A little of each?"

"Your wish is my command," he replied, grinning.

"I hope you don't mind, Buck, but I borrowed some of your hand lotion from the bathroom."

"Don't worry, it'll be on your tab."

"I hope the prices are reasonable at this establishment."

"The prices you'll find to be very reasonable. But the proprietor, alas, can be most demanding." Buck winked and turned to the stove.

CHAPTER TWELVE

THEY HAD EATEN THEIR BREAKFAST out on the deck in the bright November sun. Although Thanksgiving week was already upon them, it was still warm enough to sit outside on a calm, sunny day. Amanda did, however, borrow one of Buck's sweaters for protection against the breeze blowing off the bay. She was curled up in a deck chair, watching the water, when Buck came out from the kitchen with the coffeepot in hand.

"Would you like a little coffee to warm your insides?"

"Mmm. That'd be nice, thanks."

Buck poured them each a cup, then pulled a chair beside Amanda's. He sat down and put his hand over hers. "It's good to have you home and here with me," he said, his wide mouth smiling, his gray-flecked hair blowing in the breeze.

Amanda took his hand in both of hers. She had an urge to kiss him, to throw her arms around his neck and cling to him. "It's good to be here, Buck."

The look in his eyes was affectionate, caring, but she sensed in it a reserve, too, an uncertainty. She could tell he was wondering about his feelings for her. His expression almost seemed to ask, *What does this mean?*

Amanda could sympathize with his reaction; she felt the same way herself. Seeing the emotion on his face and feeling the loving caress of his hand, she was both moved and frightened by Buck Michaels. Despite the closeness she felt, she was still uncertain, afraid to give herself up to her feelings.

Buck turned and looked across Newport Bay, his tanned face seemingly right at home with the sun and sea air caressing it. After contemplating the scene for a moment, he swung his gaze back to Amanda. "What would you like to do today?"

"I should get home. I feel like a vagabond living out of a suitcase with nothing but tropical-weight clothes."

"How about if I drive you over to get your winter wardrobe?"

"I hardly need a wardrobe, Buck, just a change of clothes."

"Well, shouldn't you have some extra things here anyway? Never can tell when you might need them."

Amanda looked at him with surprise and uncertainty. "That sounds suspiciously like a roundabout proposition."

"I guess I am being a little obscure, aren't I?"

"What are you trying to say?"

"I don't know. I guess I'm not sure myself."

"It's probably best not to say anything. We've got to get to know each other, Buck."

"Is that what you want—to go slow? Is that what you're trying to tell me?"

Amanda sighed. "I'm not trying to tell you anything in particular. I suppose I don't know what I think."

"Well, I know I want you here with me, Amanda."

She grinned mischievously. "At least two or three changes of clothes' worth?"

"Amanda..."

She laughed. "A girlfriend of mine used to say you could always gauge the degree of a man's commitment by the number of suitcases you needed when you left him."

Buck frowned. "I don't find that amusing."

Amanda patted his hand affectionately. "Let's talk about how we're going to spend the day. That's the agenda item up for discussion, isn't it?"

"No, let's talk about tonight. I think you ought to spend the weekend here with me."

"Hmm..."

"What?"

"I guess my friend would say you're proposing an 'overnight bag' relationship."

Buck tweaked her nose. "What the hell? Bring a small suitcase."

They both laughed.

"Seriously, though, I do need to go home."

"For a change of clothes, fine, but I think we should go sailing this afternoon, have a nice relaxing dinner this evening and negotiate Sunday's agenda after breakfast in the morning."

"Tomorrow night I'll have to go home for sure. I've got to organize myself for work Monday."

"We'll talk about that in the morning." He gestured toward his sailboat tied up down at the dock. "Ever been sailing before?"

"A time or two. I'm basically a landlubber, I'm afraid."

"Well, we'll change that. Sailing clothes you'll keep here for sure." He pulled her hand to his lips and kissed it. "Come on, let's go down to the boat."

BUCK SAID THERE WASN'T TIME for a longer trip to Catalina Island or down the coast so they contented themselves with several runs up toward Huntington Beach, then down to Laguna Beach. At first, Amanda sat next to him at the wheel, letting the salt air blow in her face, watching the water, listening to the sounds of the boat's hull cutting through the pea-green waves.

Later, when the sea air began penetrating the extra clothing Buck had given her, Amanda curled down out of the wind and watched Buck navigating the craft, obviously in his element, totally free and in love with what he was doing.

He wore his sunglasses and a silly, battered captain's hat that made him look like a caricature of what he was, but it was obvious to her that he didn't care. He was doing what he wanted; he was happy. Amanda was seeing a side of him she hadn't seen before.

She realized that what she wanted—should anything ever come of their relationship—was that Buck would feel as comfortable and at peace with her as he was with his boat. That seemed to her to be the ideal foundation for a man's feelings about a woman—deep, abiding, honest acceptance.

Amanda smiled, sensing the first twinges of possessory feelings toward Buck. The comfortable companionability she felt smacked more of a relationship than anything they had shared, except perhaps their intimacy. Permitting her to see him like this was a vote of confidence; he was inviting her into the innermost recesses of his life.

"How are you doing?" he called, grinning into the wind.

Amanda nodded at him from under the hood of his sweatshirt. "Fine."

"Getting cold?"

"A little, but I'm all right."

"Well, let's head home. I could do with a bit of cognac. How about you?"

"Sounds good," she called over the clatter of the sails in the wind.

"Done!" he shouted and checked for other craft before bringing the boat around to begin tacking to wind.

By the time they reached the inlet accessing the bay, the sun was hanging over a filmy band of haze to the northwest off Point Fermin. The wind had become brisk and the motion of the boat more pronounced. Amanda felt a little queasy.

Once inside the bay, the protected water was much more placid and the wind calmer. Buck maneuvered the boat using the auxiliary engine, and Amanda sat up again, looking at the palatial homes on shore as they circled the island.

When they had tied up and disembarked, Amanda took several awkward steps on the dock, surprised at how unsteady she felt on land. She also felt stiff from sitting for so long in the cold.

"Believe it or not," Buck said, "the cure for what ails you is the same as for your fatigue last night—the hot tub."

Her lips quivered with cold as she smiled. "It sounds wonderful."

Minutes later, Amanda was luxuriating in the turbulent, steaming waters of Buck's spa when he came in wearing a navy-blue bathrobe and carrying a bottle of cognac and two brandy snifters. He put down the bottle and glasses, then stepped through the ferns to open a frosted glass panel. They looked out over the water at the oranges, yellows and pinks of the western sky.

"How gorgeous," Amanda said as a breath of cool air wafted in and caressed her face.

Buck lit several large candles on a small stand off to the side and turned off the bathroom light. Then he slipped off his robe and lowered his strong male body into the water opposite Amanda.

She had watched his movements with fascination, not feeling shyness at the sight of him unclothed as she had before. Her awareness of him took on a more elemental, physical dimension, but it still had the same comfortable familiarity Amanda had felt in the boat.

"How's my little lobster feeling now?" he asked with a crooked smile.

"Fabulous."

His foot found hers under the boiling water, and he rubbed the top of it and her toes. "You don't feel cold anymore."

"Neither do you."

His lips twisted with amusement, his eyes roamed her face and hair, which she had pinned up on top of her head. There was a hunger in his gaze. She remembered that it had been five days since they had made love. Before Buck, it had been a long time, but the deprivation then had not been nearly so great as what she was feeling now. All day, she had craved only his company. Now, suddenly, she craved only him.

"Would you like a splash of brandy?"

"Please."

Buck poured them each a little, then handed her a glass.

"To a new set of luggage," he said with a wry grin. He leaned forward and touched her glass midway over the water.

Amanda beamed at the seductive man with whom she shared a candlelit bath. She sipped her brandy, letting the fiery liquid slide down her throat and warm her. The

sensations assaulting her from all sides reminded
Amanda of their lovemaking, and she wanted him even
more.

Their legs entwined, flesh drawing sensuously and deliciously across flesh. The delicate place between her legs
was alive with awareness, keen to the nearness of his
limbs and throbbing under the roiling warmth of the water.

Putting down her glass, Amanda reached under the
frothy surface of the water and captured Buck's foot. She
held it for a time, then began massaging it expertly. She
slid partway around the oval circumference of the tub to
be nearer so that she could work the muscles of his calf.
He smiled at her, acknowledging the pleasure of the sensation. Edging still closer, her hands ran up his thigh, and
she began kneading the firm muscles there.

Buck leaned back, watching her, savoring the pleasure
she gave him. Then he touched her cheek, and his hand
dropped lazily into the water, sliding down till the back
of it pressed softly against the underside of her breasts.
He inched his body closer so that his leg was against hers.

Their faces slowly moved toward each other, and
Amanda, looking at him through heavily lidded eyes, saw
the perspiration on his skin gleaming in the candlelight.
Their lips were just inches apart when, unable to control
herself, she let her hand slide up his thigh till she found
the male length of him, hidden from her sight in the
boiling waters.

Buck moaned softly under her touch, and his tongue
traversed the distance from his parted lips to hers, entering her mouth, sensuously, delicately. In the long, deep
kiss that followed, he tasted her flavors eagerly as his excitement mounted under the coaxing caress of her fingers.

When at last the kiss ended and Amanda's excitement was as ardent as the pulsing masculinity in her hand, they rose from the water as one, their bodies steaming in the refreshingly cool air of the solarium. Buck helped her from the tub and handed her a large, fluffy bath sheet. Then they stepped into the bathroom to dry each other, stopping to kiss and hug before slipping, hand in hand, into the bedroom.

AMANDA SPENT MONDAY MORNING trying to get through the pile of mail and correspondence that had accumulated during her absence. There were also a number of phone calls to return, and the usual struggles involved in reentering the office routine. She asked her secretary, Cleo, to look through the files for a child named Lotus Moon but decided not to devote much attention to the matter herself until the afternoon when the most pressing problems awaiting her had been disposed of.

At noon, Cleo stuck her head in the door of Amanda's office to say that Buck Michaels was on the phone.

"How's my favorite Bangkok lobster?" he asked cheerfully.

"Buried in paper and unreturned phone calls but otherwise savoring thoughts of a wonderful weekend."

"Me, too. Have any plans for tonight? It's been so long since I've seen you, I thought maybe we could get together and catch up."

"Buck, I don't think it's been long enough for the water wrinkles in my skin to go away."

"Really? It seems like years to me."

"More like twelve hours."

"I don't know why I let you talk me into taking you home at midnight."

"I couldn't come to the office in my safari dress in November! Besides, everything I had with me was either wrinkled or dirty."

"Well, just don't get the idea I'm a pushover. I consider your victory in that particular test of wills to have been beginner's luck."

"Buck! You don't think you're the first man I've ever butted heads with, do you?"

"Probably the first as stubborn as me."

"Well, I have to hand you that, Buck Michaels. At least you recognize your faults."

"Faults? Who said anything about faults? I consider my stubbornness a badge of honor!"

"Lord, what have I gotten myself into?"

"Hopefully, the pleasure of Thanksgiving dinner with me and my mother. I know it's late to be asking, but mother has insisted on meeting this lovely young lady that has so thoroughly captivated her son. Could you put up with a little family 'ritual' and be my guest for Thanksgiving?"

"Buck, that's awfully sweet, but I was planning on going with *my* mother to Phoenix to spend Thanksgiving with my aunt."

"Could your mother be persuaded to let you arrive a day late? Perhaps she wouldn't mind as long as she wasn't alone."

"Well, probably not, but before I commit I should give her a call."

"Sure."

Amanda paused. "I would very much like to meet your mother, Buck."

"Well, if it can't be arranged for Thanksgiving, we'll do it another time soon, but mother enjoys her holidays and likes putting on the dog for anyone I'm fond of."

Buck's euphemism didn't go unnoticed, but Amanda was pleased anyway. Being taken home to meet his mother couldn't be a bad sign. "I'll see if I can reach my mother this afternoon, and I'll call you back to let you know."

"Sounds good. Two other pieces of business, then I'll let you go. First, dinner at seven?"

Amanda knew she had a ton of work to do at home, but she also wanted to see Buck as badly as he wanted to see her. "Okay. Seven is fine."

"Good. Second, have you found anything on Lotus Moon?"

"Well, frankly, Buck, I haven't had time to check into it, but I asked my secretary to see if she could locate her in the files."

"I see."

Amanda heard the disappointment in his voice. "But I've allocated some time for it this afternoon. I promise to have at least a preliminary report for you tonight."

"I guess I'm overanxious. Somehow I just expected her to pop right up when we got home."

There was a note of expectation in Buck's voice that made Amanda feel very uncomfortable. He was thinking of the child as though she were going to become a part of his life—she could tell. She started to caution him, but decided to wait.

Amanda felt badly—badly for Buck and badly because she feared that she was becoming a part of the problem. Perhaps it was doing a disservice to him to be cooperative. By all rights, she shouldn't become involved in this sort of exercise; there were just too many ways it could go wrong. If it were anyone else, she'd probably decline to do more than confirm that the agency had handled the case.

"Your anxiety is understandable, Buck. Perhaps I'll have something for you tonight."

"Okay," he said hopefully. "Good luck." The wistful sound in his voice was touching, and Amanda realized it was a foreboding sign.

"NOTHING," CLEO SAID in her deep, languid voice. "There's no reference to a child named Lotus Moon anywhere in the files, Amanda."

"Oh, dear, I was afraid this would happen. Maybe we should concentrate on the time frame instead of the name. Maybe by checking the little girls we handled around twelve years ago—"

"The individual files only go back five years so we'd have to get into the archives to do a thorough search on a case-by-case basis."

"God...."

"Who is this guy that it's so important to dig up information on an old case?"

"A very generous supporter of the foundation... and also a personal friend."

Cleo smiled and brushed the black curls off her face. She was in her early forties, irreverent but enormously good-hearted. Amanda liked Cleo a lot.

"How personal is 'personal,' madame director? Do we pull out all the stops, or do we go through the motions?"

"We do the best we can, spending a reasonable amount of time and effort."

Cleo nodded. "And if we still can't find anything?"

Amanda grimaced. "Then we look some more."

"I see. He's a *very* personal friend."

Amanda's look was admonishing. "Let's divide the files. It'll go faster."

They stood side by side at the cabinet pulling files. After forty-five minutes, they still had nothing. Amanda looked at Cleo woefully. "Any suggestions?"

"Well, you might call Eleanor Harbold and ask her if she remembers the case. She was director at the time the girl came through."

"Good idea. Do you have Eleanor's number? I haven't talked to her in two years or more."

"I've got a Riverside number for her, I think. The last I heard, she was still out there." Cleo went to her desk and returned a minute later with a slip of paper for Amanda.

"Thanks." Amanda retreated to her office, sat down at her desk and dialed the number.

"I'm sorry, the name is just nôt familiar to me, dear," Eleanor Harbold said a few moments later. "It's been a while, you know."

"I understand, Eleanor. I thought it was worth a try, though."

"If there was something unusual, something distinctive about the case..."

"She did have a small tattoo on her ankle, a lotus blossom and a crescent moon."

"Hmm..."

"I talked to the child's mother in Thailand. She had it done as an identifying mark."

There was silence on the line. "No, I'm afraid it just doesn't ring a bell, Amanda. There were so many children in those days, with the war and all."

"Yes, well—"

"Did you check the medical records? The doctor who examined her may have made a notation of the tattoo, even if her Thai name never made it into the file."

"That's a good idea, Eleanor, but it will mean digging the case files out of the archives and going through each one."

"Well, only you know how big a donor the gentleman is."

Amanda sighed, wishing it was that simple.

BUCK MICHAELS PULLED UP in front of Amanda's apartment building in the Belmont Shores section of Long Beach in his anthracite-gray Mercedes. The complex consisted of older garden apartments but had a lot of charm. It was not far from the ocean and a convenient place for her to live as far as Buck was concerned, being about halfway between his office in downtown Los Angeles and his house in Balboa. Just fifteen miles of coast highway separated their homes.

He got out of the car, anxious to see Amanda. Whenever they weren't together, he felt deprived, empty. He enjoyed her company, and he was going to let the relationship take him wherever it went. She hadn't disappointed him yet, and she didn't seem overanxious. He had to smile at the thought. How could she be overanxious? He hadn't given her a chance.

When Amanda opened the door in a sapphire-blue cashmere dress, Buck was stunned. He stood looking at her for a moment. "Beautiful," he murmured.

She smiled. "Thank you."

As she turned to permit him to enter, Buck's eyes fell on the nape of her neck where several errant strands of her copper hair had escaped the smooth chignon. He had an urge to kiss her there.

When Amanda had closed the door, Buck slipped his arms around her waist and pulled her up against him.

Her look was both happy and languorously sensuous. She gave him a peck on the lips.

"Is that all I get?"

"For now. I just put on lip gloss."

"Let me taste."

"Buck!"

"Did you use it all up?"

"No."

"So what's the problem? You can alway put on more, can't you?" His strong arms held her pelvis against his, but she leaned back a bit, her hands resting on his shoulders. He looked into her eyes steadily, trying to weaken her resolve.

Amanda pecked at him again, the contact only slightly more generous than before.

"Well, if you're going to be stingy with your lips, how about letting me kiss your neck?"

Amanda lifted her chin.

"No, the back of your neck."

She spun around, tilting her head slightly to the side and forward a bit so that the long, smooth arch of her nape was exposed to him. Slipping his arms around her again and clasping them over her abdomen, Buck lightly kissed her. He felt her tremble under his lips, and he breathed in deeply, taking in the sweet fragrance of her perfume. The feel of her body against his and her delicious scent aroused him, and he felt himself harden.

"It seems to me I got into trouble once before with you like this," she said over her shoulder.

"What a pleasant thought," he murmured, kissing her neck again.

"Can I turn around now?"

Buck rode his hands lightly up the front of Amanda's dress and gently cupped her breasts in his hands, but she pushed them away.

"Buck! Aren't we going out to dinner?" She turned around and faced him, as a teacher observing a misbehaving schoolboy.

"Now, Amanda, can I help it if you're irresistible?"

"I'm sure your mother didn't bring you up to take such liberties with ladies. I might just have to have a little chat with her at dinner on Thursday." She smiled at him and touched his lip with her finger.

He laughed, feeling as fond of her as he was attracted to her. "I'm pleased you'll be able to make it for Thanksgiving, by the way."

"Kelly got the message to you all right?"

"Yes."

Amanda wiggled free of his arms and walked across her comfortable and stylish living room with its leafy plants, peachy-brown carpeting and beige grass cloth on the walls. She gestured toward the chairs and love seat covered in a blue, taupe and apricot print. "Sit down, Buck, and I'll get you a drink—if we have time."

He looked at his watch. "We've got time for a quick one, I suppose."

Amanda was in the kitchen. "Scotch?"

"Please."

Buck looked around the room, liking the feel of it, thinking how it looked like Amanda. On a side table, he noticed a photograph of a young naval officer with his arms around a little girl of ten or so. Approaching the table, Buck saw that the child was Amanda—the man probably her brother. He remembered how she had spoken of him with tears in her eyes on the flight to Bangkok.

Amanda was a good person, a good human being, and he liked that. It made him desire her all the more.

After Kelly had passed on the message that Amanda would be able to join him for Thanksgiving dinner, Buck had called his mother and told her. He hadn't previously discussed with her the details of what he and Amanda had learned in Bangkok, but she had been aware of the possibility of a granddaughter for years. Buck knew he'd have to bring her up to date before he took Amanda there for Thanksgiving.

He was somewhat surprised at how calm his mother was when he told her that Lotus Moon was undoubtedly alive and well somewhere in the States. Buck himself had been far less calm when he had learned and felt himself getting more anxious by the day.

He hoped Amanda would bring the subject up soon because he had agonized all afternoon over whether, after all their effort, the trail had again grown cold. When she returned with their drinks, he'd bring the matter up though he knew she didn't approve of his ardent pursuit of the child.

Amanda reentered the living room carrying a tray, her pretty teeth gleaming like the pearls around her neck and at the lobe of each ear. "One Scotch and water," she said, putting the glass before him on the table, "and one bowl of nuts," she added, setting it down beside the drink.

"You remember all my sins."

She looked at him coyly. "Some of them are difficult to forget."

"Surely I'm not that bad."

She leaned down and kissed him sweetly on the lips. "Yes, admirably so."

Buck savored the feel of her lips and her fragrance, noting how quickly they aroused him. "Are you going to tease me all evening?"

Amanda sat in the other chair. "It's not teasing. It's being friendly."

Buck raised his glass. "To friendliness and all *your* sins."

She looked at him coquettishly and sipped her drink.

"So how was your day?"

Amanda grinned. "If that's your idea of being subtle, Buck Michaels..."

He shrugged. "At least I tried."

She shook her head. "I'm afraid I don't have a lot to tell you."

"No?"

"There's nothing in our active files on Lotus Moon. I even called the former director, the woman who was in charge of the agency when your daughter came through. Unfortunately, she didn't remember the case."

Buck felt a dark pall settle over him. "So what does that mean?"

"It means, if I'm going to investigate further, I'll have to dig into retired files, the archives."

"Will that be a problem?" he asked somberly.

"Just a lot of time and effort."

He studied her face, trying to decide if she wanted to proceed or if she was glad for the excuse to abandon the project. "What do you intend to do?"

Amanda's expression was caring, but there was concern on her face as well. "You know how I feel, Buck. I think it's important that you keep an emotional distance from Lotus Moon. But I'll do as you wish. If you want me to continue looking, I will."

"If you don't mind, I'd appreciate it if you'd look a little further. We've come this far. I'd hate to stop now."

"Okay. I'll have the old files brought out of storage. But I'd like you to ask yourself what it really is that you want and *when* you'll be satisfied."

"I just want to know what's happened to her, Amanda."

"That's all?"

It was what he thought he wanted, and he knew that's what Amanda wanted him to say, but if he were honest, Buck knew that deep down he wanted something more.

Amanda accepted the nod he gave her, and he hoped that the child wouldn't develop into a problem between them. Much as he didn't want to disappoint Amanda, he knew in his heart that he really had no choice. He had to find Lotus Moon.

CHAPTER THIRTEEN

AMANDA STOOD NEXT TO CLEO as the delivery man brought in box after box of files on a hand truck. When eight boxes had been stacked to one side of the reception area, Amanda signed the receipt and the man left.

"Just look at all this," she said with dismay.

Cleo's expression was rueful. "Sort of like when an old lover you never much cared for comes to town, isn't it?"

"Lord."

"You must have agreed to this in a moment of weakness."

"No, not exactly. I just find it very difficult to say no."

Cleo shook her head. "My mother always told me a girl who can't say no to a man's got big problems."

Amanda nodded. "Your mother was right."

"So why don't you put your foot down?"

"I know the day will come when I'll have to, Cleo. Right now, everything is going so well—except for this— that I just hate to be the one who rocks the boat."

"Is he being unreasonable?"

"No. Actually, I sympathize with what he's going through. After all, it's his daughter, his own flesh and blood that he's looking for. It wouldn't be easy for any parent to just walk away."

"What is it, exactly, that he wants?"

"That's what's got me concerned. He says he just wants to know where she is and that she's all right, but

I'm afraid he really wants more and doesn't fully realize it himself."

"So you're going to keep giving him rope until he hangs himself?"

"I'd rather think I'm going take him as far as I reasonably can, then call a halt."

"And if he gets upset and pushes you?"

"Then we'll just have to sit down and come to an understanding."

"You sure must have it for this guy, Amanda."

"That's the trouble. I'm afraid I do."

The secretary looked up at Amanda with renewed interest on her face. "Hmm..." she said, standing upright again. "How serious?"

"I don't know. I keep waiting...expecting the balloon to pop, but it doesn't. It just seems to be getting better—except for this business with the girl."

"Do you love him?"

Amanda shrugged. "I don't know. I want to be with him all the time. I'm happy when we're together. I've never felt this way before."

"And he's got big bucks?"

"Well, yes..."

"It's love."

"Cleo! That's cynical. As a matter of fact, at first I thought it would prevent us from ever having a relationship."

"Money?" Cleo asked incredulously.

"Not just his money. Everything. His life-style, his values, his attitudes, his work. When we first met, I was sure nothing would ever come of it. He was attracted to me, all right, but I thought he was just interested in a playmate. Then, after a while, it seemed to be *me* he was interested in." Amanda looked at Cleo, feeling a little embarrassed with her confession. "I suppose I sound like a silly fool."

"Not as long as it's *this* man and not just your need for *a* man that motivates you."

"Cleo, where do you get all these pearls of wisdom?"

"Are you kiddin', honey? With three husbands behind me, I know every trick in the book."

Amanda laughed. "So why aren't you happily married?"

"That's the problem—I know too much. Ignorance is a prerequisite for bliss, believe me."

Amanda's look was frankly skeptical.

"But don't let that little insight get in the way. Fairy tales can come true, as long as both of you believe in the same one!"

"Funny you say that. I think I told Buck once that life wasn't a fairy tale."

"What'd he say?"

"I don't think he took what I said very seriously at all."

"I think the guy's in love, Amanda."

She looked at Cleo, liking the sound of the words. Then she looked down at the boxes. "In the meantime, I've got this cross to bear, I'm afraid." Amanda kicked the nearest box. "Well, shall we?"

THE SEARCH THROUGH THE FILES turned out to be more onerous than Amanda had imagined. By devoting an hour or two here and there to the project during the day, she and Cleo managed to eliminate all but three large cartons of files. Much of the time, Cleo was diverted by the task of preparing the agenda for the board of directors meeting scheduled for the following week. And Amanda, in addition to dealing with the usual paperwork and getting out several pressing letters, had to devote several hours to a meeting with county welfare officials.

In the afternoon, Buck called to tell her that he had to fly up to Seattle on business and wouldn't be back until late Wednesday night. Consequently, they decided to make arrangements for Thanksgiving Day. He would pick her up at one in the afternoon. Buck's mother lived in Beverly Hills so the drive wouldn't be too long. He promised to call her from Seattle in the evening, and Amanda hung up, feeling sad at the thought of not being able to see him for a couple of days.

At four-thirty, she looked at the imposing stacks of files that remained and decided to tackle them. At first, she checked each folder, trying to determine if a case file had been set up under the name Lotus Moon. When that proved fruitless, she looked in each child's file for reference to the name. To be conservative, they had selected case files that ranged from a year before to two years after the time they thought it likely that the girl would have passed through Los Angeles. They also selected girls both younger and older than Lotus Moon's probable age at the time she was transferred to the States.

Amanda was still hard at work when Cleo left at five-thirty, and she decided to stay late and get as much done as she could that evening since she wouldn't be seeing Buck anyway. Two hours later, she had read every file twice and found no reference to the name Lotus Moon. She was getting hungry but didn't want to quit working so she decided to walk up the street and have a sandwich, then return to the office.

When she sat down at her desk again to face the mountain of files, Amanda realized that in segregating them originally, they might have inadvertently discarded

Lotus Moon's folder. So she went back through the five cartons of discarded files and managed to find two girls that met the criteria, but upon examination, neither of them appeared to be Lotus Moon.

By nine-fifteen, Amanda had concluded that the only remaining hope was to go through the medical records of each child, looking for a reference to the tattoo. The job looked as though it would take three or four hours so she decided to put it off until the next day.

Just as she was about to pick up her purse and go, the phone rang. For a moment, she ignored it, assuming it must be a wrong number. Then she remembered Buck saying he would call that evening. Amanda picked up the receiver anxiously. It was Buck.

"Well, you had me worried. Why the dedication? You after a raise?"

Amanda laughed. "No, just trying to track down a girl for a friend."

"This late? Poor thing. How's it going?"

"Not well, I'm afraid. We don't have a file identifying her by name, and I haven't found a reference to 'Lotus Moon' anywhere."

"Hmm. Doesn't sound promising," he said glumly.

"Tomorrow I thought I'd look through the medical records and see if I can find a reference to a tattoo."

"Gee, I hate to put you through this...."

"Well, I promised. Besides, I'm beginning to get caught up in the challenge of the hunt. And I'd like to find her for you, Buck."

"You're sweet." There was silence. "I miss you."

She smiled. "I miss you, too."

"It's too late for you to be out. Why don't you go home?"

"As a matter of fact, I was just headed out the door when you called."

"Good.... I'll see you Thursday afternoon, then?"

"Right."

"And Amanda..."

"Yes?"

"Be careful."

She smiled, liking his concern. "You too, Buck."

Amanda hung up and a wave of loneliness washed over her. She wished she was going home to him. Instead, she would have to content herself with a hot bath and some well-deserved sleep. Sadly, she picked up her purse and left the office.

THANKSGIVING AFTERNOON AT ONE, Buck was at Amanda's door. Seeing her, he reached out and took her hands in his. "Don't you look sensational!" he enthused, eyeing her amber long-sleeved silk dress. He pulled her to him, kissing her lightly but with tender affection.

She smiled into his eyes.

"Is it new?" he asked, admiring her again.

"Yes, I bought it just to meet your mother. Like it?"

Buck stepped back. "Let me see," he said, motioning for her to turn around.

Amanda spun around happily, her smile radiant.

"Just fabulous. You look, I don't know, elegant... beautiful."

"Oh, good. I wanted to look elegant for your mother." She beckoned him in and Buck entered, closing the door.

"God," Buck said, wrapping his arms around her, "it's so good to see you."

Amanda beamed.

"Are you ready?"

She nodded.

Buck took her hand and gazed at her in a quiet, contemplative way that made Amanda feel shy. She grabbed her brown lizard clutch purse on the entry table as they went out.

He held open the door to the Mercedes, and Amanda slid onto the smooth leather seat, feeling pampered and very elegant. When he had climbed in beside her, she took his hand, squeezing it affectionately. Buck leaned over and kissed her again before starting the car.

As they took off, Amanda turned to him. "I'd better tell you the bad news, Buck."

He glanced at her quickly. "Lotus Moon?"

"Yes. There was absolutely nothing in the files. No name, no reference to the tattoo, nothing."

Buck grimaced. "Damn."

"I went through everything at least twice, even the boys' files and older girls', thinking perhaps something had been misfiled, but I couldn't find a thing."

He seemed almost to slump at the wheel as he drove. "God, I thought for sure..." He turned to her again. "What do you think it means? Do you think she isn't in the States?"

"No, I think she is and that one of the children in our files is Lotus Moon. But without a reference to her name or the tattoo, I just can't tell which one."

"Could you find her file through a process of elimination?"

"I thought of that, Buck. I started setting aside folders that could be hers, but by the time I finished, there were forty."

"So we've got it down to one of forty?"

"It's quite probable."

They stopped at a traffic light, and Buck stared at her, thinking. "What would it take to find out which of the forty she is?"

"It would be impossible, Buck."

"Impossible?"

"Well, it would take a monumental effort, and there's no guarantee we'd have anything when we were finished." Amanda remembered her comment to Cleo about putting her foot down with Buck. She sensed the time was drawing near.

"How could it be done?"

"Buck!"

The light changed and he turned his attention to the road. "Hypothetically, I mean."

"Hypothetically?" Her tone was full of skepticism. "Buck Michaels, since when has one of your questions about this child ever been hypothetical?" She gazed at his handsome face in profile, thinking how stubborn it looked. "Has anyone ever accused you of being like a dog with a bone?"

He grinned. "No. Not to my face, anyway."

"Well, someone is now."

He looked at her, his smile slowly turning quizzical. "What are you trying to say, Amanda?"

"I think the time has come to let the matter rest, Buck. We've come to a dead end. It's time to recognize that fact and accept it."

"Is that what you want?"

"It's not a question of what I want, Buck. It's a matter of accepting facts. To torment yourself further won't do you or anyone else any good. You've lived this long without knowing every last detail about her. I think you should content yourself with the knowledge that's she's here in the States and in all probability just fine."

"But I don't know that."

"No, but it's likely."

They were entering the freeway, and Buck accelerated along the on ramp, glancing into his side mirror. When they were comfortably moving along with the flow of traffic, he spoke again. "Hypothetical or not, I'd like to know what it would take to check out those forty girls."

Amanda sighed, then stared at the highway in front of them. "First," she said after a moment's reflection, "you'd need my cooperation—that may be the biggest hurdle of all. Second, you'd need the cooperation of the placing agency—the local adoption agency. That we have no control over. Third, you'd need the cooperation of the adoptive parents, perhaps even the child. That's problematical at best. Fourth, there would have to be some identifying information in the local agency's files, like a reference to the tattoo."

"Assuming I was able to get *your* cooperation," he said with a sly grin, "don't you think it would be worth a try?"

"Buck, when will you ever be satisfied?"

"When I succeed."

"You *are* like a dog with a bone."

"You can't teach an old dog new tricks."

Amanda couldn't help smiling. "If I'd known how old you were, I'd probably have thought twice before getting involved with you."

Buck took her hand. "You know what I like about you, Amanda?"

"What?"

"I like the way you make me doubt my own irresistibility."

She gave a little smile. "There may be a lesson there somewhere."

"Yes, there probably is. But the question is, for whom?"

Buck rubbed her fingers with his thumb, and Amanda looked down at the now-familiar hand, realizing how very much she liked his touch.

CYNTHIA MICHAELS'S HOUSE was as large as any private residence Amanda had ever seen. A high stucco wall completely encircled the sumptuous grounds, and they were admitted only after Buck identified himself through the intercom system at the entrance. Amanda looked at him as the wrought-iron gate swung open, having been electronically activated from inside the house.

"Don't worry," he said, reading the uncertainty on her face, "the entrance is the worst part. It's all downhill from here. Mother's a nice lady. No pet lions or insidious-looking servants. There's only Dunstan, the butler, and his wife, Adriana, the cook. They've been with her for years."

"Just three people live in this place?" Amanda asked incredulously as they drove up the long, sweeping drive.

He chuckled. "I'm afraid so. The cleaning staff, the gardeners and mother's secretary are only here days."

Buck stopped the Mercedes at the portico.

"Oh, looks like Owen Kenner is here," he said, gesturing toward the Lincoln Continental parked farther along the drive. "He's a retired doctor, an old friend of mother's, almost like family. Owen's been a widower almost as long as she's been widowed. I don't know why they don't get married."

"Maybe they're not on the same wavelength."

Buck leaned across the seat toward her, inviting her to kiss him. She moved closer and their lips touched.

"Like us?" he asked with a mischievous smile.

She nodded slightly. "Yes, like us."

His eyes caressed her for a moment, then he reached for the door handle. "Come on, let's go smell the turkey. It's one of the things I like best about Thanksgiving."

Buck got out of the car and walked around to open Amanda's door. Through the windshield, he could see the trepidation on her face though she hadn't said anything and had maintained her poise. This had to be a difficult thing for a woman—meeting a man's mother. It was a signal to both women, really, a statement he wanted to make. Mainly, he was very proud of Amanda, and he wanted to show her off where it counted.

He opened the door on the passenger side and helped her out, marveling again at her elegance. That was the right word, elegant. It was the way Amanda said she wanted to be seen by his mother, and it was the correct choice. Knowing his mother as he did, Amanda's instincts were perfect.

"Did you grow up here, Buck?" she asked as they mounted the steps to the entrance.

"No, mom and dad bought this place when I was in college, when prices were still sane. Since then, the neighborhood has filled with Middle Eastern princes, millionaire entrepreneurs and the usual assortment of show-business types." He rang the front bell. "It's not the sort of place she'd move to now, but she doesn't want to give it up, either."

Buck noticed the slightest hint of nervousness around Amanda's mouth, but that would soon pass. He was certain they'd hit it off fine. The door slowly swung open, and Dunstan stood there in his usual black suit and tie.

"Oh, good afternoon, Mr. Michaels!" the man said warmly. "Madame," he added with a polite nod to Amanda.

"Happy Thanksgiving, Dunstan," Buck said cheerfully.

"Thank you, sir," he said, stepping back so that they might enter. "Mrs. Michaels and Dr. Kenner are in the salon."

"Thank you." Buck took Amanda's arm.

They went from the entry hall through the large, arched doorway to the left. There at the far end of the immense room and seated at either side of the fireplace was an elderly couple, both gray and distinguished looking.

Even from a distance, Amanda could see that the handsome woman wearing a French-blue silk afternoon dress was Buck Michaels's mother. She had the same wide mouth and strong jaw though on her the effect was regally feminine.

"Hello, Mother, Owen," Buck said as they approached.

The doctor rose to his feet.

"Happy Thanksgiving, darling," the woman greeted in a voice larger and stronger than her size. She was smiling at Amanda, who knew she was being examined though Cynthia Michaels was exquisitely subtle. "This must be Amanda."

"Yes. Amanda Parr...my mother, Cynthia Michaels, and Owen Kenner."

"How nice to meet you, dear," the woman said.

Amanda stepped forward and took the extended hand, which was cool, smooth and unexpectedly strong. "I'm very pleased to meet you, Mrs. Michaels."

"Oh, please, I'm old enough for it, granted, but call me Cynthia."

Amanda smiled and turned to the gentleman.

"How do you do, Amanda?"

"Dr. Kenner."

"Owen, please."

She smiled appreciatively.

"Well, sit down, children," Cynthia said. "Owen and I have done our reminiscing about bygone days. It's time for a dose of the present, don't you think so, Owen?"

"By all means," the doctor responded with a courtly smile.

Amanda and Buck sat on the couch that was between the older couple and opposite the fireplace where several logs were burning quietly, giving the room a warm, festive feel.

"Dunstan will be along with your Scotch in a moment, Preston. What would you like, Amanda?" The woman must have caught the funny little look crossing Amanda's face because she commented immediately. "Oh, you'll have to forgive me for not getting into the 'Buck' business like everyone else, but Preston was the name *I* selected, and he is my son so I'm entitled."

"I don't blame you a bit, Cynthia. I rather like 'Preston' myself."

"Since when?" Buck asked, looking at Amanda with surprise.

"Since I was told that the only one who called you that was your mother. It struck me as a rather exclusive group."

"Well said," Cynthia commented. "But, Amanda, I'd welcome you to the club, if you're so inclined."

She turned to Buck. "What do you think, Preston?"

"I think one mother is enough."

They all laughed.

Dunstan entered the room and approached the couples. "Madame?"

Cynthia ordered drinks and canapés, making a special point of having the butler remember nuts for her son.

Amanda turned to Buck. "Your reputation is known far and wide."

"Isn't it dreadful?" Cynthia said.

"Better his hips than mine," Amanda replied.

Cynthia was amused. "I'm certainly glad you came today, dear. I need a little female society."

Amanda smiled. Buck's mother was already putting her at ease.

"Now, before you arrived, Amanda, I was trying to explain to Owen what it is you do, but Preston was so vague I'm afraid I didn't get it straight."

"I'm the managing director of the Amerasian Children's Foundation in Long Beach—which is a fancy way of saying I'm the chief cook and bottle washer of a small social service agency. We repatriate Amerasian children from Southeast Asia to the United States."

Dunstan returned with the drinks, a tray of hors d'oeuvres and a small bowl of nuts for Buck.

"You actually bring the children over yourself, do you?" Cynthia asked.

"No, I make the arrangements. They're brought over by Thai, Vietnamese or Cambodian nurses, primarily because of linguistic problems."

"That makes sense," Cynthia said, picking up her fresh drink. "I propose a toast to you, Amanda," she said with aplomb, "for your fine work, your charm and . . . your good taste in men."

Buck laughed. "That sounds like a toast to me, Mother."

"Nonsense, Preston, if I had anyone else in mind, it was myself! If it weren't for me—"

"I wouldn't be here," he said, finishing the sentence for her.

Cynthia took another sip of her drink. "I must be getting old. I can see I've started repeating myself."

"No, I've just started anticipating you, Mother."

She tossed her head and looked at Amanda. "It wasn't so long ago that Preston would do well to keep up with me. I certainly hope you will succeed where I've begun slipping. He's headstrong, Amanda."

"Mother, you can't tell her all the family secrets in one day. I've carefully built an image—"

"Nonsense, a real woman doesn't respond to images, she responds to force of personality and emotion. Wouldn't you say so, Amanda?"

She reflected. "Yes, that and identity of spirit."

Cynthia Michaels smiled knowingly. Amanda saw the wheels turning and hoped the woman's unspoken reaction to her was favorable. But she knew it was too soon for Cynthia to give any concrete indication of what she thought.

Owen Kenner had been listening in bemused silence. Amanda wanted to bring him into the conversation as well. "What was your specialty, Owen?"

"Radiology."

"Oh! My father was a radiologist."

"Really?" The doctor sat up, showing interest. "Where was his practice?"

"In San Diego."

"Let's see, your surname is Parr?"

"Yes, my father was Howard Parr."

"Howard Parr...yes, the name is familiar. We radiologists are a close-knit group. Undoubtedly ran into him at a convention or conference, something like that."

"Dad did a lot of consulting in the Los Angeles area. You may have met him that way."

"Yes, that might well be. I take it he's deceased?"

"For nearly ten years. My brother was a physician, too, a thoracic surgeon. He was killed in Vietnam while working at a field hospital."

"I am sorry, Amanda. I was in Europe during the war—World War II—as a surgeon so I know what it's like in a field hospital."

"You switched from surgery to radiology?"

Owen laughed. "Well, let's say the Germans helped me switch. We were in a frantic retreat during the Battle of the Bulge, and our convoy was strafed by aircraft. My right hand and arm were hit so that was the end of the surgery."

"What a shame."

"Well, I missed the surgery, no doubt about it." He paused. "I don't know about Vietnam firsthand, but I understand your brother's generation did a great deal better in their survival ratios than we did."

"I think it was the improved evacuation techniques," Buck interjected, "as much as it was the advances in medical science."

"Yes, that's what I understand." Owen grinned at Buck. "But I wouldn't think you'd be one to laud the virtues of travel by helicopter."

"Good heavens," Cynthia exclaimed, "let's not get into that. I still have nightmares over that ordeal." She turned to Amanda. "So tell me, dear, have you succeeded in tracking down this mysterious granddaughter of mine?"

Amanda looked at Buck, not expecting the question.

"You did tell her I was aware, Preston."

"I don't believe I mentioned it, Mother."

"Well, you should have."

"No harm done," Amanda said reassuringly. "We've no secrets."

"It's not the sort of thing a son shares with a mother normally, but I've known for years—since Preston came back from Vietnam injured."

"Mother, I didn't find out Lotus Moon was mine until a few weeks ago."

"No, but you thought she was. And so did I." She turned to Amanda expectantly.

"I was telling Buck on the drive over, Cynthia, that my search has come to a dead end. I don't think it likely I'll be able to trace her now."

"Oh, that is a shame. Preston has been rather adamant, haven't you, dear?"

"Yeah," he said with an ironic tone, "like a dog with a bone." He glanced at Amanda.

"Strange way to put it," Cynthia continued, "but accurate, I suppose." She looked at Amanda. "Perhaps it's just as well, I don't see what good the exercise does, except satisfy one's curiosity, perhaps."

"There are dangers, too," Amanda said. "Emotional pitfalls, I mean."

"Yes, I would agree. You seem to be very level-headed, Amanda. I like that."

Amanda felt a surge of triumph and glanced at Buck, whose expression had grown a little black.

"What's the matter, dear?" Cynthia asked.

"I'd hoped the two of you would hit it off," Buck said ironically, "but this wasn't quite what I had in mind."

The women laughed.

"Owen, perhaps you'd better take the boy into the library and talk about the stock market. I can see Amanda and I have some things to discuss."

Buck groaned and Amanda sensed that victory was within her grasp. She smiled warmly at Cynthia Michaels and wondered, for the first time, what she might be like as a mother-in-law.

CHAPTER FOURTEEN

"YOUR PLACE OR MINE?" Buck asked wryly as he climbed into the driver's seat.

Amanda was waving out the window at Cynthia Michaels, who was standing under the porch light in the doorway of her home, a wide, gracious smile on her face. "Buck! Your mother's not twenty feet away."

"I know, I thought I'd catch you at a moment of distraction." He started the engine of the Mercedes.

"You're terrible," she said, smiling and waving as they started down the drive. "Your mother was right about you. You are headstrong."

Buck tooted the horn and waved vacantly over his shoulder. "Another badge of honor, Amanda. But to be honest, I was beginning to feel a little uncomfortable with the conspiratorial camaraderie you two developed."

"I think we see eye to eye regarding you, that's all."

"I don't quite understand that. I was hers by an accident of nature, but *you* picked me...."

Her head swung to him. "*I* picked *you*? You've got that backward, don't you, Buck Michaels?"

"I don't know. Before I met you, I was just sailing along smoothly—sort of like those male kites in Bangkok—when all of a sudden, you swooped into my life. Now here I am all snarled up in your tails." He reached over and took her hand.

Amanda laughed. "Poor baby."

He pulled her fingers to his lips and kissed them. "You were fabulous with my mother."

"You think so? She's an awfully sweet person."

"She loved you. I could tell."

Amanda smiled. "Good. That pleases me. I'm fond of her—already."

"And Owen liked you, too."

Buck continued to hold her hand as they drove in silence along a wide boulevard toward the freeway. Darkness had fallen.

"I don't mean to raise a sore subject," she said after a few minutes, "but I was pleased that your mother agreed with me about Lotus Moon. Our conversation on the drive up concerned me, and I think we should resolve what happens now—primarily for your benefit—but also for the sake of our relationship."

He shot her a glance. "What do you mean? Is Lotus Moon a problem for you?"

"Not a problem, exactly, but I feel this quest is...I don't know...standing between us, in a way."

"Not as far as I'm concerned, it isn't."

"Well, I'm in an awkward situation, Buck. I care a great deal for you, and I want to help you. I understand your feelings, but in my professional opinion, I don't believe it's right to continue this search. I really think the time has come to stop."

Buck's expression was somber.

"I'm sorry if that hurts you, but I was hoping that your mother's support of my position might be persuasive."

"My mother doesn't run my life, Amanda. Nobody does."

"No, of course she doesn't. But she loves you, and as a grandparent, she has some interest in the matter herself. Yet she sees the dangers, just as I do. I was hoping that between us we could convince you.''

''I appreciate your concern, Amanda. I really do. But I don't think you fully realize just how badly I need to know about my daughter.''

She looked at him almost imploringly. ''But I do, Buck!''

''Well, listen, I've got a proposal I'd like to make. I've been thinking about it all day, ever since you gave me the bad news on the drive up.''

Amanda felt a wave of dread come over her. His tone was familiar. It was as if he hadn't heard a word she had said.

''I've got an envelope in my pocket that I intended to give you today, before any of this came up. It's a check for a thousand dollars, payable to the foundation.''

''Buck—''

''No, let me finish. I know you've been working very hard in my interest, and it's diverted you from your other work. Let's say my intent was to compensate the foundation for lost time.'' He quickly continued. ''Now I'm not sure I understand what we're up against with these forty files, but I'd like to run them down as far as we can and, if we turn up dry after that, then I'll agree to give up.''

''Oh, Buck....'' Amanda reached over and touched his arm. ''It's so hard for me to say no to you.''

He gave her a little smile.

''But this time, I think I should,'' she quickly added.

''Before you decide, let's discuss the problem for a moment, analyze our options.'' He shot her a quick glance, then proceeded. ''Suppose, for a moment, that Lotus Moon had become a matter of life and death for you, and you had no choice but to proceed. What steps would you take to find her?"

Amanda sighed.

"Just discuss this with me, and I promise afterward we'll drop the matter and have a nice evening together. No more talk about Lotus Moon, just the two of us."

She stared ahead at the headlights of the oncoming traffic, thinking. He was staying calm. He was being polite. She almost felt an obligation to reciprocate. "Okay," she said, relenting.

"What can we do to find out which of those girls she is, Amanda? What would *you* do, if you had to find her?"

"I'd write to every agency involved with those girls. I'd ask them to check their internal files on the case that they handled and look for a reference to either the name or the tattoo."

"What are our chances?"

"I don't know. One in ten, maybe."

"Why so low?"

"These agencies are a good deal less motivated to help you than I am, Buck, and you know how reluctant I am. People in this business don't go around opening up old cases lightly. There are lives out there that could be affected."

"But I don't want to interfere."

They were on the freeway again, and Amanda was anxious to get home and have the quiet evening Buck had promised. "Your motives are not so much the issue. It's a matter of professional ethics, law and, most of all, the welfare of the child. I'm afraid it's the nature of the beast, Buck."

"How many agencies are we talking about altogether?"

"Probably a dozen."

"Okay. I'll give you a dozen checks for five hundred dollars to send along with your letter of inquiry—to cover their time and trouble. Do you think that would help?"

"It would probably get their attention. But the critical question is, what do you expect of them? If it's just verification of the case, we have a chance."

"I've just got to know she's well placed and that she's all right, Amanda."

"It might work."

Amanda could see Buck's enthusiasm rising as his plan started taking shape. "In your letter, you can tell them there'll be an additional thousand for the winner—the one who turns up Lotus Moon."

"Buck, that seems awfully manipulative. These people have their values. Their object is not profit, it's helping people."

"I'm not asking for anything improper or unethical. I'm interested in getting their attention and a little conscientious effort from them, that's all. I mean, let's face it, Amanda, they don't owe me anything, or probably you, either, for that matter."

Amanda fell silent, thinking. "I suppose you're right." She saw him beaming, and she realized to her dismay that he had won again.

They drove for a time in silence, tension in the air. "You know," Buck said, trying to lighten the mood. "I've got a little surprise for you."

"What?"

"There's a gift in the trunk."

"In the trunk? For me?" She eyed him with curiosity. "What is it?"

"Oh, I can't tell you, it's a surprise."

"Well, when do I get to find out what it is?"

"I guess when we get to your house."

Amanda felt suddenly very excited. But what could it be? "Are you going to give me a hint?"

"Nope. You'll understand when you see them."

"Them? There's more than one present?"

"In a way, yes."

Amanda thought. "Buck, I don't have the slightest idea what they could be."

"Good. Then you'll really be surprised." He laughed and it made her happy to see how much fun he was having.

Amanda couldn't remember the last time she had gotten so excited at the thought of a present. Buck took her hand again and began rubbing it affectionately as he drove. She could hardly wait to get home.

WHEN THEY PULLED UP in front of Amanda's building, she didn't bother waiting for Buck to come around and open her door. She jumped out and went around to the back of the car.

He was grinning as he walked back to the trunk. "If I'd known that you enjoy surprises so much, I'd have done this sooner."

"I love surprises!"

Buck fumbled with his keys, trying several different ones clumsily, dropping them once, obviously tantalizing her.

"Buck!"

Finally, he put the right key in the lock, turned it and lifted the lid. There, to Amanda's utter amazement, was an eight-piece set of luggage in fine, pale-blue leather. Her eyes rounded.

"Buck, it's gorgeous!"

"It's Mercedes luggage. See how it fits perfectly in the trunk?"

"But, Buck, I have a Honda."

He grinned at her, then shrugged. "Who knows, maybe someday you'll have a Mercedes. Anyway, the idea of an 'overnight bag' relationship never appealed to me."

The symbolism was more than Amanda dared contemplate at the moment so she threw her arms around him. "Thank you, Buck. I'm flabbergasted."

Cold night air was blowing in off the ocean, and Amanda shivered even as Buck held her.

"Shall we go in? I'll take in the bags, and you can fill them up with your things, if you like."

She smiled and touched his lip with her finger. "Why don't you stay here with me tonight?"

"Now that's an offer I could hardly refuse."

Moments later, Amanda was standing in her living room as Buck carried in the last of the luggage. "It's beautiful, Buck. I love it."

She hugged him again and kissed him. "Can I get you something to drink?" she asked, smiling into the sparkling cerulean of his eyes.

"I just want you," he whispered.

Amanda felt the warmth of his body against hers, and as her mouth pressed upon his neck, she smelled the faint tang of his cologne mingled with the natural musk of his skin.

His arms held her more tightly, and he kissed her hair, lovingly, softly, as though she were a fragile child. Buck seemed moved more by emotion than desire.

She sighed in his embrace, not able to cope easily with the river of feeling flowing through her. She loved him so much—she knew she did—and sensed that he loved her, too. It was all so wonderful, yet frightening.

Amanda looked up. "Can I offer you a glass of sherry?" she asked in a half whisper.

"Mmm. Sounds good." And he kissed her lower lip.

Amanda slipped from his arms and went into the kitchen, thinking how magical the evening suddenly felt. It had been a pleasant day, if a little unnerving at first, but tonight had taken on a special feeling. The unspoken messages between them were stronger than ever.

When she returned to the living room with two glasses of sherry, Buck had taken off his jacket and loosened his tie. His smile was almost joyful, touched with awe, perhaps with awareness of the currents that Amanda herself felt. He was standing by the mantel of the small fireplace as she approached. Buck took one of the glasses and ran his arm around her waist, gently pulling her close against him.

"I missed you."

"Just now?" she asked with a happy smile.

"Yes."

"I was only gone a minute."

"It seemed like forever."

She looked at him. "I like being with you, Buck."

He ran his index finger across her cheekbone, then along the line of her jaw. "When you came to see me at the office that day, did you ever think it might end up like this?"

Amanda thought of that first impression of him—the way he looked sitting at his desk with his reading glasses on his nose and the desk lamp illuminating his handsome features. "No, I never once thought of you in those terms, Buck."

"You didn't?" He looked disappointed.

"Oh, I found you most attractive right from the start. But I never thought we'd have a relationship."

"Well, I did. Five minutes into the conversation and I knew I wanted you."

"Lust."

Buck chuckled. "There was more to it than that. I was attracted to you physically, granted, but not just in the...glandular sense. Your beauty touched me emotionally." His eyes searched hers, then he smiled and pinched her chin. "It still does, as a matter of fact."

Amanda beamed and felt her cheeks coloring. "I think women must be different on the whole. I mean, a woman might notice that sort of thing in a man, but in most cases, she wouldn't draw conclusions or act on it. Like your mother said this afternoon, women are more affected by force of personality—and that requires getting to know someone."

"So when did you start getting interested in me?"

"Buck!"

"Really."

She reflected. "It was a gradual thing. A little here, a little there. A phrase, a gesture, a thought expressed. They eventually added up to interest, then...even greater interest."

His broad mouth was curved into a smile. He ran his finger over her lips, taking pleasure in touching her. "I'm glad," he whispered.

"So am I."

"Oh, Amanda." His voice was deep with emotion. He put his sherry on the mantel, took her glass and put it down beside his. Lifting her chin, he kissed her, first softly, then more emphatically, eventually coaxing a moan from her upturned mouth.

Amanda felt her heart pounding against his chest, felt her nipples hardening through the fabric of her undergarments and dress. Buck's fingers were on the zipper at her back, inching it down, eager to unclothe her, eager to get to the coveted prize of her naked flesh. When her dress was loosened, Amanda slipped from his embrace and, taking his hand, led him quietly to the bedroom.

The chamber was tiny compared to the mammoth suite at his place, but there was a charm, a femininity about it that incited Buck because of the intimacy of being in it alone with her. Filling most of the room was an antique brass bed, highly polished and gleaming in the soft light. Amanda had embellished it with a pale-blue dust ruffle, and the sheets, comforter and drapes were all in the same peach-and-blue floral print.

Beside the bed was a small round table covered with a ruffled cloth in a contrasting tone. On it was a china lamp, a small photograph of her parents on their wedding day, a vase with a single yellow rose and a scented candle in a miniature, hand-painted porcelain bowl.

Amanda left him to light the candle, and after she had struck the match, he turned off the light switch at the door. In the dim glow of candlelight, she moved to where he waited at the foot of the bed. Her face was in shadow, but the point of light behind her shone through her curls, creating a halo of burnt sienna around her delicately etched face.

Buck was moved by the quiet passivity of her expression. He put his hands lightly on her shoulders, feeling the need to verify that the apparition before him was real. "Oh, God, you're beautiful," he whispered.

Shyly, her eyes dropped from his, but her lips still carried the demure smile of her unspoken emotions. She touched his chest, toying self-consciously with the buttons on his shirt.

The scent of the candle had drifted across the small room. It was richly fragrant, suffusing his lungs and imbuing him with yearning for the exquisite creature before him. He wanted to undress her, to see her in her pristine state, to hold her in his arms. Leaning forward, he brushed her cheek with his lips, then slid her dress off her shoulders, over her hips and to the floor.

Much to Buck's surprise, under the dress Amanda was wearing a pale-peach teddy, and stockings instead of panty hose. His mouth curled with delight.

"Do you like them?" she asked, her shyness displaced by a coquettish grin.

"Fabulous. How did you know I like stockings on a woman?"

"A male friend once told me how ghastly men thought panty hose were."

"Your friend was right. When do I get to take them off?"

She tapped his nose playfully. "I thought you liked them."

"I do, but I love even more what's under them."

Amanda kissed the stubborn chin she had come to adore. "How about if I help you get more comfortable, Buck?" She began loosening his tie.

Buck smiled broadly, letting his hands settle at her waist, which he caressed through the silk film of the teddy. As she began unbuttoning his shirt, he kissed her nose. "I take it these wonderful things you're doing you discovered just by chance—a lucky guess at what the male of the species enjoys?"

Her face had the look of a gamine. "But of course."

Buck held her more tightly, but she soon wiggled free. "I'm not through yet," she objected.

He stood still, delightfully titillated as Amanda undressed him to his shorts. Next, she leaned forward and ran her lips lightly across his chest so that he felt the caressing warmth of her breath on his skin. The gesture aroused him instantly.

Amanda's hand moved toward the band of his shorts, then she hesitated.

He laughed softly. "What's the matter, lose your nerve?"

She nodded, and Buck touched her bare shoulders with his fingers, trailing them down her arms. She looked up into his eyes. Her expression was demure but vaguely suggested a feminine hunger, which, as he savored her, aroused him still more.

His fingertips moved over her chest, but when they neared the swell of her breasts, she abruptly turned to the bed and pulled back the covers, throwing the comforter over the brass railing at the foot.

Taking his hand, she crawled onto the bed and pulled him after her. He was on his elbows beside her as her head settled on the fluffy pillow, her hair a starburst of copper and wine. The shadows from the candlelight deepened her beauty, adding mystery to her allure, impelling him to possess her.

She waited for Buck to finish undressing, then she reached up, touching his gray-flecked temple. Amanda's life seemed reduced to this solitary moment of communion. She knew that she loved him.

Buck stroked her with exquisite, feathery sweeps of his fingers, yet he, too, seemed content, waiting patiently for the dance to continue, the next act to begin. "I could never get enough of you," he murmured. "You're like a goddess, just beyond my reach."

"But I'm not," she replied, grasping his arm and pulling him down so that his body was against hers. Strangely, she was alarmed at his adoration, wanting him to see and love the woman she was, not the goddess he imagined.

Buck smiled and kissed her reassuringly, then clasped her arms more as if to assure her that it was she that he adored.

Amanda's yearning for Buck moved in tandem with his desire to have her. She lay passively as he explored her teddy for a place of entry, finally finding one where it snapped together between her legs. He opened it, exposing her naked mound beneath the loose drape of the fabric.

Buck let his hand glide up through the opening of the teddy and across the taut plane of her stomach before drifting into the ruffled down of her private place. A moan of pleasure rose from her throat, and she looked at him through eyes heavy with unquenched, aching desire.

Buck rose to his knees, then took each of her hands and pulled her upright so that she sat on the bed beside him, uncertain of his plan. Taking the loose tail of the teddy, he pulled it up over her breasts, arms and head so that she was left totally naked except for the lace garter belt and stockings.

He eased her back on the bed, his own large body half over her, his face just inches from hers. Amanda felt him lightly coursing her skin, his fingers toying with the nubs of her breasts, his warm breath washing gently against her cheek. Then his hand drifted down her torso, across her moistened reservoir to her thighs and under the tops of her stockings. The heat of his breath on her face and the caress of his fingers on her legs fired Amanda's desire.

"Oh, Buck," she moaned and dragged his hand up to the pulsing caldron of her femininity.

He pressed close to her, his male essence warm and eagerly distended against her flank.

"Can I take you with your stockings on?"

"Yes," she murmured into his lips, "if you want."

"I want you, Amanda. Oh, how I want you."

The final kiss was long and intimate in its restraint and promise. As their lips parted, Buck eased over her and between her legs, which opened to receive him.

"God, oh, God," she whispered as he brushed against her, pausing at the entrance to her womanly core. Then as she arched to receive him, Buck entered her in one long, smooth thrust that penetrated to her depths.

She moaned, her chest heaving against his weight, but still he did not move. She was exquisitely pinned beneath him, her very soul crying for his storm. Totally still, he seemed to swell inside her, to fill her more completely.

"Oh, Buck, please!"

Obedient to her request, his hips rocked, and he partially withdrew, then penetrated her again. Her cries of pleasure unleashed him, and he began his rhythmic thrusts, building rapidly to a crescendo of ecstasy.

So long had she been on the edge of her pleasure that the first hint of his climax unfettered her, and she was catapulted into a frenzy of convulsion. Her cries filled the tiny room, inciting Buck to explode inside her.

Then as one, they collapsed into a sweet embrace— spent, enraptured, whole. She had become the man, he had become her.

After a long, unmeasured moment, the heaving of his
chest abated, he slipped to her side, and his lips fell
against her neck, moaning his recognition of her conquest.

"Amanda . . . Amanda."

She lay quietly, watching the shimmering dance of the
candlelight on the ceiling and listening to the throbbing
melody of her body. Pleasure enveloped her, laying on
the surface of her consciousness like a fine patina of joy.
She sighed.

Buck raised his hand, leaden with fatigue, to Amanda's moist face. He touched her cheek, gently turning her
head toward him. His face was on the pillow, just inches
from hers, his blue eyes shining darkly in the dim light.
She looked at him, feeling wonder even as she saw wonder on his face.

"I love you," he whispered.

Her heart, already full of emotion, swelled at his words
and a lump formed in her throat. So strong were her
feelings that she barely managed to reply, her words no
more than a soft murmur on her lips. "And I love you,
Buck."

He put his arms around her and gathered her closer still
to him. "Amanda, my Amanda."

And at his words, tears spurted from her eyes and ran
down her cheeks, dropping on the pillow with the same
steady beat as the pulsing of her heart.

CHAPTER FIFTEEN

THE MONDAY AFTER THANKSGIVING, Amanda was at her desk thinking how her life had taken a turn over the long weekend. She had never been happier than she was with Buck and leaving him to go to Phoenix to join her mother and Aunt Margaret had been a major depriva-tion. Though she loved her mother dearly and her aunt as well, the best part of the trip was returning Sunday night and finding Buck waiting for her at the airport.

Cleo soon popped into Amanda's office to hear the news of the big weekend. After Amanda had recounted the story of her apparent success with Cynthia Michaels, she had to deal with Cleo's questions about where it was all leading.

"Admittedly, he did take me home to meet his mother," Amanda said, trying to be circumspect, "but it doesn't mean he's on the verge of proposing. As a matter of fact, he's carefully been skirting the issue."

"No roundabout references to marriage?" Cleo asked. "That's usually how men start. They sort of like to test how the subject sounds to them, I think."

Amanda grinned. "No mention of marriage, but he did give me a set of luggage especially made for his car."

Cleo's eyes lit up. "That's it, Amanda!"

"Luggage?"

"No, his car. Men get very emotional over automobiles. Any time they involve a woman in something to do with their car, it's a meaningful development."

"Cleo, that's the craziest thing I've ever heard. Buck's a mature man, not a teenage boy."

The secretary waved off the objection. "There are certain things they never outgrow."

"This time I think you're wrong, Cleo. The gift was a result of a remark I made to Buck about luggage and commitment. A friend of mine once said that you could gauge the degree of a man's commitment by the number of bags you needed when you left him."

Cleo's melodious voice grew excited. "But, Amanda, don't you see? That's an unequivocal statement."

"Well, I know he's willing to commit eight suitcases worth, but—"

"No, silly, not that. It's the luggage *and* the car. Men always start thinking marriage at the subconscious level first, Amanda. I don't know why that is," she purred, "but it's invariably true. I think it has something to do with avoiding a shock to their system."

"I'm sorry, Cleo, but I think you're reading more into it than is there. Buck hasn't talked about marriage, and besides, we've got a big problem to resolve before that even becomes a possibility."

"You mean Lotus Moon?"

"Yes."

"He's said he wants to finish up with that first?"

"He hasn't said anything about it, no. It's just that her existence—Buck's feelings about finding her—are something that we have to deal with before we can seriously think about our relationship."

"You think *he* feels that way?"

"We haven't talked about it in so many words. But to be honest, I don't think he sees it as a problem."

"But you do?"

"Yes," Amanda replied a bit sadly. "Buck's obsessed and he doesn't know it, or at least he doesn't appreciate how destructive his obsession may become."

"Does he know how you feel?"

"I've told him I thought he was taking it too far and that it was dangerous, but I don't think he accepted what I was trying to tell him."

"Have you fought over it?"

"Not exactly 'fought.' But I'm afraid we will. His determination is unrelenting, and I just know that at some point, I'm going to be backed into a corner. There'll undoubtedly be a showdown."

"I'm beginning to understand why you're worried. It's eating at you, isn't it?"

"That's the strange thing, Cleo. Our relationship is just wonderful in every other respect. When we're not discussing this quest for the child, it's idyllic."

"Hmm . . ."

"I'm not sure what I should do . . . force the issue, let nature take its course, or what."

"Maybe things will work themselves out, Amanda. Maybe you won't even be able to find Lotus Moon."

"On the other hand, we might. And I dread his reaction if we do. I'm not convinced he'll be satisfied with a report on her."

"How about you? Are you prepared for whatever lies at the end of the trail?"

"What do you mean?"

"I mean, what happens if you find this kid and she's in a rotten situation of some kind. Say whoever's got her would be glad to have her off their hands so your fella has a chance to get his daughter. How would you feel about that?''

"I think it's unlikely..."

"But say something like that happens. Say you have to face the prospect of a stepdaughter."

"Frankly, I hadn't even thought about it."

"I don't mean to make problems where you don't have them, but it might be a good idea for you to decide how you feel about this girl yourself."

When Amanda was alone, she decided that Cleo's point had been well-taken. But she also concluded there was no reason to borrow trouble. Enough of it was lurking ahead without taking on more unnecessarily.

Amanda saw the first order of business to be writing the letters to the agencies, beginning what she hoped would be the last phase of the search for Lotus Moon. As she worked on the correspondence, doubts kept creeping into her mind. How could she justify asking another professional for help in what was turning out to be a rather personal crusade?

Amanda struggled with the draft, working and reworking it until it met her standards for honesty and integrity yet was likely to bring the results she desired. When she had finished, she read it again, asking herself how she would react if she were to receive such a letter. Amanda honestly didn't know the answer.

That night when Buck gave her the checks to send along with the letters—eleven in all—he seemed positively euphoric. "I have a feeling this is going to work," he enthused.

Why? Because money talks? she wanted to ask, but she didn't. Amanda knew she was beginning to resent the unknown child and that worried her, too. It was important that she maintain a constructive attitude in the matter, doing her best to help Buck regardless how things turned out. If marriage was ever to come of their relationship, how could it be successful if they couldn't handle a problem like Lotus Moon together?

Once the letters and the checks were sent off, Amanda tried to forget about them, but they always seemed to be at the back of her mind. Buck was being rather taciturn, sensing that it wasn't something she liked to discuss.

On Wednesday he left for Washington on business and, just as before, Amanda felt bereft at his absence. Thursday night he called her.

"Heard from any of the agencies yet?" he asked hopefully.

"It's only been two days since the letters went out, Buck. It's much too early."

"Well, I thought maybe someone might have gotten your letter and called."

"It's not a race against the clock, you know. I'm sure the possibility of an additional thousand dollar donation is appealing, but there can only be one 'winner,' and no one else is as anxious as you." Her words were a little more pointed than she had intended. And in the brief silence that followed, she began to feel badly.

"You don't like it that I'm anxious to find her, do you?"

Amanda could see that she had hurt Buck's feelings. His question was a legitimate one, but she knew that now wasn't the time to discuss it. "I'm sorry, Buck. I didn't mean it that way."

Fortunately, he let the matter drop, and the conversation moved on to other topics, ending with plans for Amanda to spend the weekend with him at Balboa. She hung up the phone, relieved.

The next afternoon, Amanda received a call from the
director of an agency in Pennsylvania. The woman told
Amanda none of the six children that her agency handled had a tattoo, according to their files. Nevertheless,
she indicated a willingness to contact the adoptive parents to see if the tattoo might have been missed. Amanda
was surprised and wondered if Buck's strategy might not
be working after all.

She debated all afternoon whether to tell Buck, when
he returned from the East Coast, about the call she had
received. Amanda finally decided that she had an obligation to keep him informed even though she would have
preferred to spend an evening without discussing Lotus
Moon.

"Well," he said on hearing the news that evening at
dinner, "sounds like our strategy is working. Tell the
truth," he said good-naturedly, "do you think you'd
have gotten that phone call if we hadn't sent those
checks?"

"Always having been optimistic about human nature,
I'd like to say yes."

"I believe in human nature, too," Buck said with a
laugh, "but I like to help it along wherever I can."

Amanda smiled politely at Buck's remark, but he
could see that she was hiding her feelings. He realized his
search for Lotus Moon was troubling her. Although they
were coming down to the wire and he was certain the
matter would soon be settled one way or another, it
seemed to be even more of a problem for Amanda than
before.

Buck wondered if there might not be something in the
situation, some factor, that he had missed. Was there
some kind of jealousy or resentment? He couldn't see
why. But for some reason, she saw his search as an inter-

ference in their relationship, which struck Buck as strange since his quest for the child was what brought them together in the first place.

Everything seemed fine between them as long as they avoided the subject, and Buck knew that he loved Amanda too much to let an insensitivity on his part spoil what they had going. He hoped the girl would turn up soon so that they could concentrate on their own relationship.

Buck had been watching her as they sat across from each other in a little seafood restaurant. She had been avoiding his eyes though he could tell by the way she looked around and by the expression on her face that she was aware of his gaze.

Finally, he reached across the gingham tablecloth and covered her hand with his, hoping the affection would bring her back to him. Amanda looked up, her smile a little wistful, a little distant.

Buck lifted his wineglass to Amanda in toast, thinking it would be very wise of him to avoid the subject of Lotus Moon if their weekend was to be as pleasant as the last.

"AMANDA," CLEO SAID, "if your weekends with that man are responsible for that Monday morning glow of yours, you may as well go ahead and marry him. Why waste the weekdays?"

"Cleo, he hasn't asked me to marry him. Besides, you and I have been over that ground already."

"All right. So raise my spirits and tell me about your weekend," she purred, her eyebrows twitching provocatively.

"Sailing around Catalina Island Saturday. Walking on the beach in the fog and leisurely brunch at Laguna on Sunday."

"Well, at least he didn't make you watch football with him. That's a good sign." Cleo thought for a moment. "What's on the agenda this week?"

"Board meeting's the big item. Then at the end of the week, I have two boys coming in from Bangkok from the Christian Mission Orphanage."

"That's the same one that Lotus Moon came from, isn't it?"

"Yes, but let's not get into that again. We've spent too much time on that case already."

Cleo rolled her eyes. "If you'll excuse me, I think I hear the phone ringing," she said, turning.

It wasn't, but Amanda saw the opportunity to tease her a bit. "You'd better watch your step," she called after Cleo. "Staff salaries is one of the items on the agenda for the board meeting."

"I know," Cleo said over her shoulder as she retreated from the room. "I was the one who put it on."

Amanda couldn't help laughing.

The week went by quietly. On Tuesday, the woman from the agency in Pennsylvania called to say that none of the children handled had a tattoo. Amanda felt curiously ambivalent.

The following day, she received two responses to her letters of inquiry. One simply reported a negative result regarding its three children, and the other returned the check with a note saying their charter prevented them from disclosing the requested information. Amanda worried that Lotus Moon might have been one of the two children handled by that agency and wasn't sure whether she felt disappointment or relief.

She reported the results to Buck as they came in, and he seemed to take them with equanimity though his initial optimism was clearly waning. Amanda worried that he might become depressed. Though they talked once or twice a day, they didn't see each other during that week. Amanda had to spend every available minute preparing for her board meeting Wednesday night.

"So when do I get to see you again?" Buck lamented Thursday morning when he called.

"Whenever you like."

"I like all the time, but one or the other of us always seems to be busy."

"I'm free this evening. . . ."

"Well, I've got that dinner with the editorial staff tonight."

"Unfortunate," she said, teasing.

"And tomorrow evening you're busy."

"Yes. I've got to meet a flight from Bangkok with two Amerasian children—those two boys. Remember the ones we saw when we went to visit Mrs. Pakorn?"

"Sure. I talked to the older one for quite a long time while you were inside playing Mrs. Michaels."

Amanda reddened at Buck's reference to their deception. At the time, it seemed far less adventurous than it did now.

"Say, Amanda, is there any reason that I couldn't go with you to the airport? It would be nice to see the boys again."

She hesitated, thinking that anything that might remind Buck of their search for Lotus Moon would be problematical. Then she realized that she couldn't shield him forever. Besides, it was her life's work; the subject matter couldn't be a problem for them if they were to have a relationship. "I suppose it would be all right, if you'd enjoy it. I'd certainly like your company."

"What time do I pick you up?"

THE MAIL BROUGHT another returned check, two more negative reports involving a total of eight children, and a letter requesting further information regarding the purpose of Amanda's inquiry. The last was a source of irritation, but rather than leave it hanging over her head for the weekend, she decided to get out an immediate response.

That afternoon, she called Buck to give him a report, but he was tied up in meetings so she left a message with Kelly. Forty-five minutes later, he called back.

"Not looking so good, is it?" he asked sadly.

"We've heard from seven of the eleven agencies I wrote to, Buck, so there are four yet to hear from. The one asking for clarification is still a possibility, too."

"How many of the girls are accounted for?"

"Twenty-six. But five are with the agency wanting clarification, meaning half of our original group are still possibles."

"But two agencies won't cooperate with us. How many girls did they handle?"

"Four."

"Hmm. Ten percent."

"Yes."

"God, I hope she's not one of the four. That would be tragic, wouldn't it?"

"Frankly, I'm surprised I haven't gotten more like that. Let's just hope one of the bigger agencies doesn't fall into that group as well. That could eliminate five or six girls in one blow."

"I guess all we can do is wait...."

Amanda could almost see Buck's disappointed face, and she felt badly for him. She wished he was there with her so that she could put her arms around him and comfort him. "You know we're well into December," she said, trying to distract him, "and I haven't done a bit of Christmas shopping. Would you like to go together this weekend?"

"Sure. I'd like that."

"When do you usually decorate your house?"

"The past few years I've had a professional do it."

"How uninspired."

"It's a big house...."

"Well," Amanda said resolutely, "I'm not going to let you get away with that this year. Why don't I help you with your place, and you can help me with mine?"

"Okay."

"This weekend we can take inventory of your decorations and buy whatever we'll need."

There was a pause.

"I've missed you this week, Amanda."

"I've missed you, too."

"Why don't you bring two or three bags this weekend instead of that small one."

"Goodness, you *are* sounding serious," she teased.

"I am. So... why don't we go to my place right from the airport tomorrow night?"

"Okay, if you'd like."

"I'd like very much."

Amanda hung up feeling happier than she had in days.

Friday morning, she was reviewing the documentation for the two boys who would be arriving from Thailand that evening when Cleo came in with the mail. "Looks like more responses to your letters," she said, handing Amanda three envelopes.

"Thanks." Amanda eagerly picked up her letter opener as Cleo retreated from the room.

The first was from a large agency in New York that had handled seven children. They reported there was neither a name nor a reference to the tattoo in any of the files.

The second letter was from an agency that had handled three girls and indicated their need to have further information on the purposes of the investigation before responding. Amanda groaned.

The final letter was from a small agency in Kansas City. Amanda opened the envelope and was shocked with the first sentence she read.

Dear Miss Parr:

In response to your letter of inquiry, we are pleased to report that our case is very likely the one you are seeking to verify.

The child's medical records contain a reference to a small tattoo—a blossom and a crescent moon on the left leg just below the anklebone on the interior side. The girl's age and general description correspond to the child you are trying to locate.

Per your request, I am pleased to provide the following information as permitted under our administrative guidelines and state law. The child is now thirteen years of age and in good health as of our last contact with the adoptive family three years ago. The name given her by her adoptive parents is Laura. She resides with both parents in the state of Kansas. (There are no other children in the family, either natural or adopted.)

Laura is of above-average intelligence, has scored well in her standard tests, and is interested in music and dance. She is well adjusted socially, and there is no indication of problems of any kind due to her mixed heritage and racial background. Her adoptive family's income is above the mean for their community though they would not be considered wealthy. Every indication is that Laura is in a wholesome environment.

Any further information you or your client may require can be released only with the consent of the parents. I would be happy, however, to forward any requests to them that you may have.

I hope the information provided has been useful to you. Please extend my appreciation to your client for the very generous donation to our agency.

Sincerely yours,
Madeline Wagner, Director

Amanda reread the letter, hardly believing that at last Lotus Moon had been located. She knew that Buck would want to know immediately, but she felt the need to let the news sink in a bit—to consider just what it meant to them. First and foremost, the uncertainty would be over. The letter was more detailed and explicit than Amanda had dared hope. Perhaps Buck would be satisfied with it.

As she sat at her desk contemplating the turn in events, she thought about the best way to tell Buck. She would have liked to be with him and have him read the letter himself, but in a way, it might be better to let him savor the information in private, to let it sink in before she saw him.

She picked up the telephone and excitedly dialed Buck's number. He was as shocked as she.

"My God, somehow I never thought it would happen," he said after she read him the letter.

"Aren't you pleased?" she enthused.

"Yes...I'm...relieved, I guess. I've been afraid of the worst, yet hopeful for so long, I don't quite know what to think."

"Well, I'm really happy for you, for Lotus Moon—Laura."

"Do you think we should call her Laura? I've gotten so used to thinking of her as Lotus Moon that Laura seems strange."

"Laura is how she thinks of herself so I would think that's the name to use. Do you like it?"

"Yes, I've always liked the name Laura. But not knowing her, I frankly have trouble relating it to anything." He paused. "You know, the funny thing is I've always pictured her as looking like Dameree."

"Dameree's a beautiful woman. Laura would do well to look like her mother."

"Yes, I suppose so."

There was a silence, and Amanda wished she knew what Buck was thinking. "Do you still want to go with me tonight to meet the boys at the airport?"

"Oh, yes. I've been looking forward to it."

"Five-thirty still all right?"

"Yeah, fine."

"Okay, Buck, see you then." Amanda hung up wondering what wheels had been set in motion.

BUCK SAT IN A VINYL ARMCHAIR in the immigration office at the Los Angeles International Airport as Amanda reviewed the documentation for her two orphans with an official. He tuned out their patter, thinking again as he had all afternoon about Lotus Moon, Laura.

Reaching into the inside pocket of his suit coat, he pulled out the photocopy of the letter Amanda had read

to him on the telephone that morning. He liked the name
Laura. He mused. Laura Michaels. But that wasn't her
name. It was Laura something else. What would she
think to know that her real father was right here in the
country with her, a newspaperman from Los Angeles?
Would it frighten her, or would she be intrigued?

The girl was thirteen. The only parents she had ever
known were these people someplace in Kansas. Laura
had been one when she left Bangkok—she would have no
recollection of that, nor the orphanage there, nor Dameree. What's more, he did not exist, either, as far as she
was concerned. Maybe someday she'd be curious, but
thirteen-year-olds thought about other things, surely.
Things like music and dance.... Buck wondered if she
sang or played an instrument. Probably the piano. That
was really American.

He pictured a little clapboard house in a small town in
Kansas with a cozy parlor and an upright piano against
the wall. A girl with long black hair and features that
were half Dameree's and half his was sitting there, playing to the beat of the metronome. Tears spontaneously
welled in his eyes.

Buck folded the letter and put it back in his pocket.
Amanda was just finishing her conversation with the official, and Buck tried to listen dispassionately. Nevertheless, the image of the girl at the piano burned at the back
of his brain.

When Amanda got up, Buck rose to his feet, too. They
left the office, the immigration officer escorting them
through customs toward the gate where the flight was due
in about twenty minutes.

Once they were alone at the gate, Amanda turned to
Buck with an expectant, eager expression on her face.

"I've done this dozens of times during the past few years, but it always excites me," she said, beaming.

"Why?"

"I don't know, the thought of bringing them home, I suppose, finding a good home for them." She took Buck's hand and squeezed it.

He could see that her feelings were sincere, but he wondered if she felt relief at the news about Lotus Moon. It had been more of a burden for them than he had himself realized. Now the uncertainty was over—at least most of it.

"What were you thinking about just then, Buck? You had the most thoughtful expression on your face. Was it Laura?"

He nodded, feeling a little guilty.

"You are pleased, aren't you?"

"Oh, yes, pleased and grateful to you, Amanda."

"I'm just interested in your happiness and peace of mind. It was good news—the fact that she's in a good home, I mean."

"Yes."

"You don't sound very sure."

"Well, it's too bad they haven't had contact with her in such a long time. I mean, problems could have come up since their last follow-up." Buck could see by Amanda's doleful expression that it was not a popular tack to take. He decided to back off. "But then, I suppose there'll never be enough certainty, will there?"

"We got an awfully thorough response, considering."

Buck turned and looked out the window toward the darkened airfield. He realized that he, too, felt expectation at the arrival of the two boys, but emotionally it was more akin to awaiting the arrival of his own child, Laura.

For the first time, he saw the danger that Amanda had warned him about, but he couldn't help it. He knew deep inside that he would have to see his child.

CHAPTER SIXTEEN

OVER THE WEEKEND, the weather turned cold and rainy. The first storm of the season came blowing in off the Pacific. Buck and Amanda spent a quiet Saturday morning at his house reading and watching the rain pelting the large windows. They both put on bulky sweaters, Buck fixed a fire in the fireplace and Amanda made coffee, carrying two large mugs into the living room where he was lying on the couch in his stockinged feet.

"You look the picture of contentment," she said, squeezing his knee.

Buck took Amanda's hand and pulled her down beside him on the couch. "I feel good when I'm with you," he responded.

"It does seem like the perfectly natural thing, doesn't it?"

He nodded and took the mug of coffee she handed him.

"You know, you were wonderful with the boys last night. Speaking Thai with Lon put him at ease. I think you've made a friend."

"Poor kid seemed scared. I just wish I'd remembered more. I've forgotten most of the Thai I used to know."

Outside the wind gusted, blowing sheets of rain against the windows with great force. They looked out, barely able to see the houses lining the shore across the bay.

Amanda shivered and Buck stroked her arm affectionately.

"It's a good day to be indoors.... Remember those
hot, balmy nights in Bangkok?"

"It's hard to believe that was just over a month ago."

Buck ran his fingers up Amanda's spine to the bare
skin on the back of her neck, which he caressed lightly.
"It *is* hard to believe. And in just a few weeks it will be
Christmas."

Amanda sighed.

"Were you planning on being with your mother?" he
asked.

"We usually spend Christmas Day together."

"Would it be too adventuresome to invite her over
here?"

She looked at him with uncertainty.

Buck shrugged. "Well, it's a time for families to be
together. Maybe we could invite my mother, too—make
a real day of it." He laughed a little sadly. "All we'd be
missing is children."

He didn't mention her name, but Amanda knew he
was thinking of Laura. She looked at his wistful blue
eyes, never having seen them so nostalgic before. "It
would be nice with both our mothers—I'm sure they'd
get along—but I think it might be a little much, Buck."

"Why? We care about each other and want to be together, and we care about them. It seems reasonable
enough to me."

Amanda pictured the four of them eating Christmas
dinner together. The notion *was* appealing. "Well, let's
think about it, Buck. But the first order of business is
deciding how we're going to decorate this house. Tell you
what. Let's have a look at all your decorations and plan
what we're going to do to make this place really festive."

Buck grinned at her provocatively and pulled her hands to his lips, kissing them softly. "Sure you wouldn't just like to relax and worry about all that later?" he asked with a suggestive lilt to his voice.

"Oh, no, you don't, Buck Michaels! No diversionary tactics. We're going to get this house whipped into shape this weekend. And I'm going to get you into the holiday spirit if it kills me."

Buck laughed and pulled her closer. She resisted for a moment until the soft caress of his lips became too much.

AMANDA HELD BUCK'S HAND tightly as they walked down the festively decorated mall aglow with bright lights and the reds, greens, silvers and golds of Christmas. The shopping center was crammed with people and awash with the chatter of children and the refrains of carols and holiday tunes.

"Feeling the spirit of Christmas yet?" Amanda asked, beaming at him hopefully.

He chuckled. "Frankly, shopping doesn't do it for me."

"When we do the decorating you'll get in the mood."

They walked along, hand in hand, until they came to the Santa's village that had been set up for the children, the main attraction being Santa Claus himself. Amanda and Buck looked in the window at the toddler who had just been placed on Santa's lap. The little girl's eyes rounded, and she obviously was on the verge of tears. Amanda looked up at Buck with amusement on her face but found him staring at the scene with a distant, detached expression. Her heart sank. She took his arm and they walked on.

Several minutes later, they came to a toy store, and after pausing, Buck said, "Let's go in here for a minute."

Amanda followed him in and watched as he wandered around. "Do you have any kids on your Christmas list?" she asked as he peered in a glass case at the dolls.

"No, I guess I don't."

They quietly left the store, and Amanda realized that the letter from Kansas City, rather than being the end, apparently was another beginning.

MOST OF THE DRIVE HOME was in silence. Supposedly they were listening to the tape of Christmas music Buck had inserted into the tape deck, but Amanda didn't really hear it. Her mind was busily turning over the troubling new development in Buck's behavior. When they entered the kitchen from the garage, he dropped all the packages on the kitchen table.

"Would you mind getting me a glass of sherry, Buck? If you don't mind, I'd like to sit down and talk with you for a few minutes."

She went into the living room, and a moment later, Buck followed with two glasses of sherry. He dropped down in the chair opposite Amanda, his face indicating that he knew what was on her mind.

They stared at each other. "It's Laura, isn't it, Buck?" He nodded.

"What is it? What do you want?"

"I can't get her out of my mind, Amanda." He paused. "I want to see her."

His words didn't surprise her, but her heart dropped nonetheless. She watched him, unable to speak, fighting her irritation, feeling betrayed, but understanding his pain and frustration all at the same time. She looked down, and her eyes closed before finally looking up at his sober face. "I won't do it, Buck. I can't."

He continued to stare at her, his expression implacable but unaccusing. He was neither demanding nor imploring, but it was obvious he couldn't deny his feelings. She figured he didn't like the way he felt any more than she did, but there wasn't much he could do about it. Amanda knew it was up to her.

"I hate to deny you, but I must."

Still, he said nothing.

"Can you accept that, Buck? Do you hate me because of it?"

"No, of course I don't hate you."

"But obviously you're not pleased."

"No, I suppose not."

"Do you understand my position? I've already gone five times further than I would have for anyone else. If it weren't for my feelings for you, Buck, I wouldn't have done even this. I think it would be bad for the child, bad for her parents and bad for you."

"But I've told you I don't want to interfere. I just want to see her, even if it's only at a distance."

"No, Buck! Put it out of your mind. Please!"

"Would it hurt to ask?"

"I refuse to do it. As a professional, I'm convinced it's wrong, and it would be irresponsible of me to let my feelings for you interfere in my judgment."

His eyes flickered with irritation. "How can it hurt to ask? If Laura or her parents are against it, they'll say so, but why should you decide for them?"

"I would have to ask the director of the Kansas City agency first, and I'm sure it would never get past her."

"She said in her letter that she would be happy to relay any requests for information."

"But this is not a request for information."

"All they can do is say no."

Amanda felt herself getting upset. His stubbornness had a way of getting to her—especially when he backed it up with dispassionate, logical arguments. She was beginning to feel heartless and arbitrary even though she knew she was right. "Buck, you can be so frustrating at times!"

"What is it you're afraid of?"

"I don't want anyone hurt—including you!"

"I'll worry about me, and let's let the people in Kansas worry about themselves."

"What is it you *really* want, Buck? Don't you see that you're never satisfied? Every time I do something for you, you ask for more. There's no end to it. To be honest, I don't think you'll be satisfied until the child's living here with you in this house." Amanda felt her cheeks flush. Her words had been harsher than she had intended.

"Am I that bad, Amanda?" he asked in a low, calm voice.

She looked at him. He was a master at undermining her convictions although she knew he meant no harm to anyone. "I'm sorry, Buck. I don't mean to attack you personally."

"Look, I know I keep asking for more, and I know from your standpoint it looks like I'm double-crossing you, but I'm not. I want the same thing now that I've wanted all along. I want to make sure she's all right. I want to see with my own eyes."

"You haven't said *that* before, Buck."

"I know. I guess I haven't realized that whatever I've learned is inadequate until I get there. Every time I learn something new about my daughter, it just raises more doubts. I've got to find out for myself."

"Well, I understand that, but it's an idle wish. This sort of thing is just not done, and I am personally against it."

"So that's it, then. You won't help anymore."

"Not with that, no."

They looked at each other across the narrow space separating them. Never had a little gap seemed so far to Amanda. She hated the situation so much that she felt as though she'd cry. She stared at Buck, loving him through her disappointment and anger.

"I guess that's the end of it, then," he repeated, his voice flat, cold.

"Buck, this is tearing me up. I can't bear your resentment any more than the pressure," she said, her voice almost pleading.

"I don't resent you."

"You can hardly feel very kindly toward me."

"I'm disappointed, but I understand."

"Do you?" She felt the tears begin to well.

"Of course."

Amanda studied the face of the man she had come to love. This was destroying them. "I don't believe you," she said, as her control began slipping. Her mouth twitched with emotion.

"Amanda..."

It was too late. The tears began to fall, and she dropped her face into her hands.

Buck went to her immediately, kneeling at her feet. "Amanda, I'm sorry. I was being selfish. I shouldn't have said anything."

"You can't help it," she sobbed. "Not if you feel that way."

"Come on, lady, I love you. And that's a lot more important."

"No, it isn't. What could be more important than your own child?" she asked, wiping her cheeks with the back of her hand.

Buck gave her his handkerchief. "I was not thinking of you and your feelings, Amanda. I was wrong."

"No, you weren't wrong. It's only natural," she said, looking at him through tear-soaked lashes.

He pinched her nose. "What are we going to do, fight over why the other person is right?"

Amanda blew her nose. "I didn't say you were right, I just said I understood why you feel the way you do."

They laughed.

"Well," Buck said, stroking her cheek, "let's forget about it."

And Amanda wished with all her heart that they could.

ALTHOUGH BUCK AVOIDED the subject for the rest of the weekend, Amanda couldn't forget. Every time she looked at Buck's face, she felt terrible, as though she had perpetrated a great injustice even though she knew that the position she had taken was the right one.

Monday morning she sat in her office, thinking about Buck and about Laura, a young girl somewhere in Kansas oblivious to the turmoil she had created in the lives of two unknown people in California. If it hadn't been so sad, she would have found it amusing.

Amanda tried to analyze the situation as dispassionately as she possibly could. One thing was clear to her above all else—she had to find a way to satisfy Buck about Laura's well-being. The chances of him being allowed to see her were one in a million, but she wondered if *she* might be permitted to meet the girl. Since she was a professional whose agency had been involved in the case originally, perhaps the parents might agree to her visiting the family home. On an impulse, she called Madeline Wagner in Kansas City.

"I don't know, Amanda. We don't normally conduct follow-up investigations ourselves this long after the placement. But . . . I suppose I could ask."

"I would appreciate it, Madeline."

"I think it would be best if I'm very frank with the adoptive parents."

"Certainly. I understand. Anything you can do would be appreciated."

Amanda decided not to tell Buck about her initiative. It seemed to her a long shot at best, and she didn't want to disappoint him if nothing came of it. During the balance of the week, they got together once for lunch and twice for dinner. Buck had a heavy schedule so they stayed together only one night after going out, but the mood had been a little melancholy and tentative.

They didn't make love that night; Buck just held her in his arms. After he had dozed off, she cried herself to sleep, wishing it could be like it had been before.

Their disagreement the previous weekend was hanging in the air, and though nothing was said directly, it affected both of them—or at least Amanda sensed that it did. She was tempted to tell Buck about the overture she had made to Laura's parents, but she held back. She couldn't rely on anything so tenuous to lighten the mood so she just waited to see what would come out of Kansas City. Perhaps, too, a little time and distance between them would be a good thing.

On Friday, Madeline Wagner called with surprising news. "I don't believe it myself, Amanda," she said, "but Laura's parents have agreed to a visit. They suggested a week from Saturday. Would that be convenient?"

That was just a few days before Christmas, but Amanda didn't hesitate. "Certainly, Madeline, that would be perfect."

"They have some conditions. No one is to know their identity but you."

"That's certainly acceptable."

"Good. I suggest you come to Kansas City first. I can brief you here. The family lives in Northeast Kansas, only a few hours' drive away."

Amanda hung up feeling ecstatic, almost as though she had been given a reprieve. She contemplated how she was going to tell Buck about her good fortune—their good fortune. Not on the phone. She wanted to make it more personal than that. She wanted to see the expression on his face.

They had a tentative date for dinner out that night, and Amanda decided that she would have him come to dinner at her place instead. She would make it a special occasion, a candlelight dinner, perhaps get a bottle of champagne, then tell him the good news. The prospect excited her, and she hurried to call him with the invitation.

"SO WHAT'S THE SPECIAL OCCASION?" Buck asked, smiling at her across the table with a little of his old sparkle.

"What makes you think it's a special occasion?" Amanda teased, enjoying the mood. "Isn't the chance to see you reason enough to have some champagne?"

"Have I been neglecting you that much?"

"No, I'm just feeling happy tonight."

"Why?"

"I've got some good news."

"Really? What is it?"

She beamed. "Next weekend I'm going to Kansas to see Laura and her parents."

Buck sat for a moment, dumbfounded. "How did you arrange that?"

After she had told him the story, Buck shook his head in disbelief. "Amanda, you amaze me."

"Aren't you pleased?"

"Of course," he said, smiling broadly. "It's practically as good as if I were going myself."

She looked at him. "I know you'd like to go, Buck, but this is the only way I could arrange it."

"I understand."

They opened the champagne, and Amanda offered a toast to Laura. Buck countered with a toast of his own. "To you, Amanda, the woman I love."

After they had finished eating, they took the rest of the wine into the bedroom and finished it between kisses. The fog that had been lying over them for a week dissipated, and Amanda felt she had regained the man she loved.

BUCK MICHAELS SAT in the conference room, listening to his editors discussing the front page of the afternoon edition of the *Tribune*. Occasionally, someone would glance at him, looking for a reaction to a comment, but they knew that his heart and mind were not in the work, not the way they usually were.

He caught himself daydreaming about Amanda and Laura, the family he carried in his thoughts, and forced himself to concentrate on what was being said—at least long enough to ask a halfway intelligent question to let them know that he was there.

When the meeting finally broke up, Buck approached Kelly's desk. "Any calls?" he asked.

"No, Boss, she hasn't phoned yet this morning." There was a mischievous grin on her face, which he ignored, walking past her into his office.

A moment later, Kelly entered, carrying his cup of coffee. She put it down on his coaster and stepped back but didn't leave. Finally, Buck noticed and looked up at her quizzically. There was a look on her face that told him she wanted to talk. "You have something you'd like to say, Kelly?"

"No, but I thought you might. What's bugging you, Buck?"

"Is it that obvious?"

She nodded.

"I guess I've been distracted recently."

She gave a little laugh. "Is it love or the girl?"

He picked up his coffee and sipped it. "I suppose both." Then he told her about Amanda's upcoming trip to Kansas.

"You ought to be pleased."

"I am, but I'm also as frustrated as hell."

"Because you can't go along?"

"Yes."

"It must be tough sitting by, knowing how close you came to finally seeing her."

"If it weren't for Amanda, I'd just take matters into my own hands and find the child. At least have a look at her from a distance."

"If it weren't for Amanda, you wouldn't have gotten this close."

"I know, that's the hell of it. Almost from the beginning, it's been a problem for us both. Nemesis and friend rolled into one."

"So what are you going to do?"

"Grin and bear it. I haven't any choice."

As the week went by and the time for Amanda's departure drew near, she began feeling more and more tense. By all rights, it should be a welcome event, but she was coming to dread it, not because she didn't want to go but because Buck wasn't going. Reason told her that what she was doing was right, but her heart chafed at her own logic.

Buck was being good about it, but she knew that he, too, was suffering. He was caught between his love for her and his respect for her decision, and his desire to see Laura. Amanda feared she was both his ally and his enemy.

One afternoon toward the end of the week, Cleo came in with the sandwich Amanda had asked her to bring back when she went out to lunch. She dropped the paper sack on the desk. "I forgot whether you said mustard or mayonnaise so I got both."

"I like both."

"Good. I'm allergic to bland myself. Always better to err on the side of excess."

"Interesting philosophy."

"Experience. I've had three bland husbands."

Amanda laughed. "You've gained more wisdom from marriage than any woman I know, Cleo."

The secretary grinned. "None of them had two nickels to rub together so I suppose I was destined to get something out of it."

The women looked at each other, both knowing Amanda's feelings were going unexpressed.

"What's bothering you, honey?" Cleo finally asked in a low, intimate voice.

"I don't know what to do."

"About the trip?"

"Yes."

"Your mind telling you one thing, your heart another?"

"Something like that."

"Any way to compromise?"

"Not that I can see."

Cleo thought. "Are you going to marry this guy?"

"Things are moving that way," Amanda admitted, "but it's too early to say. We've got to get this behind us—that much I'm sure of."

"I don't know what's right and what's wrong in situations like this, Amanda, but I do know that if a relationship is to mean anything, it's got to take precedence over everything else. Sometimes you have to sacrifice, do things you wouldn't normally do. Put your fella first, I guess is what I'm saying."

"He'd like to go with me to Kansas, I know, but there's no way that would work. It would end in an ugly scene—I'm sure of it."

"Is there a chance you could talk the people into letting Buck see the girl?"

"They've made it clear they don't want that, Cleo. And even if I could, I'm not so sure it's a good thing for the child. And maybe not for Buck, either."

"Is there any harm in asking? Besides, the girl doesn't have to know who he is, does she? Isn't what he's after just to see her?"

"That's what he says."

"Maybe you can find a way to arrange it."

Amanda pondered what Cleo had said. "Yes," she said vacantly, "you may be right."

THURSDAY NIGHT, another storm blew in, bringing more rain. Amanda stood at Buck's living room window looking out at the dark bay through the sheet of water rippling down the glass. Behind her, in the corner, was the tree she and Buck had trimmed the previous weekend. It was large and well proportioned. She had grouped candles and poinsettias throughout the room, giving it a cheerful yet elegant feel.

Amanda saw Buck's reflection in the glass as he returned from the kitchen with mugs of hot chocolate. He put them down on the table, then walked over behind her, slipping his arms around her waist. "What's so interesting out there?" he asked, kissing her ear.

"I was just watching the rain, listening to it drumming against the window."

He held her tightly, and Amanda loved the feel of his arms around her. She had been agonizing all evening how to raise the subject of the trip, and she knew by the way Buck had been watching her that he was aware that something was amiss. It was better when he held her, though. It somehow gave her strength.

After they had stood at the window for a long time watching the rain and the twinkling lights across the bay, she turned around and looked up at him. He waited patiently, giving her time to find her courage.

"Buck..." she whispered, her voice faltering, "would you like to go to Kansas with me?"

He stared into her eyes for a long minute, trying to understand the implications of her question. "I thought I couldn't."

"Well, technically you can't, but I'm trying to find a way for you to at least see Laura—if I can arrange it."

"What do you mean?"

"I thought I would ask Laura's parents if it would be all right if you saw her. If I can convince them and you're available, then . . ."

"Amanda, are you sure you want to?"

"There's no guarantee, Buck. They may not agree. And I'll have to have your solemn promise not to interfere. If you come with me, you'll have to do exactly what I say and no more. The temptation and the frustration might be unbearable, but I'll need your word."

His face was somber. "What made you do this—change your mind, I mean?"

She kissed his stubborn chin. "I love you."

"Did you just discover that?" he asked with a wry smile.

"No, I just discovered the implications. If I can't trust you, Buck, then our relationship is in trouble. I'm going to do the best I can for you and trust you to see that I don't hurt anyone else in the process."

"I wouldn't want to see Laura hurt. Or her parents, either."

"I know you wouldn't." She pulled his face down to hers and kissed him deeply. Then looking into his twinkling blue eyes, she felt a sheen of tears well in her own. "Together, Buck, we'll do the best we can."

He took her face in his hands, smiling before covering her mouth with his own. "I love you, Amanda. I love you so much."

CHAPTER SEVENTEEN

THE FLIGHT TO KANSAS CITY was strangely reminiscent of the flight they had taken together to Bangkok, and yet it was so very different. Instead of the blue Pacific below them, there were snow-covered mountains and flat, barren plains. Instead of heading to an exotic, tropical setting, they were flying to America's heartland. Instead of going in search of an elusive, mysterious child, they were going to see a thirteen-year-old girl in Kansas who liked music and dance—Buck Michaels's daughter.

Buck held Amanda's hand tightly as the plane touched down in Kansas City. They rented a car and hurried to the unpretentious building in Roeland Park that housed the adoption agency. Having decided there was no point in making Madeline a party to their plan, Amanda went in alone while Buck waited in a coffee shop on the corner.

An hour later, Amanda and Buck left for Hiawatha, Kansas, a small town in the extreme northeastern corner of the state. They drove north on U.S. 73, through Leavenworth, Atchison, over to Horton, then along a long, straight stretch of highway through gently rolling terrain covered with cornfields.

On either side of the road, the fields were strewn with brown and broken stalks, remnants of the last crop. Dotting the landscape were farmhouses and barns, many clustered under the boughs of trees that were skeletal and desolate looking under the slate-gray sky of winter.

The towns, however, were little oases of civilization, festively decorated with great plastic snowmen, Christmas stars and Santas on the lampposts. The residential sections were festooned with green wreaths and red ribbons on doors, Christmas lights and an occasional crèche scene in the middle of a parched brown lawn. Darkness was falling as they entered Hiawatha. Buck drove through the town, past the town square and county courthouse to the outer limits before turning back again.

"Well, it looks like we have a choice of two motels," he said. "What appeals to you, the Sunflower Motel or the Best Western Lodge?"

"You choose."

Buck picked the Best Western Lodge because the sign said Color TVs. They went to their room, which was spacious and clean. It reminded Amanda of her travels with her parents as a child.

"Not quite the Oriental," Buck said with a grin after peeking into the bathroom, "but there's a sanitary strip of paper over the toilet seat, and that's all that matters."

Amanda sat on the bed, exhausted from the long day. "Bed's nice."

"Feel like some dinner before we settle down to our color TV? The motel restaurant looked pretty nice."

"Sounds good to me," she said, glancing up at Buck.

He touched her cheek affectionately, then went to the window and gazed out. "Sure is a wholesome-looking place, isn't it? I bet in the fall all those maple trees are just gorgeous. And I wouldn't be surprised if they had a championship football team." He turned and looked at Amanda. "Do you suppose Laura might be a cheerleader or the baton twirler with the band?"

Amanda smiled and shook her head, marveling at Buck's sentimentality and thinking how glad she was that

she had brought him. Just visiting the town would have
to give him some peace of mind.

After freshening up, they put their coats back on and
walked to the restaurant. The air was very cold and a
wind had come up, cutting right through Amanda's
clothing. She held Buck's arm and pressed against him as
they walked. By the time they reached the doorway, her
cheeks were rosy red.

The inside of the restaurant felt warm, and most of the
tables were full, creating a most hospitable atmosphere.
People turned and looked at the unfamiliar couple, and
for a moment, the chatter in the room dropped to a hush.
"Big city slickers," their looks seemed to say, but they
were friendly faces. Some people smiled.

A middle-aged waitress approached as soon as Buck
and Amanda had slid into a booth by the window.
"Good evening," she said, placing a glass of ice water
and a menu before each of them. She smiled through her
glasses at Amanda. "Getting pretty brisk out, isn't it?"

Amanda rubbed her hands together, still feeling the
chill. "Seems awfully cold to me, but then I'm not used
to it."

"Where you folks from?" the woman asked in a sweet,
midwestern drawl.

"Los Angeles," Buck replied.

"My goodness, you have come a long way."

Amanda could see that the woman's curiosity had been
aroused and that she was contemplating another overture but decided against it. "Well, I'll give you folks a
few minutes to look at your menus," she said hospitably
before turning away.

After a leisurely meal of salad, chicken fried steak,
mashed potatoes and mixed vegetables, they had some
apple pie à la mode.

"Mmm," Buck said as he finished his pie, "if this sort of thing is passed along by genes, Laura has apple pie here every chance she gets."

Amanda smiled at him warmly. At that moment more than at any time since she had met him, Amanda saw Buck as a father, picturing him with his little Amerasian daughter. She hoped, for his sake, he would have a chance to see the girl before they left.

THE NEXT MORNING while Buck went out for a walk, Amanda called the home of Laura's parents, Jay and Betty Springer, at the number Madeline had given her. She made an appointment to visit them at one-thirty that afternoon.

After lunch, Buck and Amanda walked back to the motel from the restaurant, interested in the somewhat different face the town presented by daylight. Once in their room, Buck turned on the television to watch a football game, knowing Amanda would be leaving soon. He propped himself up on the bed, trying to look casual and at ease, but Amanda realized that he must be suffering terribly with frustration.

She gathered her things and went to the door.

"Good luck," he said evenly and watched her as she stepped out into the cold December day.

Amanda got in the car and drove to a street just south of the town square, as Betty Springer had directed. Turning onto Minnehaha Street, she drove until she came to the address she had been given. The Springer home was a frame house set on a deep, narrow lot. Maple trees, now completely barren of leaves, lined the driveway.

Amanda stared at the house for a moment, amazed that a search that had begun in a conversation with Buck Michaels atop an office tower in downtown Los Angeles three months ago had ended here, on Minnehaha Street in Hiawatha, Kansas. In between, there had been Bangkok, that lovely garden at the Panan Cherng Temple in Ayudhya, Kupnol Sustri, Mrs. Pakorn, Dameree, Madeline Wagner, and now Jay and Betty Springer.

Amanda gathered her thoughts for a moment before getting out of the car, wondering what the Springers would be like, wondering what Laura would be like. Madeline had told Amanda that Jay owned a television and appliance repair shop in Hiawatha and that Betty worked part-time as a dressmaker. Laura was now in her last year of junior high school. Betty had said she would make sure that the girl would be home for her visit.

Taking her briefcase, more to give herself an official-looking appearance than for any other reason, Amanda got out of the car and walked to the entrance of the house. There, on a brass plaque below the bell, she read, Jay, Betty and Laura Springer. She knocked softly.

A moment later, the door was opened by a woman in her late thirties. She had short dark hair and rosy cheeks and a rather wide, prominent mouth. Only slightly plump, she had apparently dressed up for Amanda's visit, wearing a brown wool skirt and beige nylon blouse with a large, loose bow at the neck. She smiled. "You must be Miss Parr."

"Yes. And you're Mrs. Springer?"

The woman nodded. "Please come in."

Amanda stepped into a small but cozy living room, decorated for the holidays with a tinsel-laden Christmas tree topped by a silver-winged angel. Over the doors of the room were Christmas cards hanging from a string, interspersed with pieces of plastic mistletoe.

A man who had been sitting in an easy chair with a newspaper folded on his lap put his paper aside and rose to his feet, shifting his weight rather stiffly as he grinned at the new arrival. He wore a fresh white shirt and a pair of wool slacks. He was a rawboned man but had a kind, pleasant face.

"Jay, this is Miss Parr from the adoption agency," Betty said as they walked over to him. "This is my husband, Jay Springer, Miss Parr."

Amanda extended her hand to the man, who shook it in a shy, yet friendly way. "Please call me Amanda," she said, looking at each of them in turn.

"We're Betty and Jay, then," the woman replied. "Here, Amanda, sit on the couch. It's the most comfortable place."

Amanda sat down, smiling at them both, trying to put them at ease. "It's awfully good of you to let me visit, especially at this time of year, just before the holidays and all."

"It's the best time for visiting," Betty replied, sitting down next to Amanda. "People have the Christmas spirit. Leastwise they should."

Jay nodded in agreement.

"In a nice town like this, I'm sure it's especially true," Amanda said.

"Where are you from, Miss...Amanda?"

"Los Angeles. Long Beach, actually."

"I knew it was Los Angeles or San Francisco, one," Betty said. "Miss Wagner told me when she called, but I forgot."

Jay scratched his head. "You come all the way out here just to see us?"

"Yes, there is virtually no follow-up on our cases, and I thought this would be a particularly good one to check up on since I know Laura's natural father and met her mother in Thailand while I was there recently."

Betty looked at Amanda warily. "They aren't having second thoughts, are they?"

"Oh, no, it's nothing like that."

"But they wanted to know about her?"

Amanda was surprised at how quickly things had gotten down to the basic points. "Yes, there's curiosity, a strong interest in your daughter's welfare. Both the mother and the father have changed. They recognize that she will never be a part of either of their lives. I think the uncertainty about Laura's circumstances has been the biggest problem for both of them."

"So you just want to be able to tell them that Laura's fine?"

"That's one purpose for my visit, yes, but I have a professional interest in seeing how Amerasian children fare in the long run as well. May I ask you some questions regarding Laura?"

"Sure," Betty replied.

"A major concern for me has always been how a racially mixed child fares as she or he gets older. I would think that Laura would be rather unique in a community like this. Have there been any problems?"

"Well, this town sure isn't modern in attitudes like the cities," Betty replied, "but most of the people are decent. In my way of thinking, one person who's different fares better than a minority group. We've had no problems, Amanda. Laura's treated same as all the other children in town."

"Better, maybe," Jay added.

Betty agreed. "She's always been very popular with the other children. Has as many friends as any other girl her age—more than most, I'd say."

"That's wonderful," Amanda enthused. "I take it she's healthy and happy?"

"Oh, yes. You can meet her in a while. She's visiting a neighbor. We wanted to talk to you a spell first."

"I'm glad you did. How much have you told Laura about her background, and is she aware of the purpose of my visit?"

"We've told her everything we know about where she came from, which isn't much. To be honest, we didn't think her father was known. When Miss Wagner told us he was in California, it came as quite a surprise."

"Frankly, the whole story has just unraveled over the past few months. The father was aware that the mother had a child, but they were separated during the war, and he only recently found out the child was his for sure."

"We haven't told Laura that her father is known and lives in California. We thought she was just too young to deal with that sort of information." Betty looked at Jay. "We've been discussing it but haven't decided just when she should be told. Probably when she's old enough to decide for herself whether she ever wants to see him."

Amanda's heart sank. She had expected this reaction, even thought it best, but still had harbored hopes that Buck might get to see Laura during the trip. "Laura's natural father would be interested in meeting her, of course, but he knows that the decision is completely up to you."

"We feel she's just too young, Amanda."

"I understand."

"We sort of figured this," Betty said, "and got together some of Laura's school pictures, thinking he might like them to know her by." She got up and walked to the dining table at the other side of the room, picked up an envelope and returned, handing it to Amanda. It was sealed.

"That's very thoughtful and considerate," Amanda said, feeling touched by the gesture.

"There's room for more than just Jay and me to love her, Amanda."

The man nodded.

"He'll treasure these, I know."

"We didn't know the mother was interested, too, so maybe you can send a few to her."

"We can have copies made," Amanda said, thinking of her promise to Dameree.

"Would you like to see Laura's room?" Betty asked. "It might be better than when she's here so she's not embarrassed. Thirteen-year-old girls are young women, you know. They're proud." The woman stood and led Amanda through the adjoining hallway to a bedroom.

It was the typical room of a young American teenager. There were posters on the wall, pictures of puppies, horses, a popular rock group, and there was an especially large poster over the bed of a ballerina. Stuffed animals and dolls were still in evidence, but Amanda could tell they were receding somewhat in prominence. Laura was indeed at that critical point between childhood and young adulthood.

Hanging from a hook on the closet door was a tutu. "I understand Laura likes music and dance. Is that one of her costumes?"

"Yes, she's dancing in a school performance. It's this evening."

"Betty made the dress for Laura," Jay said from behind them in the hallway.

The woman went over and took it off the hook, holding it for Amanda to see, obviously very proud.

"It's lovely, Betty. I understand you're a seamstress."

"Yes, I do special things mostly, like wedding dresses." She hung the tutu back up and looked at her husband. "Why don't you call the Ducketts, Jay, and have Laura come home and meet Amanda?"

He went to the telephone as the women returned to the living room. Several minutes later, the front door opened, and Amanda watched with anticipation as a lovely young girl with glossy black hair and a bright-red parka entered the house. She glanced shyly at Amanda, then smiled, exposing shiny braces. She was beautiful, taking the best of the two races in her parentage. Her complexion was milky white, and her eyes, while almond shaped, were a smoky blue in color, yet she had the exotic, Oriental beauty of her mother.

"Laura, honey," Betty said, "this is Miss Parr from the adoption agency in California."

"Hi," she said shyly.

"Hello, Laura. I'm very happy to meet you." Amanda found herself staring at the child, seeing her through Buck's eyes.

"Take off your jacket and sit down with us," Betty said.

Obediently, Laura went and sat on the couch, with Amanda and her mother on either side.

"I understand you're going to be in a dance tonight," Amanda said to the delicately beautiful girl beside her.

Laura smiled, a little embarrassed. "Yes," she replied timidly. "We're doing *The Nutcracker*."

"How lovely. What role are you dancing?"

"The Sugar Plum Fairy," she said self-consciously.

"Laura's been taking dance for six years," Betty interjected. "Her teacher says she's one of the best she's ever had."

"That's quite an achievement," Amanda commented, touching the girl's hand. She agonized, thinking what it would mean to Buck to be here at this moment. How sad it was he couldn't see her. At least there were the pictures. It was an awfully thoughtful thing for them to do.

They chatted for a few more minutes, then Amanda realized that it was time to go. She thanked the Springers, complimented Betty on her lovely home, then got up. The others stood, and Amanda touched Laura's shoulder. "Good luck with your performance tonight."

"Thank you," Laura said, coloring a little.

"Are you going back to Kansas City this evening?" Betty asked.

"No, I'll probably leave in the morning."

"Would you like to come to the performance? It's here in town. Laura's school, the junior high, is over in Robinson, but they're putting on the ballet at Hiawatha High, on the east side of town."

Despite her convictions, Amanda saw in the invitation an opportunity for Buck to see Laura. She couldn't resist. "I'm traveling with my fiancé. Would it be possible to bring him along?"

"Sure, if he can afford the price of a ticket. It's fifty cents."

They all laughed and Amanda bid them farewell, thrilled that Buck would finally be able to see Laura, if only on stage. She hurried back to the motel. He was waiting where she had left him, sitting on the bed in front of the television set, an expectant expression on his face and having no idea whatsoever the score of his game.

THEY ARRIVED EARLY at the high school auditorium, hoping to get seats close to the stage, but the theater was already half full, leaving them near the middle of the audience. Amanda held Buck's hand as they sat in silence, listening to the chatter of the townspeople and feeling conspicuous, obviously strangers.

At the motel, she had recounted her entire visit with the Springers from the brass plaque under the bell to the tutu on the closet door and the braces on Laura's teeth. Then she had taken the envelope from her purse and handed it to Buck, watching as he tore it open and stared at the half dozen photographs. She sat next to him on the bed and looked with him, commenting on Laura's beauty, sharing his awe as he fingered the pictures of the daughter he had never seen.

Then when she had told him about the performance that night and the fact that, as her fiancé, he could go, too, Buck had thrown his arms around Amanda and given her a fierce hug. Sitting beside him now, she could feel his eager anticipation at the prospect of seeing his daughter for the first, and perhaps only, time.

The auditorium filled, the usual tension before a performance was in the air and the curtain finally went up. They waited impatiently for the scene where the Sugar Plum Fairy first appears.

Eventually, Laura danced onto the stage wearing the tutu Amanda had seen that afternoon. She was lovely, a feminine young woman moving with youthful grace. Amanda thought her quite good and glanced up at Buck, whose face was transfixed as though it were a miracle he were witnessing, not a school performance of *The Nutcracker*.

When the scene ended and Laura left the stage, Amanda looked again at Buck. His eyes had filled with tears and one overflowed, running down his cheek until he brushed it away with his hand. She held his arm tightly, letting her head touch his shoulder, fully aware now of the gift she had given him.

When the ballet was over, the audience began slowly moving out of the auditorium though many people, being related to the performers, lingered behind, waiting to see their child and extend the requisite compliments. Buck and Amanda had reached the aisle when a voice called out to her.

"Miss Parr!"

She turned to see Betty Springer in a bright-red dress, moving through the crowd toward them. Jay was behind her in a blue suit and tie.

"Did you see Laura?" she asked, her face filled with pride.

"Yes, she was sensational!"

"Didn't she look nice in the dress Betty made?" Jay asked, joining his wife.

"Beautiful, just beautiful." Amanda glanced at Buck. "Betty and Jay, I'd like you to meet my fiancé, Buck Michaels. Buck, these are Laura's parents, Betty and Jay Springer."

They shook hands.

"Did you enjoy the performance, Mr. Michaels?"

"Very much. Your daughter is an outstanding ballerina."

Betty smiled, acting the proud mother she was. "I know it must seem pretty small town to you and all, but the kids worked real hard."

"For their age, they did an excellent job," Amanda replied. "It was a very ambitious project."

There was a brief, awkward silence. "Are you making a vacation out of the trip, Mr. Michaels?" Betty asked.

"Yes, Amanda asked me to come along. I know Kansas City, but I've never been in your part of the state."

"There's not much here but farming," Jay said. "It's the principal industry. Only one, really."

"It looks to be mostly a corn area—I noticed as we were driving in."

"Yeah, the wheat's farther west. There's more rain in these parts so corn does well. That and alfalfa."

"Here comes Laura," Betty said, and they all turned toward the front of the auditorium and watched the girl making her way up the aisle.

Amanda glanced at Buck, whose eyes were fixed on the slender young girl. She felt a clutch of fear, worrying that with them actually face-to-face, something might go wrong. A glance at Betty Springer told Amanda that she, too, had read something in Buck's expression, but the woman turned to her daughter.

"You were just terrific, honey," Betty said as she hugged the girl.

Jay patted her shoulder. "First-rate."

"Hello, Miss Parr," Laura said, looking at her and at Buck.

Amanda took the girl's hand. "Congratulations on an outstanding performance, Laura. You were just beautiful."

"Thank you." She bit her lip self-consciously.

"Laura, I'd like you to meet my fiancé, Buck Michaels."

"Hello, Laura," Buck said, extending his hand.

The girl hesitated, then put her slender fingers in his. Amanda glanced at Betty, whose face was showing a touch of alarm. Was it wariness of a stranger, or had the woman sensed something?

"I thought you were awfully good," Buck was saying. "I've never seen *The Nutcracker* done better, nor by a lovelier ballerina."

Laura turned and looked at her parents, blushing with pride. Betty put her arm around the girl's shoulders, but her eyes were on Buck. He didn't notice, though, his full attention being on the child.

"Are you going to be a ballerina when you grow up, Laura?" Buck asked.

"I like dancing a lot," she replied, "but you have to be pretty good to do it for a job. I think I'd like to be a writer."

"That's a good occupation," he said. "I know a little about it, being in the newspaper business. Maybe you'll be a reporter someday."

"I think that would be fun."

Buck glanced up at the parents and seemed to notice the uncomfortable silence.

"Maybe you'd better change," Betty said to Laura in a low voice.

The girl nodded. "Nice to have met you," she said sweetly, looking at Buck, then at Amanda.

"Nice to have met you, too," Amanda said.

Buck's face was full of emotion, and Betty Springer seemed as aware of it as Amanda. But his only reaction was to smile as the child turned and made her way down the aisle.

Amanda's heart was in her throat. Betty was staring at Buck, whose eyes were glued on the girl as she left the auditorium. By the expression on Betty's face, Amanda could tell that the pieces had fallen into place.

"Mr. Michaels," Betty finally said, her voice quivering, "you're Laura's father, aren't you?"

"What?" Jay exclaimed.

Buck shot an anxious look at Amanda. For an instant, their eyes locked, neither of them moving, their faces filled with dismay and uncertainty.

Jay bristled. "What the hell...I thought you a-greed—"

The woman took her husband's arm, calming him. "It's all right, Jay." She turned to Buck. "I know what you did just now, and I'm grateful you didn't say anything to Laura," Betty said softly. "It was not an easy thing to do, I know." Her own eyes, like Buck's, filled with tears. "Thank you," she whispered. "Thank you for letting Laura go."

Buck reached toward Betty tentatively, unable to speak. She stepped over, embraced him briefly, then looked up as a tear ran down her cheek. "Someday, perhaps Laura can know you as her father." She turned to Jay.

Silently, the man shook Buck's hand and nodded to Amanda. Then taking his wife's arm, he walked with her out of the auditorium.

WHEN BUCK AND AMANDA STEPPED out into the cold December night, there were snowflakes in the air. The parking lot was still jammed with cars and pickup trucks making their way toward the exit so Buck took Amanda's hand and pulled her in the other direction. "Shall we walk a bit?" he asked. They went behind a building and headed across an open field as the snow swirled around them. Amanda slipped inside the circle of his arm, holding him tightly about the waist. They walked in silence until they came to the track and football field. Buck stared up into the night sky, breathing deeply of the crystal air, sending billowing vapors from his breath into the darkness.

As the wind cut through her, Amanda studied Buck's face, his mouth turned up in a half smile. "Was it wonderful seeing her?" Amanda whispered.

"Yes. It was what I needed."

"Do you feel better?"

"Much. As though the weight of the world had been lifted off my shoulders." He turned and looked at her. "I knew it had been a problem for me, but I hadn't realized how much."

She searched his eyes in the darkness of the winter night. Snowflakes brushed his face, settling on his black hair and lashes, but he was smiling. She felt reassured. "I'm glad we came—that you got to see her."

"It was a wonderful gift, Amanda. I'll always be grateful."

"How do you feel now?" she asked fearfully, uncertain.

"Wonderful." His eyes sparkled.

"What do you plan to do?"

They started walking again, across the football field. "I thought it might be nice to establish a trust fund with Betty and Jay to help with Laura's education, if they'd accept the help."

"I'm sure they would. They want what's best for her."

"Yes, I could tell they were good people."

"Are you content, then, with Laura's situation?" Amanda asked hopefully.

He stopped and faced her. "Yes, very content." He lifted her chin and kissed her softly on the lips.

When the kiss ended, Amanda opened her eyes and found his expression happy, almost whimsical. He grinned.

"What, Buck?"

"For the past year, I've wanted to find Lotus Moon more than I've wanted anything. Happy as I've been with you, and as much as I love you, Amanda, this has been a tremendous ordeal for me."

"I know it has." She pressed her face against his neck and held him, enjoying the warmth of his body and the familiar scent of his skin. "Oh, Buck, I love you so."

He held her face in his hands, looking deeply and lovingly into her eyes. "Amanda, darling," he whispered, his voice choked with emotion, "will you marry me?"

"Oh, Buck!" she exclaimed, pressing her lips against his, closing her eyes and letting the snow-flecked night air take them again. "Yes, Buck. Oh, yes."

They both laughed and, with their arms around each other, they began spinning on the frozen turf, slowly at first, then faster and faster until they were dizzy and breathless, their laughter echoing through the crystalline night air.

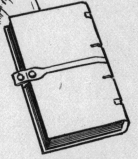

Take 4 books & a surprise gift FREE

SPECIAL LIMITED-TIME OFFER

Mail to   **Harlequin Reader Service®**

In the U.S.   In Canada
901 Fuhrmann Blvd.   P.O. Box 2800, Station "A"
P.O. Box 1394   5170 Yonge Street
Buffalo, N.Y. 14240-1394   Willowdale, Ontario M2N 6J3

YES! Please send me 4 free Harlequin Superromance® novels and my free surprise gift. Then send me 4 brand-new novels every month as they come off the presses. Bill me at the low price of $2.50 each—a 10% saving off the retail price. There are no shipping, handling or other hidden costs. There is no minimum number of books I must purchase. I can always return a shipment and cancel at any time. Even if I never buy another book from Harlequin, the 4 free novels and the surprise gift are mine to keep forever.

134-BPS-BP6S

Name _____ (PLEASE PRINT)

Address _____ Apt. No. _____

City _____ State/Prov. _____ Zip/Postal Code _____

This offer is limited to one order per household and not valid to present subscribers. Price is subject to change.

DOSR-SUB-1R

Harlequin Intrigue

WHAT READERS SAY ABOUT HARLEQUIN INTRIGUE . . .

Fantastic! I am looking forward to reading other Intrigue books.

*P.W.O., Anderson, SC

This is the first Harlequin Intrigue I have read . . . I'm hooked.

*C.M., Toledo, OH

I really like the suspense . . . the twists and turns of the plot.

*L.E.L., Minneapolis, MN

I'm really enjoying your Harlequin Intrigue line . . . mystery and suspense mixed with a good love story.

*B.M., Denton, TX

*Names available on request.

Harlequin Intrigue

Because romance can be quite an adventure.

Available wherever paperbacks are sold or through

Harlequin Reader Service

In the U.S.
901 Fuhrmann Blvd.
P.O. Box 1325
Buffalo, N.Y. 14269

In Canada
P.O. Box 2800, Station "A"
5170 Yonge Street
Willowdale, Ontario M2N 6J3

INT-6R